John D. Baltz

Hon. Edward D. Baker, U.S. Senator from Oregon

Colonel E.D. Baker's Defense in the Battle of Ball's Bluff, and, slight biographical

Sketches of Colonel Baker and Generals Wistar and Stone

John D. Baltz

Hon. Edward D. Baker, U.S. Senator from Oregon
Colonel E.D. Baker's Defense in the Battle of Ball's Bluff, and, slight biographical Sketches of
Colonel Baker and Generals Wistar and Stone

ISBN/EAN: 9783337161903

Printed in Europe, USA, Canada, Australia, Japan

Cover: Foto ©Raphael Reischuk / pixelio.de

More available books at **www.hansebooks.com**

HON. EDWARD D. BAKER

U. S. SENATOR FROM OREGON,

ONE OF

America's Heroes, formerly in Congress from Illinois, Colonel 4th Illinois Regiment and Commander of General Shields' Brigade in the War with Mexico; Colonel 1st California or 71st Penna. Vol. Regiment, Organizer and Commander in 1861 of the Philadelphia Brigade; Appointed Brigadier-General Volunteers August 6th, 1861, to rank from May 17th, 1861, which he declined August 31st, 1861; Appointed Major-General Volunteers, September 21st, 1861, which he had neither accepted nor declined at the time of his death. General McClellan was then the only other officer in the Army of the Potomac holding the rank of Major-General.

COLONEL E. D. BAKER'S

Defense in the Battle of Ball's Bluff, fought October 21st 1861, in Virginia,

AND

Slight Biographical Sketches of Colonel Baker and Generals Wistar and Stone.

BY

JOHN D. BALTZ,

LATE LIEUTENANT.

FORMERLY A PRIVATE, CO. H, 71ST PENNA. VOLS.

PUBLISHED FOR THE AUTHOR.

INQUIRER PRINTING COMPANY, LANCASTER, PA.

1888.

CONTENTS.

PAGE

CHAPTER I.

Biographical Sketch of Colonel E. D. Baker, United States Senate, Organizer of the 1st California Regiment. His Service and Death. Dedication of Monument at Gettysburg in the Presence of Pickett's Division 9

CHAPTER II.

Biographical Sketch of Brigadier General Isaac J. Wistar, and Early History of the 1st California or 71st Penna. Volunteers 29

CHAPTER III.

Biographical Sketch of Brigadier General Charles P. Stone, Colonel of the 14th U. S. Infantry 48

CHAPTER IV.

Forecast of Colonel Baker's Defense. Topography of the Country. Stone's Means of Defense. He Prepares a Flotilla. His Advance upon Leesburg 53

CHAPTER V.

Official Reports and Communications Previous to the Battle. Charges Made Against Colonel Baker and Misstatements Answered 68

CHAPTER VI.

Stone's Official Orders and Instructions for the First Advance. The Movement of Troops. The Hour Fixed when Colonel Baker took Command. His Orders. . . . 95

(3)

CHAPTER VII.

The Movement of Troops—Their Condition, Number, and Orders at Edward's Ferry. A Commander Wanted. Testimony of Generals Lander and Dana, Colonel Tompkins, Majors Mix, Bannister, Dimmick, and Philip Hanger, with Comments. 121

CHAPTER VIII.

A Glimpse at the Confederate Forces and their Movements from Fort Evans and Edward's Ferry to Attack Colonel Baker. General Evans' Report. Colonel Barksdale's Report. They take Prisoners, and Fire upon those in Retreat. Stone's Troops held by One Company, 13th Mississippi 146

CHAPTER IX.

Colonel Baker and Lieutenant Colonel Wistar on the Bluff. Stone, in Command at Harrison's Island, Instructs Baker to hold the Bluff. Baker's Position very Perilous. "All was going well up to Baker's Death." General Banks' Testimony, Colonel Van Allan's Testimony, General Lander's Testimony, Colonel Devens' Testimony, and Captain Bartlett's Report. Colonel Baker's and General McClellan's Generalship Contrasted. Stone's Peculiarities. Colonel Cogswell Ordered to take charge of the Artillery. He gave the Order to Retreat. McClellan Exonerates Stone. McClellan's Subsequent Testimony. McClellan All-Potent. 154

CHAPTER X.

General Stone before the "Joint Committee on the Conduct of the War." His Arrest and Imprisonment. Testimony as to his Loyalty. The Committee's Opinion of Stone's Conduct. Orders to Colonel Baker Authenticated. Colonel Baker's Presentiment. Orders which Stone said were Spurious 183

CHAPTER XI.

General Stone Released. His Arrest as Viewed in Halls of Congress. He does not Demand a Court of Inquiry. His Report of the National Casualties at the Bluff and Statement not Corroborated 200

CHAPTER XII.

General Stone again appears before the Committee. Supplies Omissions and Corrects some of his Mis-statements. General McClellan Approves of the Crossing. Transportation Sufficient. Colonel Van Allan's Testimony. McClellan's and Stone's Dispatches. Stone's Opinion of McCall's Movements. His Reason for not Demanding a Court of Inquiry. He does not think the Committee Solicited his Arrest. Committee's Final Conclusion. Names of Senators and Representatives of whom the Committee was Composed. 214

CHAPTER XIII.

Concluding Comments and Testimony—General McClellan's Report, and his Testimony. McClellan's Position and Prospects. He Supplies the Missing Link. Stone Reduced, Resigns His Commission. General Grant's Opinion. General McCall's·Testimony 229

ILLUSTRATIONS.

Portrait of Colonel E. D. Baker (Frontispiece) . . , ... 8
Cut of Regimental Monument at Gettysburg 25
Portrait of General Isaac J. Wistar 28
Map of the Battle Field and Position of Troops at Ball's Bluff. 94
Sketch of Cliff at Ball's Bluff, showing Troops Crossing . 157

PREFACE.

HAVING looked anxiously during the past, but in vain, for a full account of the Baker tragedy in, and the Stone episode growing out of, the affair at Ball's Bluff, with conclusions definitely drawn from reliable data, clearing up the mystery surrounding that affair, and feeling dissatisfied, not only with the published errors, so apparent to those who had been upon the field, but also with the meagre accounts that occur in many of our publications, while the ominous silence in other works seem to lend a deeper shade to the enigma, tending rather to sharpen an already keen desire to follow the principal actors, step by step, through the various details of the whole affair, I concluded to delve into the National and Confederate official reports, and the testimony taken by the "Committee on the Conduct of the War," for my personal gratification, hoping to find therein some convincing data, more in keeping with the views entertained by many of the participants. After having made a careful examination and study of the whole subject, from that and other sources, I found that errors much greater than I had anticipated had been given to the public, and were currently passing for truths, for want of a more thorough knowledge of the whole matter; therefore, I thought I might at least expose some of the errors by contrasting them with offical reports, despatches, and reliable testimony. With such thought in view, I finally commenced the arrangement of this data, with comments as contained in this publication, for the information of my comrades, and those most interested. Hoping that the views therein contained will prove to be just, if not pervaded with so much charitable silence as some might deem proper, I dedicate this volume to the survivors of the 1st California Regiment, organized by Colonel E. D. Baker, whose life and reputation they hold most dear. In the preparation of this volume, I am indebted for some specific information to Comte de Paris' "Civil War in America," and other authorities therein named, and for some general information to "Martial Deeds of Pennsylvania," "Twenty Years in Congress," by Mr. Blaine, an address by General Wistar to the survivors of his old regiment, and the "Civil War in America," by Lossing.   J. D. B.

April 2, 1888.

SLIGHT BIOGRAPHICAL SKETCHES

OF

SOME OF THE PRINCIPAL ACTORS

IN THE

BATTLE OF BALL'S BLUFF.

CHAPTER I.

COLONEL E. D. BAKER.

EDWARD DICKINSON BAKER, late a member of the United States Senate, a soldier distinguished in two wars, was born in England about 1808, of poor but worthy parentage, members of the Society of Friends, who with their children sought the hospitable shores of America, landing at Philadelphia when Edward was about nine years old. After the lapse of a few years, by the death of his father, he became the sole dependence of the family, and thus while a boy his native force of character, and self-reliance marked his career. Among the earliest recollections of his youth by which he was impressed, was the splendid pageant attending the funeral of Lord Nelson. With the surviving members of his small family, he removed to the then far West, the land of hope and promise, and settled in Springfield, in the State of Illinois, then a fledgeling of the Republic, where at an early age he joined the sect of "Christians or Disciples of Christ," largely known as "Campbellites," then in their infancy, whose only

(9)

"book of doctrine or discipline is the Bible," and before he attained to his majority, he became one of their
most eloquent and renowned speakers. This quiet and
peaceful profession failed to satisfy the restless activity
and ambition of his youth. He turned his attention
to the more stirring and lucrative profession of the law.
Having fine natural gifts, which he improved by close
attention to his profession and extensive reading, he
soon attained eminence at the Illinois bar. He was
not only well read in the law and general literature of
the day, but he especially delighted in studying the
principal historical campaigns of the Old World—those
of the most famous of the ancient Greek warriors, and
of the more modern generals, Frederick the Great,
Marlborough and Napoleon, all of whom he re-read
carefully, and with whose historic marches and battles
he was absolutely familiar.

In 1846 he was elected from his district to Congress,
where he became distinguished in debate.

When war was declared against Mexico, he at once
returned to his home and raised the 4th Illinois Regiment of Volunteers, with which he joined General
Scott's army on its march to the City of Mexico.
While en route upon a transport a mutiny broke out
in a Southern regiment, in quelling which he was severely wounded by a shot through the throat, from
which he recovered and served in the field to the conclusion of the war, winning great renown at Cerro
Gordo, where General Shields was wounded, leaving
Colonel Baker in command of his Brigade as Senior
Colonel, which he led successfully against the Mexican
position. Upon his return to Illinois at the close of
the war, he was re-elected to Congress, where he served
his State with great brilliancy and bade fair to become
one of the leaders of the House.

The Whigs of the Northwest presented Colonel
Baker for a seat in the Cabinet of President Taylor,

upon whose death and over whose remains, he delivered an eulogy typical of the great soldier, which immediately took rank as one of the most ornate, and classic orations delivered in the American Capitol.

His failure to receive a Cabinet appointment was a sore trial to him, causing him to think that his political career in Illinois was broken; and in 1852, after the close of his service in Congress, he joined the throng who were seeking fortune and fame on the Pacific slope.

When leaving Washington he said to a friend that he should never look on the Capitol again unless he came bearing his credentials as a Senator of the United States, with which he did return in eight years.

After leaving Illinois he was attacked by fever on the Isthmus, narrowly escaping with life, which left him prematurely aged, and his rugged constitution permanently impaired.

At the California bar, at that time an exceptionally able one, adorned with remarkable men from nearly every State in the Union, he speedily took a leading place, and as a jury advocate had no superior, being continually sought for in most of the leading criminal cases of the day, some of which remain landmarks in the jurisprudence of the Pacific Coast. It was there he became acquainted with Senator Broderick of California, a supporter of Douglas, who was antagonized by the Democratic followers of William M. Gwin, his colleague in the Senate, which in the heat of the campaign of 1859 led to a duel with Judge Terry, a prominent Democrat of Southern birth, in which Broderick was killed in the first fire—at which the Nation was profoundly affected, the excitement being greater throughout the country than ever attended a duel, except when Hamilton fell at the hands of Burr in 1804.

The oration over the remains of the dead Senator was delivered by Colonel Baker in San Francisco, in which he drew a realistic picture of the bloody tragedy and portrayed the characteristics of the participants so graphically, with irresistible power and eloquence, that violence was feared from the stirred multitude, which upheaving of the masses added greatly to the influence of the political party most concerned, and contributed in no small degree to Lincoln's triumph in California the ensuing year.

Colonel Baker again changed his place of residence, locating in Oregon, where he was elected to the United States Senate, and spent the winters of 1860–61 in Washington, then overflowing with treason, discord and turbulence. Though firm in his views, he was by no means a bitter partisan, many of his warmest personal friends belonging to the defeated party. He gave full credit to the sincerity of Southern statesmen, and with his positive and ardent nature scorned the talk of peaceful adjustment, maintaining that the differences were unadjustable except by war, and that a great war was certain to take place upon the inauguration of the new President, and earnestly advised the arming and disciplining of troops for the inevitable struggle. When the telegram startled the Nation with the announcement that the old flag had been dishonored and lowered from Fort Sumter, the upheaval of the North which followed met an enthusiastic response in the breast of Edward D. Baker, who was shortly thereafter commissioned by President Lincoln to raise for the service of the United States a regiment of infantry, with himself as Colonel, which was recruited during the months of April and the early part of May, 1861, at Philadelphia, for "three years or the war." This regiment was the first enlisted of the three years' troops, being organized April 29th, 1861, under the immediate charge of Lieutenant-Colonel Isaac J. Wistar, and mustered into the service for "three years or the war," the pay of some of the companies dating from April 16th, although the authority for so long a muster is not clearly defined under the following order:

WAR DEPARTMENT,
WASHINGTON CITY, *May* 8, 1861.

COLONEL E. D. BAKER, Senate.

Sir: You are authorized to raise for the service of the United States a regiment of troops (infantry) with yourself as Colonel, to be taken as a portion of any troops that may be called from the State of California by the United States, and to be known as the California Regiment. Orders will be issued to the mustering officer in New York to muster the same into the service as soon as presented.

In case the proper government officers are not prepared to furnish clothing for the men of your regiment at the time you find it necessary, you are authorized to purchase for cash their outfit of clothing, provided the same is properly charged in the muster-rolls of your command.

I am, Sir, very respectfully,
Your obedient servant,
SIMON CAMERON,
Secretary of War.

Under this order Colonel Baker had his regiment furnished by purchase, with an excellent outfit of clothing at their headquarters in Fort Schuyler, at the junction of East River and Long Island Sound, where they were drilled eight to ten hours a day, and subjected to strict discipline and guard duty at the Fort, before marching into Virginia. Of the movements of this regiment, led by Colonel Wistar during the greater part of its early history, we will have occasion to speak hereafter. Colonel Baker was always solicitous for the welfare of his men, and by many kind and thoughtful acts endeared himself to them. On one occasion, just previous to the first battle of Bull Run, while the regiment was on the Peninsula, and before moving out toward Richmond on that side in co-operation with McDowell's movement, the men were addressed by Colonel Baker as follows:

"My men! I want you all to listen to what I have

to say to you, for it may concern some of you, but I hope not many. I know that there are many men who enlist at times under excitement of different kinds, and after the excitement has passed they regret the step. Now if there is any one here who feels that he has not the courage to do a soldier's duty, let him give his name to his Captain, who will bring him to my head-quarters to-morrow morning, and I will see that he is furnished free transportation to his home. And I warn any man who hoots at those embracing this offer, that he will be summarily punished. I love and respect the man who has the moral courage to acknowledge the truth, if he has not the physical courage to face the foe."

The following day 35 out of 1500 men came forward and were sent quietly to their homes.

This regiment was not recognized by the State of California, and was compelled at first to make its re-turns to the War Department, the same as the regi-ments in the regular service, but was finally placed upon the roster of the Keystone State as the 71st Reg-iment of the Pennsylvania line, having served several months, and lost a number of men in action before many of the regiments bearing prior numbers were in service at all, or had completed their muster.

Colonel Baker, whose sagacity told him that the war could not be settled in three months' time, had the honor of commanding the first "three years' regi-ment" that entered the volunteer service in the great Rebellion, to which he subsequently added the 69th, 72d and 106th Pennsylvania Volunteers, forming a brigade with himself as its Commander, shortly before he fell in battle, of whom Mr. Blaine writes:

"On the 1st of August, while performing the double and somewhat anomalous duty of commanding his regiment and representing Oregon in the Senate, Mr. Baker entered the chamber in the full uniform of a

Colonel of the United States Army. He laid his sword upon his desk, and sat for some time listening to the debate. He was evidently impressed by the scene, of which he was himself a conspicuous feature. Breckenridge took the floor shortly after Baker appeared, and made a speech, of which it is fair criticism to say, that it reflected in all respects the views held by the members of the Confederate Congress then in session at Richmond. Colonel Baker evidently grew restive under the words of Breckenridge. His face was aglow with excitement, and he sprang to the floor when the Senator from Kentucky took his seat. His reply, abounding in denunciation and invective, was not lacking in the more solid and convincing argument. He rapidly reviewed the situation, depicted the character of the Rebellion, described the position of Breckenridge, and passionately asked, 'What would have been thought, if in another Capitol, in a yet more martial age, a senator with the Roman purple flowing from his shoulders had risen in his place, surrounded by all the illustrations of Roman glory, and declared that advancing Hannibal was just, and that Carthage should be dealt with in terms of peace? What would have been thought, if after the battle of Cannæ, a Senator had denounced every levy of the Roman people, every expenditure of its treasure, every appeal to the old recollections and the old glories?' Mr. Fessenden, who sat near Baker, responded in an undertone, 'He would have been hurled from the Tarpeian Rock.' Colonel Baker, with his aptness and readiness, turned the interruption to still further indictment of Breckenridge; 'Are not the speeches of the Senator from Kentucky,' he asked, 'intended for disorganization? Are they not intended to destroy our zeal? Are they not intended to animate our enemies? Sir, are they not words of brilliant polished treason even in the very Capitol of the Republic?' It is impossible to realize the effect of the words so eloquently pronounced by the Oregon Senator. In the history of the Senate, no more thrilling speech was ever delivered. The striking appearance of the speaker, in the uniform of a soldier, his superb voice, his graceful manner, all united to give the occasion extraordinary interest and attraction. The reply of Mr. Breckenridge was tame and ineffective. He did not repel the fierce characterizations with which Colonel Baker had overwhelmed him. He did not stop to resent them, though he was a man of unquestioned courage."

The course of Mr. Breckenridge was in direct hostility to the prevailing opinion of his State. The Legislature of Kentucky passed a resolution asking that he and his colleague, Lazarus W. Powell, should resign their seats, and in the event of a refusal, that the Senate would investigate their conduct, and if it were found to be disloyal, expel them. Mr. Breckenridge did not wait for such an investigation. In the autumn of 1861 he joined the Rebellion, and was welcomed by the leaders and the people of the Confederacy with extravagant enthusiasm.

Among the earliest acts of the next session was the expulsion of Mr. Breckenridge from the Senate. It was done in a manner which marked the full strength of the popular disapprobation of his course.

Of the surroundings, and the scene attending the death of Colonel Baker, General Wistar spoke substantially as follows, in addressing the survivors of his old regiment: "Baker constantly traversed the line, watching for an opportunity for a movement. Twice wounded myself, he was the first at my side on both occasions. He was not then touched, although a small bush was cut off between us as we talked."* When the "fire

---

* "The enemy's fire increased as their reinforcements continued to arrive. For us there could be no reinforcements, and it was almost certain death to bring up ammunition."

of the enemy had enveloped three sides of your position," while on the fourth was the turbulent and swift-
flowing Potomac, movements were almost impossible;
"nothing remained but the exaction of all, and more,
than the position no longer tenable was worth, but to
surrender, of which no one thought," although officers
and men were falling, as leaves of autumn, before the
bullets whistling around them, like driving sleet from a
winter's sky. "But in looking back to those stirring
scenes, whatever we may think of the plan or object of
that enterprise, none ever doubted Baker's signal coolness and gallantry on the field of battle. His courage
kindled as he saw the end approach, and knew it must
be disastrous. Several incidents during the heat of the
action showed that he fully understood the situation.
One of his remarks was: 'The officer who dies with
his men will never be harshly judged.'" The idea of
leaving the field seems never to have entered his mind,
preferring death to retreat. In this sublime temper
the warrior feels invulnerable—he heeds not sword or
missile, nor the on-rushing steel of the foe. He has
already conquered death; and while resolved to die on
the field, fights like one of the immortal gods of
old. Under favorable conditions such courage, such a
victory over death, would bear along with it the prestige of success, and carry an army with the shout of
triumph, conquerors over the hard-fought field.

"After it seemed to both of us that ruin was certain,
in response to a remark that a quick and easy death
was the best thing left us, he replied: 'The bullets are
kindly seeking for you, but avoid me.' That generous
and noble heart, sympathetic with all around him, had
abandoned hope, although resolved upon duty to the
last, while calmly anticipating the stroke which alone
should separate him from his men. But I believe that
you, who are the survivors of that and many other
bloody fields, will agree that if Baker had lived until

2

the last man, such was the affection and confidence he had inspired, he would have continued to hold your line firmly while there remained a soldier to mark it and a cartridge to fire.

"When I was at last personally disabled by the third shot, it was Baker who picked me up and had me conveyed to the boats. It was their last trip. Immediately afterward, Baker, sword in hand and face to the foe, fell dead" pierced with several balls while encouraging his men, and by his own example sustaining the obstinate resistance they were making. Under the heavy and continuous fire of the enemy the line receded, "and after your successful counter charge in which you brought off Colonel Baker's body, our troops were forced over the bluff, and though for a long while afterwards a desperate resistance was made as skirmishers, the cohesion as a manageable line was lost." Colonel Baker had told a number of the men of his old regiment, that if he should fall, and he evidently thought he would, in the battle then imminent, not to let the Confederates have possession of his body. They recovered his lifeless form after his coat had been stripped from his person; raising the precious burden in their arms, they bore it away amid a shower of bullets.

The brave and loved commander, who was a model in camp, genial without familiarity, dignified without stiff formality, maintaining the profoundest respect and winning the warmest admiration of all, was voiceless. His body was safely and tenderly carried to the river's brink, and thence over to the opposite shore. After crossing the river to Harrison's Island, and clambering up the bloody bank, wet and slippery, the scene was a more orderly one of death, but more profoundly sad. The wounded and dying strewed the ground, among whom the surgeon's knife, by the weird light of the tallow candle, was busy severing the shattered limb or extracting the ball from the maimed, while the nurses were applying bandages and staying the flowing of blood, from many to whom the tumult of battle was almost hushed, while the wild thrill of the strife was fast ebbing away in the death echoes along the shore. As the limp form of the venerable Baker, was borne along the line of his Brigade, they looked upon the blood-stained corpse with tearful eyes, and with suppressed voices and sorrowful hearts they whispered : "Father Baker is dead ! His brigade loved him."

The indignation, the intense and general emotion, excited in all classes of society by the death of Baker as the sad event of the bloody tragedy suddenly flashed upon them, was an instinctive and with many an involuntary homage to his distinguished loyalty and eminence. "The falling of the column revealed the largeness of the space it had occupied in the public eye," and the Nation was startled as it viewed the magnitude of the void in the fore-front of its resolute defenders.

A great calamity had befallen the Nation ; one of the most charming of orators and ablest of statesmen of the time, "who thoroughly comprehended the great issues and the horrible crime of the conspirators," was forever silent—having proven upon the field, that he had the courage to die for his country, among the first of the 750,000 which he predicted upon the rostrum, in his eloquent and prophetic speech, might fall, delivered by the side of President Lincoln at a grand Union meeting, April, 1861, in New York, *i. e.*

"Young men of New York * * * Young men of the United States ! You are told this is not to be a war of aggression. In one sense, that is true ; in another not. We have committed aggression upon no man. In all the broad land, in their rebel nest, in their traitor's camp, no truthful man can rise and say that he has ever been disturbed, though it be but for a single moment, in life, liberty, estate, character, or honor. The day they began this unnatural, false, wicked, rebellious warfare, their lives were more secure, their property more secure by us—not by themselves, but by us—guarded far more securely than any people ever had their lives and property secured, from the beginning of the world. We have committed no oppression—have broken no compact, have exercised no unholy power, have been loyal, moderate, constitutional and just. We are a majority of the Union, and we will govern our own Union, within our own Constitution, in our own way. We are all Democrats. We are all Republicans. We acknowledge the sovereignty of the people, within the rule of the Constitution ; and under that Constitution, and beneath that flag, let traitors beware. * * * I propose that the people of this Union dictate to these rebels the terms of peace. It may take thirty millions. It may take three hundred millions. What then? We have it. Loyally, nobly, grandly do the merchants of New York respond to the appeal of the Government. It may cost us seven thousand men, it may cost us seventy-five thousand men in battle. It may cost us even seven hundred and fifty thousand men. What then? We have them. The blood of every loyal citizen of this Government is dear to me. My sons! My kinsmen! The young men who have grown up beneath my eye, and beneath my care—they are all dear to me; but if the country's destiny, glory, tradition, greatness, freedom, government, written constitutional Government, the only hope of a free people—demand it—let them all go. I am not here now to speak timorous words of peace, but to kindle the spirit of manly, determined war. * * * I say my mission here to-day is to kindle the heart of New York for war. The Seventh Regiment is gone! Let seventy and seven more follow. * * * Civil war for the best of reasons upon one side, and the worst upon the other, is always dangerous to liberty, always fearful, always bloody. But fellow-citizens, there are yet worse things than fear, than doubt, and dread, and danger, and blood. Dishonor is worse. Perpetual anarchy is worse. States forever commingling, and forever severing, is worse. Traitors and Secessionists are worse. To have star after star blotted out—to have stripe after stripe obscured—to have glory after glory dimmed—to have our women weep and our men to blush for shame throughout generations yet to come—that and these are infinitely worse than blood."

* * * "And if from the far Pacific, a voice feebler than the feeblest murmur upon its shore may be heard to give you courage and hope in the contest, that voice is yours to-day; and if a man whose hair is gray, who is well nigh worn out in the battle and toil of life, may pledge himself on such an occasion and in such an audience, let me say as my last word, that when amid sheeted fire and flame I saw and led the hosts of New York as they charged upon a foreign soil for the honor of your flag, so again, if Providence shall will it, this feeble hand shall draw a sword, never yet dishonored, not to fight for distant honor in a foreign land, but to fight for country, for home, for freedom, for humanity, and in the hope that the banner of my country may advance—wheresoever that banner waves, there glory may follow and freedom be established."

Mr. Blaine writes: "The Second Session of the 37th Congress opened in December, 1861, under the shadow of a great disaster at Ball's Bluff, in which the eloquent Senator from Oregon, Edward D. Baker, lost his life; * * * a man of extraordinary gifts of eloquence, lawyer, soldier, frontiersman, leader of popular assemblies, tribune of the people. In personal appearance he was commanding, in manner most attractive, in speech irresistibly charming. Perhaps in the history of the Senate, no man ever left so brilliant a reputation from so short a service."

The day after the battle General McClellan announced the death of Colonel Baker, and spoke of him having "many titles to honor," a patriot, "zealous for the honor of his adopted country," cut off "in the fulness of his power as a statesman, and in the course of a brilliant career as a soldier distinguished in two wars," who "died as a soldier would wish to die, amid the shock of battle, by voice and example animating his men to brave deeds."

The Senate appointed a day for the consideration of the death of their distinguished member; President Lincoln was in attendance, and participated in the mournful proceedings. Most touching eulogies were pronounced by the dead hero's compatriots of the Senate. From that body resolutions were sent to the House of Representatives, where like proceedings were held, and all over the country the grief was general and profound, over the fall of that noble man who had become endeared to all. Amid which the funeral cortège, with solemn and measured tread, moved in mournful procession along the draped streets of the cities, en route to his far western home ; while the muffled tones of the bells sounded out their solemn cadence, from city to city, and tolled off another hero who had gone to his final rest.

Upon the slope of the far Pacific the news of his death created a like profound sensation. It reached San Francisco on the 25th of October, a few days after the battle, when the line of telegraph between the Atlantic and Pacific had just been completed and opened for use; and while preparations were being made in San Francisco to fire a salute on the following day in honor of this important event, a dispatch from the East announced the death of Baker. Rejoicing was turned into sadness and mourning, and the celebration was deferred out of respect for the lamented statesman and loyal soldier.

At the bloody angle on the battle-field of Gettysburg is erected a beautiful and imposing granitic monument, twelve feet high and six feet square at the base, upon the cap of which is inscribed, "California Regiment," and upon the base, "Second Brigade, Second Division, Second Corps." This monument was unveiled and dedicated by the survivors of Colonel Baker's old regiment, the 71st Pennsylvania Volunteers, on the 3d of July, 1887, in which ceremony, by special invitation, the survivors of Pickett's Division participated, of which General Burns (U. S. A.), an old commander of the brigade, said, in an address on that occasion:

"*Baker's California Regiment:* Called into being by the inspiring eloquence of the great orator whose name you bore, how could a 'dumb servitor' of the State master such glowing sentences to vibrate a rythmic sound in your ears, or stir a throbbing pulse in your hearts?

"I came to you when in the deepest mourning for your dead father—stricken on the field of battle before your eyes—when your hearts refused to be comforted. Like the Israelites in Egypt, you felt that I was a Pharaoh, who knew not Joseph, and oppressed you—strangers in a strange land. You had been reared under patriarchal rule: I brought the iron autocratical rule of stern discipline. How you hated the despot! who, if not an usurper, used all the forms of tyranny.

*   *   *   *   *   *

"Why these reminiscences of other fields than Gettysburg? My farewell order enjoined strict adherence to discipline. The god of war did not, like Minerva, spring full equipped from the head of Jove. You were preparing for the culminating test of discipline. You were destined to fill a space in a line of battle with the world for spectators, where the typical élan of the cavalier was to hurl its momentum against disciplined

courage—the staying qualities of the cooler North—
where the waves of the highest tide of war were to
dash upon the rocks of the Union, that echoed in the
roar, 'Thus far, no further;' and the mighty ocean of
strife was to ebb back into the bed of peace. Pickett's
charge will live in song, and its sad requiem will echo
'the Philadelphia Brigade.' 'When Greek meets
Greek, then comes the tug of war.' Here upon this
historic field Americans can say the same of Americans. Which can claim superiority, when perhaps
chance turned the scale? Had some other brigade
been here, without your staying qualities—had not
the prescience of your colonel seized upon the guns
loaded and capped, left by the dead and wounded of
the day before, and piled here opportunely at hand,
whereby he multiplied the force of your fire many
times your numbers, and by so placing his right behind walls as to enfilade the advancing mass—had
not the one piece of cannon been seized by the aid of
your infantry, and run into the angle of wall to be
loaded to the muzzle with broken shells, balls, and
bayonets, hurtling its deadly contents into the stagger-
ing mass at close range—had not your brothers of the
69th wheeled to face the breach opposite, and take the
foe in flank, while the 72d and a part of the 106th advanced to meet his front—what might have been the
result at that weak centre?

" These unique and terrible resources might well
have astonished and broken the hearts of exhausted
manhood. They exhibited the genius of war in con-
centrating on strong points, and opening a trap to
choke in a defile. The God of battles alone can know
why the centre of our army was not pierced on that
day. But we now know that it was the second time in
the history of the war, that the Army of the Potomac
owed to the Philadelphia Brigade the safety of its
centre. The fact that less than a hundred Confeder-

IN MEMORY OF THE FALLEN.

ates crossed that stone wall, proves that the force of the charge was broken by the cross-fire beyond, and these could well be cared for by the reserve of the brigade. Batchelder's map shows the great space between your brigade and that on your right, the thinnest of the line. You claim only to have done your duty, but the time, place, and opportunity were yours. God, in his all-wise providence, decided events. We are now united, never again to be divided; our Union is cemented with our blood. Those who fell are honored as heroes; those who remain are brothers in arms, dedicating here mementoes of valor, not of strife.

"The Philadelphia Brigade fraternizes with Pickett's Division. They recognize each other's bravery, and respect each other's fame. The world will applaud both alike, and history will record their deeds together. This memorial of a regiment's deeds is a memento-mori of those who fell on both sides, and will be a guide-mark on the route of fame for the future American soldier.

"The fortunate few who fought here that day, must wear the wreath of greatest glory, for the most conspicuous hand-to-hand encounter. That honor is shared by the 71st Pennsylvania Volunteer, as a member of the Philadelphia Brigade, which received the force of the gallant charge of Pickett's Division. It is not invidious to speak of this regiment and that brigade, for it was the key of the position, and it was the fate of war.

"Other regiments and other brigades did their duty, and assisted in the fight; but here was the point of attack, here the rain of shot and shell centered, and fell in torrents long before the charge. Here is the historic spot, and around it a halo of glory will ever cluster, and the aureole encircle the brows of those who here fought, with the light of undying fame.

"It is *fiat justitia* that Pennsylvania's sons should here defend their native soil."

The tablet on the front of the monument has inscribed upon it:

> *Seventy-First Pennsylvania,*
> *Commanded by*
> *COLONEL R. PENN SMITH,*
> *Carried into action : 24 officers, 307 enlisted men.*
> *Casualties : killed, 2 officers, 19 men ; wounded, 3 officers,*
> *55 enlisted men ; missing, 3 officers, 16 enlisted men.*
> *Total, 98.*

On the left tablet:

> *The Seventy-first Pennsylvania participated in all of the principal battles of the Army of the Potomac, and most of the minor ones until mustered out at the expiration of its term of service, July 2d, 1864. It numbered during its service nearly 2300 men, the total loss during that period being about 1800.*

On the rear tablet:

> *To the left of this point, on July 2d, the 71st Pennsylvania assisted in repulsing the famous attack of Wright's Georgia Brigade. During the terrific cannonading of July 3d, the regiment occupied a position sixty yards in the rear of this spot, a number of the men voluntarily helping to work Cushing's disabled battery. As the enemy emerged from Seminary Ridge the regiment was ordered forward, the left wing to this point, the right wing to the wall in the rear. When Pickett's Division rushed upon the left wing in overwhelming numbers, it fell back into line with the right, thus bringing the whole regiment into action, with the additional use of a large number of loaded muskets gathered from the battlefield of the previous day. The regiment captured a large number of prisoners and three flags.*

On the right tablet:

> *This regiment was organized April 29, 1861, being the first three years regiment to complete its organization. It was enlisted in Philadelphia by Senator E. D. Baker and Isaac J. Wistar, by special authority from the War Department, to be accredited to the State of California, and was known as the "California Regiment." After the death of Colonel E. D. Baker at Ball's Bluff, October 21, 1861, it was claimed by its native State and became the Seventy-first Pennsylvania.*

Of Colonel Baker and the service of his regiment, General Wistar said, in the address alluded to, "How his heart would have swelled, and his eye kindled, could he in his last moments have foreseen the future career of the regiment he loved so well—that it was destined to stand the peer of any in the glorious Second Corps, to cover the retreat of Pope's routed columns, charge Jackson's veterans at Antietam, receive on its steady bayonets the shock of Pickett at Gettysburg, and that after blazoning on its standard the historic names of the Peninsula, Fredericksburg, Chancellorsville, Spottsylvania, and innumerable minor engagements, it should, after the acknowledged expiration of its term, and before re-enlistment, volunteer at the call of its corps commander to assault the works at Cold Harbor, where you lost 100 men actually ordered home for discharge; and finally, that of the 2200 men who, from first to last fought under your flag, 119 was the remnant for the last muster out. That look into the future was denied him. But who shall say that during those after years his memory, precept and example, were not mustered under your flag when it led the advance, and cheered the last moments of dying comrades who fell out of your ranks forever in the shock of battle."

A still more glorious scene, in which his old regiment participated, of peace and reconciliation over the grave and burial of the dead feuds and issues of the war, in which he would have delighted, was also "denied him."

At the same time, and upon that historic spot, the late Confederates, survivors of Pickett's grand Division, clasped hands with the survivors of the " Philadelphia Brigade," where they had glared at and met each other in the deadly conflict of July 3, 1863, the healing and mellowing effect of time, having not only obliterated and covered all traces of blood and carnage upon the field, but also effaced from the hearts and minds of the surviving actors all thoughts and feelings of hatred. They met as friends, as kinsmen, beneath the ample folds of the old flag, without "one star blotted out" or "one stripe obscured," and there extended and received across the old stone wall, shattered and riven by shot and shell, the right hand of brotherhood, and thus by greetings of peace, concord and good-will, showed that all enmity had been buried with the dying flash of the last gun from the South, and there proved to the nations abroad, that they were one in name, one in heart, of one nation, with one govern-ment, and but one flag, which gracefully waved over the whole land, purchased by the patriotic valor and blood of their forefathers, by whom their homes and their land were made free and independent.

This heroism and noble magnanimity, which mu-tually attracted conqueror and conquered, is truly the greatest in historic annals. What an imperishable cap-stone, what a crowning of glory, the blessings of an enduring and heartfelt peace, following the baptism of blood not shed in vain! How momentous the event in its relation to future history! What a revela-tion to hand down to posterity, to be hallowed in per-petuity by the ages to come! That reconciliation and fraternal greeting, of the magnanimous and brave will be cherished, a sacred legend, around the camp-fires that shone brightly upon the blue of the North, and the grey of the South, long before the dying embers have smouldered away and quite gone out, and ever after rise from the ashes, in odorous incense an oblation to the God of peace. If the spirits of the illustrious departed, participate in the affairs of this world, will there not be traced upon this scene, with a pen of re-fined gold, the benediction of the venerated Father of our country, who "was first in peace, first in war, and first in the hearts of his countrymen?"

"He whose patriotic valor universal homage won,
He who gave the world the Union, the immortal Washington."

BRIGADIER GENERAL WISTAR, U. S. V.

CHAPTER II.

GENERAL ISAAC JONES WISTAR, the youthful trap-per, frontiersman, commander of Indian rangers, and distinguished soldier, was born on the 14th of November, 1827, in the city of Philadelphia. His father, Caspar Wistar, M. D., also born in Philadelphia, was a lineal descendant of Caspar Wistar, of Heidelberg, Hesse Cassel, who came to this country in 1696, and purchased large tracts of land in Philadelphia county, and throughout the Province of Pennsylvania. His mother, Lydia Jones, was also a native of Philadelphia. Their son Isaac was educated at Westtown boarding-school, Chester county, and at Haverford College; who, from his early youth, showed great fondness for manly sports, especially those of hunting and fishing, over mountain and stream, and at the age of sixteen crossed the Rocky Mountains, to the far Pacific, then almost a trackless wilderness, inhabited only by Indians and frontier settlers, where he remained until about 1860, witnessing many changes and struggles for supremacy over the red man, and the primeval solitude, spending part of the time trapping in the territory of the Hud-Bay Company in the Arctic regions, and in the Rocky mountains.

In 1850 and 1851, then but 23 years of age, he commanded a body of Indian rangers and scouts, with whom he fought the hostile tribes of savages on the borders of California and Oregon, and gained considerable experience in the warfare incidental to the early settlement of the Pacific coast, after which he studied law, and was admitted to practice at the California

(29)

bar, composed of able jurists from nearly every State in the Union, and it was there he became the law partner of Honorable E. D. Baker, in 1853. During the winter of 1860–1861, while the subject of our sketch was in attendance on the Supreme Court of the United States, he was called to the staff of General Cadwalader, in Philadelphia, and was busily employed in organizing the militia for three months service; but agreeing with Senator Baker that the war was not to be settled in a three months' campaign by the militia, he turned his attention to recruiting and organizing in the city a regiment of volunteers for three years service, which Colonel Baker had been specially authorized to raise by President Lincoln, to be called the "First California Regiment," and to be accredited to that State in case of a call for troops from the Pacific coast, whose militia was not called upon for the three months service.

The major part of this regiment was recruited during the month of April, 1861, it being organized as a regiment on the 29th of the month with E. D. Baker, Colonel; Isaac J. Wistar, Lieutenant-Colonel; and Robert A. Parrish, Jr., Major; being sent by companies during the month of May to Fort Schuyler, on Long Island Sound, to be drilled and perfected in discipline.

After they had been drilled and thoroughly disciplined as a regiment, they were ordered to Fortress Monroe by the way of Philadelphia to reinforce General Butler, who had been repulsed at Big Bethel. As the regiment marched in column through the city of Philadelphia, it reflected the greatest credit on its officers, and elicited the heartiest applause from the citizens, who crowded the line of march. In every step and movement they gave evidence of fine drill and discipline. Notwithstanding the captured rebel grey suits in which they were uniformed, and the name of the State of the far Pacific on their regimental flag, the Philadelphians recognized in the regiment marching to the

seat of war, hundreds of young men from the Quaker
City. They took cars for Baltimore, and upon nearing
that city, received ball cartridges for the first time.
Placing their baggage under special guard, they ar-
rayed themselves in light marching order, then called
California style, consisting only of pants and shirt,
with the tails outside, over which the cartridge boxes
were strapped, with muskets loaded ready for use.
This precaution was thought necessary on account of
their being the first regiment to march through the
city of Baltimore by that route since the 6th Massachusetts had been fired upon.* They marched through
the crowded streets, and reached the boat on the Pa-
tapsco without being molested, and embarked for
Fortress Monroe, where they arrived early the next
morning, and debarked upon the sacred soil of "The Old
Dominion." The regiment marched out toward Hamp-
ton Village, and encamped on the Peninsula, where
they scouted and did picket duty, in the vicinity of Big
Bethel, preparatory to an advance on Richmond from
Fortress Monroe. When General McDowell was ordered to advance upon Manassas, General Butler prepared to move his small force up the Peninsula toward
Richmond. Artillery was brought from the fort,
rations prepared and issued, and an advance made toward Little Bethel, waiting on the way for word that
all was going well with McDowell at Manassas; but instead of receiving word to advance farther, they were
ordered to Washington, to help turn the insetting tide
of Confederates after the defeat of the three months
men at Bull Run, who had disintegrated, and no
longer existed as an army. The regiment embarked
at Fortress Monroe, regretting the loss of at least one
of their number,† who had been mortally wounded

* The three months men having passed through Maryland by
other routes after the riot.

† Corporal Joseph Sargster, Co. "H."

while on guard.   After arriving at Washington, they
learned more of the details of the defeat and retreat of
General McDowell's army, which had been composed
largely of the bravest and truest patriots of the North,
and also of some indifferent material who had volun-
teered under the firm conviction that there would be no
serious fighting.   Some of the regiments, principally
three months' men, were badly officered; many of
whom gave way, and scattered or fled to their homes
just when they were most needed, thus disorganizing
and causing confusion throughout the whole army,
which ended in dire disaster.   "Never before had so
black a day as that black Monday lowered upon the
loyal hearts of the North" as was witnessed when the
crowds of fugitives from the grand army were pouring
into Washington, a heedless, worthless mob, who had
thrown away their arms and equipments, and abandoned all semblance of military order and discipline.
It seemed as though the accumulating forces of the enemy encompassed the National capital darkly as the
horizon of despair.

But still there were some few effective batteries and
solid battalions that had marched back in good order,
depressed, but unshaken and dauntless, one of which
was afterwards affected by the contagion.   The men
of the —————————, a two years' regiment, after returning from the battle field, where they had suffered
in killed and wounded, encamped on Meridian Hill, in
the suburbs of Washington, and there became discour-
aged and demoralized.   When they were ordered to
march into Virginia again, they positively refused, and
broke out in open mutiny.   No persuasion could induce
them to return to duty, until they were finally surrounded by Regular infantry, cavalry and artillery,
with orders to open fire upon them.   They then, seeing that resistance was useless, reluctantly obeyed, and
moved across the river, escorted by the Regulars, where

they performed good service, and became one of the best regiments in the army. The contagion was not confined to this regiment alone, of the two years' men in McDowell's army; but it was there more pronounced. Great dissatisfaction having existed as to the general-ship displayed in the short campaign they had just gone through.

The California Regiment, led by Colonel Wistar, marched through Georgetown, and crossed the Chain Bridge, to the south bank of the Potomac, where the toils and hardships of war were met and endured afresh;* at times under fire on the picket lines;† in retal-

---

* While companies H, I, and P, were on picket duty, some firing was heard along part of the line, and rifle shells were fired from our batteries in the rear, after which Captain Strong, of an Indiana regiment, came in through the California posts wounded and bleeding freely. He claimed to have encountered several of the enemy, and to have killed two and wounded one of them, and was himself shot through the cheek and some part of the body. This detail from the California regiment was relieved the next day by the 79th New York, and returned without loss.

† The firing of small arms in the direction of Lewinsville, was explained one morning by the return of a detachment of the 79th New York, under Captain Ireland, consisting of 160 officers and men, who had marched at 1 a. m. by various by-paths, without disturbing the enemy's pickets, to a designated point, where they arrived at day-break. The command was divided into two wings, and lay in ambush for a force of the enemy that were likely to fall back from Lewinsville after a night's foray upon our pickets. They did not wait long: soon a body of cavalry endeavored to pass the ambuscade, when they were fired upon and put to flight. Previous to their retreat, the enemy fired upon the left wing of the ambuscade, killing one private—John Dowee. The lowest estimate of the enemy's loss was 4 killed, 2 wounded, and 1 prisoner; and they left in the hands of the right wing a major of Colonel Stuart's Cavalry, who fell wounded. The alarm having been sounded in all of the enemy's camps in the neighborhood, the National-ists retired, and arrived in camp at 10:30 a. m., bearing in a litter the body of John Dowee.

iation of incursions upon the enemy, where fell Captain Lingerfelder, of the 2d Battalion, then called to the support of the masked battery; or moving off on the double-quick, while the Confederate shells were bursting around, to reinforce General Smith's reconnaissance,* attacked by the Confederates under Colonel Stuart,† at Lewinsville, where the Nationals lost 6

* General Smith ordered about 2000 troops of all arms "to cover and protect a reconnaissance of the village of Lewinsville and vicinity, to determine all the facts requisite for its permanent occupation and defence," which movement was commenced at 7:30 a. m., and the reconnaissance was completed about 2:15 p. m., at which time the National forces were ordered to retire; when about moving to the rear, were attacked by Colonel J. E. B. Stuart, with cavalry, infantry, and artillery, who opened a brisk fire upon the retiring forces, which was replied to principally by Captain Griffin's Battery, from different positions while retreating. In the afternoon, while the California Regiment was busily plying the pick and shovel in the intrenchments, they were startled by the screaming and bursting of shells near by. Then a courier rode into camp in great haste with orders, and the bugle sounded the assembly. The men dropped the picks and shovels and ran to their pieces, kept stacked in line ready for use, and were hastily formed, and double-quicked by Lieutenant-Colonel Wistar in their shirt sleeves toward the bursting shells. As they reached the direct road, they met the driftwood from the field that spoke plainly of the encounter—first the inhabitants fleeing for their lives, then some wounded men limping to the rear in advance of the ambulances. The California Regiment reached the line held by the 79th New York and 19th Indiana, in support of Captain Mott's battery, which had just come into action. They passed on to the front and deflected to the left, forming line of battle along a picket fence skirting a cross-road, which they held until the National batteries, by a well-directed fire of shells, had silenced the Confederate guns, and scattered some of their forces—when the National forces again retired, after which the California Regiment marched leisurely back, (covering the rear) to their work in the intrenchments.

† General Stuart, the most famous cavalry General of the Confederacy, who was killed in 1864, while resisting one of General Sheridan's raids.

killed, 12 wounded, and 3 prisoners. At another time
on the skirmish line and foraging expedition,* driving

* The California Regiment, under Colonel Baker, accompanied General Smith, who marched from his camp at 9 a. m., on a
foraging expedition toward Lewinsville—the right wing under
Colonel Taylor—leaving on the hill commanding Langley, one
section of Captain Mott's battery, supported by three companies
of the 19th Indiana, advanced on the road to Lewinsville—on a
knoll covering the right, the centre section of the same battery,
with four companies of the 2d Wisconsin—and one mile farther
on the remaining section, under the immediate command of
Captain Mott, the 33d New York, and a company of Kentucky
Cavalry, all at Mackall's house. The 3d Vermont and the remainder of the 19th Indiana being thrown out as skirmishers on
the left, supported by a reserve formed of Captain Barr's Pennsylvania battery and five companies of the 6th Maine, about 300
men ; and in advance to their right one section of Captain Griffin's battery, with three companies of the 5th Wisconsin, and in
the edge of the woods the *2d battalion of the California Regiment, under Major Parrish.* Captain Griffin's remaining sec-
tions occupied the hill about one and a half miles from Lewinsville, covering the country to the left and the road in front with
the *1st battalion of the California Regiment, under Colonel
Baker.* Five companies of the 5th Wisconsin, the Berdan
sharpshooters, *two companies of the Philadelphia Zouaves,* and
Lieutenant Drummond's Regular Cavalry forming the centre ;
six companies of the 79th New York half a mile in advance as
skirmishers, supported by the two remaining companies of the
79th and the 2d Vermont; in all, 5100 infantry, sixteen pieces
of artillery, and 150 cavalry. There being at that time no
sign of the enemy, with the exception of a few cavalry scouts,
the quartermaster loaded his wagons, 90 in number, all of
which was accomplished by 3 p. m., and the National forces
were being drawn in, when word was received that the enemy
were approaching from over the hills from Fall's church road.
Then, in full view, what seemed to be a large regiment marching rapidly in close column, and others deployed as skirmishers
with the apparent intent of turning the National flank. At the
same time they opened fire with apparently but one gun on our
extreme left, when the centre section of Griffin's Battery came
back to the California Regiment in the woods. At 4:30 they
had placed two guns in position on our right, and opened on

back the Confederates and silencing their guns; while taking their farm products, and occupying much of the ground lost by the Nationals after the disaster at Bull Run, almost without a casualty. Then again in the stealthly night march and skirmish before Munson's Hill,* causing the Confederates to withdraw

Mott's section at Mackall's, which was at once replied to by Griffin's and the rifle piece of Mott's section. After firing some thirty rounds, some of the shells exploding right among the enemy, they limbered to the rear, the dust marking their line of retreat. General Smith reported, "The conduct of the troops was all that I could desire, standing with perfect coolness while the enemy's shot was falling, as it did at one time, all about them; *one shell bursting over the California Regiment* wounded one man slightly in the arm, and their cheers must have been heard by the enemy every time our shells seemed to reach their mark." After the Confederates retired, the Nationals shortly thereafter fell back with all their forage and some prisoners. The California Regiment, forming the rear guard on their front, did not arrive in camp until about 8 p. m. After dusk the Confederates brought a piece of artillery to the cross-roads, and fired four or five shots into Langley, and after delivering this parting salute, fell back again.

* *The 1st battalion of the California Regiment* relieved the 19th Indiana from picket duty, but were recalled at 4 p. m. the next day, and ordered to camp for rest preparatory to a night's march, so accurately described by Lieutenant-Colonel Wistar to Colonel Baker commanding brigade, dated September 29, 1861, "In compliance with orders received last evening from General Smith, during your absence, I marched with my regiment about 9:30 p. m., arriving opposite Vandeburgh's house about 11 p. m. Here I was detained about two hours from the necessity of clearing away a number of trees felled across the road. During the interval, *I took the head of the column as directed by General Smith, with the 1st battalion of my regiment, consisting of nine companies: I was followed by a battery of four guns, and then by my 2d battalion of seven companies, under Major Parrish.* My instructions from General Smith were to proceed without advance guards or flankers until I should pass Colonel Burnham, who, with his regiment, was near the next cross-roads, and after passing him, he being the most advanced of

from that much dreaded and supposed stronghold, with
a loss to the right battalion of the 1st California of 4

our forces, to throw out three companies, deployed as skirmishers across the road, and follow them with my column at a distance, say one hundred and fifty yards, connecting the head of the
column with the centre of the skirmishers by a file of men at inter-
vals of ten paces. This had just been accomplished when General
Smith, with his staff, overtook me, and the command was put
in motion. After proceeding a short distance, I was surprised
to find a picket guard of a New York regiment, having supposed
we had passed all of our out posts. At the first turn to the
right, which occurred within a quarter of a mile, after the de-
ployment of my skirmishes, they began to come in collision
with picket guards, who said they belonged to the 4th Michigan. The road at this point was lined with thick woods on both
sides. At the turn of this road there was stationed a picket
of about 20 men, thirty yards beyond was another of about 6
men, and the head of the column had not progressed more than
fifty yards past the latter when a regular volley was fired into
the 2d and 3d companies (H and N) of my line from immediately behind the fence which lined the woods on my left. The
head of the column having now passed the woods on our right,
the latter was replaced by open fields, exposing us to the light
of the rising moon, while from the woods on our left, whence
an invisible enemy continued to pour his fire, was in deep shade.
Nothing was visible in the woods but the flashes of their guns;
convinced the firing was the mistake of friends, I rode between
my men, who had instantly faced towards the woods whence the
firing proceeded, vainly calling upon all parties to cease firing.
At that moment my horse was shot and rendered nearly unmanageable. Notwithstanding my exertions, a fire was delivered by my own men, who could bear it no longer, and continued perhaps, for a few minutes, when the party in the
woods retired. I now ordered my killed and wounded to be
carried to the rear and dressed my line, and was endeavoring
to reassure all parties when the parties in the woods having returned suddenly, threw in another volley, from not less than
forty pieces, which my men instantly returned without orders,
the distance being the width of the road, say six yards. This
time the firing extended nearly as far back in the road as the
rear of my 1st battalion, producing a panic among the artillery
horses, which turned and dashed off to the rear, breaking loose

men killed and 14 wounded, and finally in the role of
the sapper and miner, making secure for those to come,
by earthworks, the ground thus gained at Camp Advance, which stood as a lasting monument to their
comrades fallen in deadly strife during this short but
active campaign, whom they laid to rest with the
honors of war on the pine-clad hills of old Virginia.

While the 1st California and other regiments were

from the guns, and producing great confusion in my 2d battalion, by rushing over them at full speed. A number were shot,
and the remainder were turned off the road, and order was soon
restored. *After sending my killed and wounded to the rear, I
put my command in the woods, which concealed the firing
party, whoever they may have been, thoroughly scoured and
took possession of it,* and with the aid of Adjutant Newlin,
formed line of battle along its front to hold the road, and at the
same time stationed my 2d battallion, under command of Major
Parrish (who was of very great assistance during the whole
night, and whose perfect coolness during such general confusion
was very gratifying,) in the woods at the right, *so as to cross
fire with the 1st battalion, on the road in front,* and then
after rallying my skirmishers, and distributing them as pickets
all around our front, reported these dispositions to General
Smith, who was pleased to approve them. On the following
afternoon at 4 p. m , I left the position by General Smith's
order, and marched back to camp, where I arrived without
further incident at dark. My loss was 4 killed (Sergeant Phil-
son, Company N, privates Pascoe, Payran, and White, of
company H) and 14 wounded.

Major Parrish prevented further loss of life by restraining the
captain of a battery, who was about firing his guns heavily
charged with grape and canister, upon the 1st battalion of the
California Regiment, then dressed in grey uniforms, while
moving to take the woods from which they had been fired upon.

While this blundering scene was being enacted in the hearing of the enemy, they silently retired from Munson's Hill,
which was taken possession of by the Nationals.

Colonel Baker reported, "As the California Regiment was
most exposed, I deem it proper to speak in terms of high commendation of Lieutenant-Colonel Wistar commanding, who
evinced peculiar coolness and intrepidity."

thus engaged at Camp Advance, General McClellan was organizing and disciplining the Grand Army of the Potomac, which was ever thereafter standing an impassable barrier between the Confederate and National capitals, or thundering at the defences of Richmond until the Confederate capital fell, and with it the Army of Northern Virginia. As an evidence of the strict discipline enforced in the new army, the troops at Camp Advance, during the early part of September, were called upon to witness the death of Private William Scott, of the 3d Vermont Regiment, for sleeping on picket post, having been tried by court-martial, and ordered to be shot to death by musketry. He was taken from the guard-house to the place appointed for his execution, and while kneeling upon his coffin, by his newly-dug grave, facing the firing party, ready to fall—an example of military severity—a carriage drove up in haste, bearing a pardon from the Secretary of War, and thus a really brave soldier was saved, to fall a few months later under fire from the enemy—so graphically described by Francis de Haes Janvier:

THE SLEEPING SENTINEL.

'Twas in the sultry summer time, as War's red records show,
When patriotic armies rose to meet a fratricidal foe—
When from the North, and East, and West, like the upheaving
    sea,
Swept forth Columbia's sons, to make our country truly free.
  *   *   *   *   *   *   *   *   *   *
Where, dwelling in an humble cot, a tiller of the soil.
Encircled by a mother's love, he shared a father's toil—
Till, borne upon the wailing winds, his suffering country's cry
Fired his young heart with fervent zeal, for her to live or die.

Then left he all—a few fond tears, by firmness half concealed,
A blessing, and a parting prayer, and he was in the field—
The field of strife, whose dews are blood, whose breezes War's
    hot breath,
Whose fruits are garnered in the grave, whose husbandman is
    death!

Without a murmur, he endured a service new and hard;
But, wearied with a toilsome march, it chanced one night, on
    guard,
He sank, exhausted, at his post, and the gray morning found
His prostrate form—a sentinel, asleep upon the ground!
   *   *   *   *   *   *   *   *   *   *   *
And this poor soldier, seized and bound, found none to justify,
While War's inexorable law decreed that he must die.
   *   *   *   *   *   *   *   *   *   *   *
Within a prison's dismal walls, where shadows veiled decay—
In fetters, on a heap of straw, a youthful soldier lay:
Heart-broken, hopeless, and forlorn, with short and feverish
    breath,
He waited but the appointed hour to die a culprit's death.
   *   *   *   *   *   *   *   *   *   *   *
'Twas morning—on a tented field, and through the heated haze,
Flashed back, from lines of burnished arms, the sun's effulgent
    blaze;
While, from a sombre prison-house, seen slowly to emerge,
A sad procession, o'er the sward, moved to a muffled dirge.

And in the midst, with faltering step, and pale and anxious
    face
In manacles, between two guards, a soldier had his place.
A youth—led out to die—and yet, it was not death, but shame,
That smote his gallant heart with dread, and shook his manly
    frame!

Still on, before the marshalled ranks, the train pursued its way
Up to the designated spot, whereon a coffin lay—
His coffin! And, with reeling brain, despairing—desolate—
He took his station by its side, abandoned to his fate!

Then came, across his wavering sight, strange pictures in the
    air—
He saw his distant mountain home; he saw his parents there;
He saw them bowed with hopeless grief, through fast declining
    years;
He saw a nameless grave; and then, the vision closed—in tears!

Yet, once again. In double file, advancing, then, he saw
Twelve comrades, sternly set apart to execute the law—
But saw no more—his senses swam—deep darkness settled
    round—
And, shuddering, he awaited now the fatal volley's sound!

Then suddenly was heard the noise of steeds and wheels ap-
proach—
And, rolling through a cloud of dust, appeared a stately coach.
On, past the guards, and through the field, its rapid course was
bent,
Till, halting, 'mid the lines was seen the nation's President!

He came to save that stricken soul, now waking from despair;
And from a thousand voices rose a shout which rent the air!
The pardoned soldier understood the tones of jubilee,
And, bounding from his fetters, blessed the hand that made
him free.*

With the advent of the invigorating month of October, 1861, the California Regiment left their booths at
Camp Advance, beyond Chain Bridge, Virginia, bearing
with them the proud distinction of having been honorably mentioned and especially commended by their
superior officers for their coolness and soldierly conduct
while in action. The regiment marched out to picket
the fords of the upper Potomac for the winter, which
was fast approaching, as indicated by the cold nights
and depicted by the beautiful but fast-falling foliage.
They took up the line of march from Fort Ethan Allen
(afterward called Fort E. D. Baker), a work of their
own construction, bivouacking in the fields adjacent to
the roadside by huge fires of rails from the neighbor-
ing fences, which made a cheerful warmth and light in
the gloaming, and lulled the weary and foot-sore soldiers into deep slumber at their different bivouacs,
until they reached their destination, by the way of
Chain Bridge, Great Falls, Rockville and Seneca Mills.
October 3d they reached a point about four miles beyond Poolesville, Maryland, and went into camp, having
arrived at their objective point without being shelled

* During the siege of Yorktown, the 3d Vermont charged
across the Warwick river, to the enemy's works, and Scott was
among the first who crossed, and there fell mortally wounded,
and died with his face to the foe.

or meeting with opposition, and reported to Brigadier-General Charles P. Stone, who was about forming a special corps of observation, on the right flank of the Army of the Potomac, with his headquarters at Pooles-ville, a short distance from Conrad's and Edward's ferries, on the Potomac river, in the department of Major-General Banks, whose troops were holding the Maryland side of the river, from Darnestown to Williamsport. Near Conrad's ferry, on the Virginia shore, were the heights of Ball's Bluff, distant about three miles from Leesburg, the capital of Loudon county, Virginia, where the Confederate left, under General N. G. Evans, who had figured quite conspicuously on the battle-field of Bull Run, was strongly intrenched, commanding the approaches to the village of Leesburg, at the terminus of the Alexandria, Loudon and Hampshire Railways. The troops under General Stone confronted these forces of the Confederate army under General Evans. Edward's ferry was about five miles down the river from Conrad's ferry, and between them was Harrison's island dividing the river, where some thrilling events took place before October had faded into the more sterile November. A short distance from the river the 69th, 72d and 106th Pennsylvania were brigaded with the California Regiment, forming the third brigade of the Corps of Observation, where they settled down under canvas, picketing and guarding Conrad's ferry and other points along the Potomac, at times encountering the fire of the Confederate pickets so fittingly expressed in the "Picket's Last Watch:"

> "All quiet along the Potomac," they say,
> "Except now and then a stray picket
> Is shot as he walks on his beat to and fro
> By a rifleman hid in the thicket."
> 'Tis nothing—a private or two, now and then,
> Will not count in the news of the battle.

Not an officer lost, only one of the men,
Moaning out all alone, his death-rattle.
* * * * *
All quiet along the Potomac, to-night;
No sound save the rush of the river.
While soft falls the dew on the face of the dead.
The picket's off duty forever.

Colonel Baker acting as Brigadier-General, in command of the brigade, left Lieutenant-Colonel Wistar in command of the regiment. About midnight October 20, 1861, Colonel Baker received, at brigade headquarters, the following order, and directed Colonel Wistar to put it into execution:

HEADQUARTERS }
CORPS OF OBSERVATION,
EDWARD'S FERRY, Oct. 20, '61, 11 P. M.

COLONEL: You will send the California Regiment (less the camp guard) to Conrad's ferry, to arrive there at sunrise and await orders. The men will take with them blankets and overcoats and forty rounds of ammunition in boxes, and will be followed by one day's rations in wagons. The remainder of the brigade will be held in readiness for marching orders (leaving camp guards) at 7 o'clock a. m., to-morrow, and will all have breakfasted before that hour.

Very respectfully,
Your most obedient servant,
CHAS. P. STONE,
Brigadier-General, commanding.

Colonel E. D. Baker, commanding Third Brigade.

This order was delivered by Captain Candy, Assistant Adjutant-General, and was followed by a verbal one, by the hands of Dr. J. L. Mackie, volunteer aid-de-camp, cautioning Colonel Baker to have the march conducted as silently as possible, with unloaded arms. Colonel Wistar, commanding the California Regiment, acted promptly in carrying out this order. While his encampment was wrapped in deep slumber, the silence unbroken save by the resolute tramp of the alert sentinel as his footfall echoed upon a chance wakeful ear, the shrill, clear peals of the bugle sounded the call "To arms," which suddenly aroused and animated every soldier to action. Every man grasped his gun, hurried on his equipments, and the once sleeping host was armed and in martial array awaiting orders. After partaking of hot coffee and hard tack, and receiving one day's rations, with cartridge boxes refilled, they moved off the field and disappeared in the darkness. As the cold, grey haze of morning broke on the horizon, the road on which they marched and various objects were faintly revealed. The first battalion, consisting of A, C, D, G, H, L, N and P, all the companies that were in camp at that time (the second battalion under Major Parrish being then on picket duty along the Monocacy river), reached Conrad's ferry about 7 a. m., and reported their arrival to General Stone by a mounted officer, and were ordered there to await further orders unless heavy firing was heard across the river, in which event to cross and support the Massachusetts troops on the Virginia shore. On the opposite side of the river, beyond Harrison's island, loomed up the gigantic heights of Ball's Bluff to be scaled, with the treacherous Potomac flowing swiftly but noiselessly at its base; and everything seemed wrapped in silence and mystery, at first broken only by the word of command, the marching of companies to their assigned positions for crossing, followed by the distant reports of small arms and the occasional echo of a bursting shell thrown from our guns on the island, as the low, sullen boom reverberated across the river. Of the crossing and the action that followed we will have occasion to speak hereafter.

At the battle of Ball's Bluff, Colonel Wistar was twice wounded; when he received his third wound, he was carried from the field, and was so near the borders of death that the bed sheets under him could not be changed for several weeks, considerable time elapsing before he was convalescent.

Upon his recovery, he was commissioned Colonel, for gallantry in action, although previous to that time the command of the regiment had devolved principally upon him. When General McClellan advanced up the Peninsula, in 1862, Colonel Wistar was again with his regiment, although not fully recovered from his wounds.

When the regiment moved out from the woods, in which they had been held all night, facing the enemy's works at Yorktown, as many supposed, with orders to charge the works at the first dawn of light, Colonel Wistar was helped upon his horse, and led the regiment in full view of the enemy's works, and continued on duty during the siege, and until after the battle of Williamsburg. While still suffering from his old wounds, he was taken down with the Peninsula fever, and remained in a critical condition for some time.

He was able to rejoin his regiment in time to take part in the battle of Antietam, where he led his men into the action, on the right of the line, about 10 o'clock on Monday, the 17th of September, in the neighborhood of the Dunkards' church, where the carnage became fearful, and death's harvest most bountiful, in the midst of which he fell seriously wounded, while advancing with his regiment to drive the enemy from a strong position. For hours afterward, the battle raged furiously over this ground, the contending troops swaying back and forth with varying success.

Colonel Wistar was at three different times within the enemy's lines, but was finally rescued by our forces gaining ground, and was carried off and cared for, having previously received both kind and questionable attention from some Confederate officers, then unknown to him, but whose names have since been learned.

While lying upon the field, losing blood freely, a lieutenant from a Georgia regiment demanded his sword. Colonel Wistar informed him that his sword

was in the possession of one of our officers, and that if
he wanted it, he had better join his regiment, and assist in capturing it. The lieutenant then demanded
his parole, and this the Colonel also refused to give,
stating that it was very possible he would again fall
into the hands of his friends. At that moment Generals
James A. Walker and J. E. B. Stuart, accompanied by
their staff, rode up, and Colonel Wistar beckoned to
the officers for assistance, when General Walker ordered
a young captain on Stuart's staff to go to his aid.

The young captain gave the tourniquet on the Colonel's arm an extra twist to stop the flow of blood, and
endeavored in other ways to make him comfortable,
and when he had learned how the Georgia lieutenant
had annoyed the Colonel, he reported it to General
Walker, who immediately ordered the lieutenant to his
regiment, accusing him of skulking. The young captain who so kindly offered this assistance was Mosby,
who afterward became notorious as a guerrilla.

Colonel Wistar was again promoted for gallantry,
this time to the rank of Brigadier-General, and, although both his arms were permanently crippled from
wounds, he continued in the service of his country.

In February, 1864, he commanded a column of cavalry and infantry, about 1500 strong, with orders to
raid upon Richmond, and release the Union prisoners
there. He pushed rapidly northward from New Kent
Court House to the Chickahominy, intending to cross
that stream at Bottom's Bridge, which he found too
strongly guarded, while beyond there appeared too
many evidences of strength to warrant him in attempting to cross—the enemy having been warned by a
culprit, who escaped from prison by bribery. He returned to New Kent without loss, his infantry having
marched eighty miles within fifty-six hours, and his
cavalry one hundred and fifty miles in fifty hours.

In the operation before Petersburg, he led a brigade,

and in the bloody battle at Drury's Bluff, his brigade formed the only part of General Butler's line, composed of the 10th and 18th Corps, which was able to hold its ground against Beauregard's sorties, and finally, when it retired, it did so under orders leisurely, with all its guns and colors.

He participated in all the operations of his corps down to and including the capture of Richmond, and was always at the post of duty. During the whole war few officers showed more skill and determined bravery, and but few suffered more from wounds received in battle.

CHAPTER III.

GENERAL STONE.

BRIGADIER-GENERAL CHARLES P. STONE, a gradu-
ate of West Point Military Academy, from the State of
Massachusetts, was accomplished and scholarly, a scion
of the Puritan stock of that commonwealth, which had
been honorably represented in every war in which the
American people had engaged. He, having served as
a lieutenant in the Mexican War with high credit, was
brevetted captain for meritorious service on the field.
In 1855 he resigned his commission, and became a citizen of the State of California. In the latter part of 1860,
while mutterings were loud and angry, just before the
breaking out of the Rebellion, we find Captain Stone
in Washington City, and in response to a request from
his old commander, General Scott, he rallied around
him the, loyal men of the District of Columbia, in defense of the Capitol, then thought to be in imminent
danger, especially so after the demonstration of the
mob in Baltimore.

As early as January, 1861, he was made Inspector-
General of the District, and at once commenced organizing and instructing volunteers. When Fort Sumter
was fired upon, he had under him not less than 3,000
well-organized troops fit for service, and on the 2d of
January, 1861, he had the honor of being the first man
mustered into the service for the defence of the Capitol,
commanding all the troops in Washington during the
dark days at the close of April, when the city was cut
off from the loyal people. During those seven days, he
slept but three hours in his bed, all other rest being
taken in his military cloak. All the outposts around

Washington were under his command, until the passage of a portion of the army into Virginia in May, in which some of his troops were the first to encounter the pickets of the enemy. His management and conduct was so warmly approved by the President that, when he directed the organization of eleven new regiments in the regular army, he appointed Captain Stone to the colonelcy of the 14th United States Infantry, and he afterward commanded a brigade under General Robert Patterson in his advance through the Shenandoah Valley in July, 1861, while General McDowell was advancing upon Manassas. After General McClellan had been called to the active command of the Army of the Potomac, General Stone, then commissioned Brigadier-General of volunteers, was selected to command a division of the army, to occupy the valley of the Potomac above Washington as a corps of observation. His orders from General McClellan contained the following expression of confidence: "I leave your operations much to your own discretion, in which I have the fullest confidence." He made his headquarters at Poolesville, Maryland, near Edward's Ferry, opposite to General Evans' headquarters at Leesburg, Virginia, where we find these two commanders guarding their respective sides of the Potomac, dividing their forces before the battle of Ball's Bluff.

4

DEFENSE

OF

COLONEL E. D. BAKER.

IN THE

BATTLE OF BALL'S BLUFF,

FOUGHT OCTOBER 21, 1861, IN VIRGINIA.

CHAPTER IV.

A BRIEF FORECAST OF COLONEL BAKER'S DEFENSE.

IN DEFENSE OF THE LATE COLONEL EDWARD D. BAKER, A
SENATOR OF THE UNITED STATES OF AMERICA, WHO
LOST HIS LIFE WHILE ENGAGED IN AN ADVANCE
UPON LEESBURG, UNDER THE DIRECTIONS
OF GENERAL CHARLES P. STONE.

OUT of respect to one who commanded the love and
affection of his followers as filially as any revered
parent could that of his children, I propose, as a
slight tribute, to recount some of the errors which have
crept into the public records, as insidiously as the silent
exhalations of the noxious miasma, affecting Colonel
Baker's character as a discreet and obedient military officer, at the battle of Ball's Bluff. If I can trace to its
source the hidden main-spring from which first trickled
in devious courses, with uncertain strength, the malevo-
lent data, gathering force as the channel deepened and
broadened, bearing on its bosom the evils of calumny, and
expose it to the light of day, how salutary the effect, if
corroborated by documentary proofs and incontrovertible
testimony! If in defense of truth and candor it becomes
necessary to speak plainly of another, when the evidence of wrong is undeniable, to lay open the secret re-
cesses of duplicity, or to unmask the dissimulations of
injustice, under such circumstances, the rising of a generous indignation can be excused, if not wholly approved. It is true that Stone has gone to his final rest,
and is no longer able to meet criticism. That was
equally true of the honored and gallant Baker, when
charged with misconduct, who had many admirers and
powerful friends, to whom the result of his one hasty

(53)

interview before the battle was never by him unfolded, for he could not then speak in his own defence. Unlike Stone, he never had "his day in court," although he left gaping wounds to appeal for him, had they but tongues, "poor, poor, dumb mouths" to speak for the silent one so eloquent—while Stone not only gave his ample time and talents to his defense, but exhausted all argument and device in support of his cause on many occasions, which are of public record. It is not my purpose to raise new issues, but simply to expose to the light of day that which has been said and printed, including much from Stone's pen, that produced false impressions, and so passed into history, without many facts in the case being made to appear. I trust that any honorably conceived desire to do justice to an old and loved commander, by presenting his side of the cause for the consideration of historians, with malice to none, will be favorably received. I propose to narrate some incidents and facts of very apparent preparation for an advance upon Leesburg, made by General Stone in compliance with the expressed desire of General McClellan, and as nearly as possible to fix the hour when Colonel Baker assumed command of the National troops at Ball's Bluff, after General Stone had made his preparations for, and had advanced at two points a considerable body of troops into Virginia, and to show how limited was the time given for deliberation before Colonel Baker was called into action—aye! he arrived amid the din and shock of battle, while from the field of deadly strife there came appeals for help from his countrymen to him most dear, National troops in great peril—a call which no brave man could resist, although under the existing circumstances, many would have paled at the thought of the perils by the way. Every pulsation of the heart urged the chivalrous Baker, nature's nobleman, to the rescue, and most nobly and wisely did he advance and do his whole duty to the last. Had another officer proved as devoted, intrepid and true, all would have been well. As dangers more thickly environed him and his devoted band, his courage grew, while others became hopeless; and when he saw that defeat was inevitable, and that a retreat must be disastrous and even more harrowing than the bloody scene before him, in a somewhat dejected, but deeply sympathetic spirit, he remarked to Colonel Wistar, "The officer who dies with his men will never be harshly judged." Would that it had been so! I propose to show by whose authority he acted on that sad and eventful day, and the true cause of the disaster, and upon whom should mainly rest the odium; and as far as it may be compatible with the liberty of discussion, reveal the cause which impelled the division commander to pursue the unenviable course which he mapped out, and the consequent effect thereof upon him up to the time he felt constrained to resign his commission in the army of the United States, and sail for distant shores.

It is apparent from the drift of some recent publications, that the baleful influence of the circumstances attending the arrest and imprisonment of General Stone, on the charge of disloyalty, coupled with his official utterances, have so worked upon the minds of writers as to cause them to give General Stone the place, in some of the historical works of the day, of that of the martyr in the disaster at Bull's Bluff, instead of that of the victim of his own acts and folly, which caused dire disaster to the troops of his command.

It is not with General Stone the suspect, suffering in close and solitary confinement, held for treason, deprived of his pocket money, and denied even an interview with the partner of his bosom, said to be in the deepest anguish, while the armed sentinel paced before his prison door, that we have to deal; but rather with Stone the general, his acts and deeds upon the field, and his official utterances and ulterior purposes affecting the reputation and character of the defenceless and honored dead, against whom he directly charged the cause of the disaster, and thus attempted to hold up to public gaze a pure, ardent and obedient officer as one who had distinctly violated the orders and instructions of his superior. Such a challenge requires courage and should be supported by the strongest facts and the severest logic—the most ample and unquestioned proof—when made against one whose highest ambition and glory was in the service and preservation of his adopted country, even to the shedding of his life's blood in her defense upon the field of battle. No mere technicality or subterfuge will suffice; the whole evidence must be facts clear and unquestioned, or the person thus essaying to divert attention, presumably in an effort to shield himself, not only courts the severest criticism of the public, but richly merits such condemnation as the circumstances of the case will warrant.

If General Stone, the commander, is adjudged blameless, for a blunder so plain that he who reads can see it, in which he sacrificed almost one thousand men, the pride and flower of the States from which they came, and thus cast discredit upon the national arms, the evidence of his innocence should be made apparent; he should not be acquitted by ex parte statements, by so shallow and fallacious a defense as he sets up in his official reports and utterances made use of by writers, in which he calls attention to the "distinct violation, by Colonel Baker, of his orders and instructions," without having these charges corroborated by facts, which of itself would indicate plainly the utter weakness of the defense, while a motive for such charges may be strongly presumed. Is such evidence permissible, while the accused is physically unable to reply in his defense? If so, the proceedings would be more arbi-

trary, and far less creditable, than the proceedings, so
much deprecated, under which General Stone was arrested and imprisoned for treason. Upon such evidence and by such means shall Colonel Baker be made
the scapegoat, while the real blunderer escapes to pose
as a martyr? Before coming definitely to a conclusion
whether it be General Stone, or Colonel Baker, that
should be most blamed for this blunder, and how far
General McClellan contributed thereto, let us look at
the facts and the evidence in the case. And while depre-
cating the summary arrest and incarceration of General
Stone, without allowing him the privilege of facing his
accusers and the right of self-defence, thus denying
him the inherent right of the humblest citizen of the
republic, we should not be so far carried away in sympathy for General Stone under harsh treatment—for
which Colonel Baker was wholly blameless—as to lose
sight of the facts attending the battle, and the conse-
quences of General Stone's official reports thereon,
affecting Colonel Baker's character, and what might be
the reflex therefrom.

We find that Colonel Baker is speechless in death,
while General Stone, the sole survivor of their one
hasty interview before the battle, is able to tell his tale,
and if so disposed, has the power to profit by the circumstances. He commands the division containing all
the troops that were in or near the engagement, with
autocratic rule, and by the friendly aid and approval
of his chief, he is master of the situation, equalled only
by the military despotism of Europe, if his plans and
purposes be not interfered with by a civil tribunal. All
the reports thereon must pass through his hands, and
the officers under him well know that it would be at
least an unpleasant thing to confront their superior
with distasteful facts; and if he be a regular army officer, it may be attended with many difficulties, as evi-
denced by Colonel Hinks' report to General Lander, and

forwarded by him to General Stone,* which contained the following: "I cannot close this report with justice to our troops, who fought valiantly, without commenting upon the causes which led to their defeat and complete rout. *The means of transportation (furnished by Stone), for advance in support or for retreat, were criminally deficient,* especially when we consider the facilities for creating proper means for such purposes at our disposal. The place for landing upon the Virginia shore (designated by Stone), was most unfortunately selected; * * *in fact no more unfortunate position could have been forced upon us by the enemy, for making an attack, much less selected by ourselves.*" It is needless to add that immediately upon the receipt of this report, General Stone had Colonel Hinks censured, in "General Orders, No. 24"† containing words of caution to other officers, *i. e.,* commanding officers are cautioned against making unnecessary and rash statements in their reports * * as from such statements not only great injustice may be done, but ill-will, most prejudicial to the good of the service, is certain to be engendered." "And also by the testimony of Captain Richardson, of the 7th Michigan Regiment, who, in answer to a question, testified,‡ "It is a military rule that a man must keep mum or have his head taken off. Our Major wrote a letter home, which unluckily happened to be published, in regard to the means of crossing we had (at Edward's Ferry) at the time of the Ball's Bluff affair. That letter got back somehow, and General Stone had him arrested for complaining about the facilities for crossing the river, though the letter did not mention General Stone at all. Through the instrumentality of our Colonel, he was not cashiered, but

* Official Records, Series I, Vol. V, page 314.
† Official Records, Series I, Vol. V, page 317.
‡ Report of Committee on Conduct of War, Part II, page 345.

was allowed to resign and go home. But there is no doubt that it was that unfortunate letter that was the cause of his having to go home." Therefore, officers must be deferential and discreet, in all things and at all times, whether it be in making official reports or in testifying before a civil tribunal; otherwise they will incur the ill-will and enmity of their commander. General Stone himself must prepare, from the reports of his subordinates, the principal and final report of the whole affair. Can we in justice to the honored dead, and to precedents of equity, rely wholly upon General Stone's reports? Should we not rather seek for facts and testimony to corroborate or disprove them, and likewise as to his ability and fitness to command, as shown on that occasion?

With such intentions in view, let us first glance at Stone's orders from General McClellan upon assuming command, August 12, 1861,* "Make such arrangements as will enable you, in the event of an attack in force, to fall back on General McCall, or to enable him to move up to your support at some strong position, which we can hold with the force at our disposal. *Should you see the opportunity of capturing or dispersing any small party by crossing the river, you are at liberty to do so, though great discretion is recommended in making such a movement.* * * I leave your operations much to your own discretion, in which I have the fullest confidence." And also at the topography of the territory where this scene was enacted, as viewed by well-known military men.

The battle-field at Ball's Bluff is distant from Leesburg, the objective point, about three miles, and at its base flows the Potomac river (dividing Maryland from Virginia), which runs almost north and south between Conrad and Edward's ferries, inclining to the eastward, with the Chesapeake and Ohio Canal skirting the

* Official Records, Series I, Vol. V, pages 557–559.

Maryland shore, on an elevated bed, on the east side
of the river—the ferries being about five miles apart,
between which, in the river, is Harrison's island, a
low, flat strip of ground, about three miles long, very
narrow, and about three hundred and fifty yards wide
opposite the bluff—the distance from the Maryland
shore to the island across the river below Conrad's
ferry, being from three hundred and fifty to four hundred yards, and that from the island to the Virginia
shore from two hundred to two hundred and fifty yards
wide, as marked by the courses of the boats.   Opposite
Harrison's island, on the Virginia shore, the ground
rises with great abruptness, for a distance of about one
hundred and fifty yards, and is studded with trees,
rocks and undergrowth, making it entirely impassable
to artillery or infantry in line; at the summit the surface is undulating, overlooking Harrison's island at an
altitude of about one hundred feet, from which the
island can be completely commanded and raked with
artillery and rifles at very short range, and likewise the
Maryland shore by artillery, for some distance inland.
At Edward's Ferry, these conditions were reversed;
the Maryland Heights completely commanded the Virginia shore and the adjacent ground for some distance
inland.   Edward's Ferry (like Conrad's ferry) was a
regular crossing place, as indicated, where the water
spread out, meeting no unusual obstruction, while
along the sides of Harrison's island the whole volume
of the stream, being crowded into narrower channels,
deepened the water and caused it to flow with greater
velocity, from three to five miles per hour, according to
the rainfall.

At the time General Stone's troops crossed, the river
had been swollen by recent rains, causing it to flow with
greater rapidity.   Viewed as crossing places for military operations, we find that troops could be embarked
at either Edward or Conrad's ferries, and debarked

upon the Virginia shore; while, at Harrison's island, crossing, they must disembark on the island, march across it, say three hundred and fifty yards, then re-embark for the Virginia shore, with all the attendant difficulties, disadvantages and loss of time at the additional landings, consuming about double the time required in crossing at either of the two ferries named. This is the place to which General Stone referred in his report,* *when he misstated that Colonel Baker was upon the field quite early in the morning, thereby producing a wrong impression,* i. e., "Colonel Baker, having arrived at Conrad's ferry with the First California regiment at an early hour in the morning, reported to me in person at Edward's ferry, stating that the regiment was at its assigned post" * * * "I decided to send him to Harrison's island to assume command." *Colonel Baker did not arrive with the California regiment; his orders were, "You will send the California regiment"—which he did. "The remainder of the brigade will be held in readiness for marching orders."* It was Colonel Wistar who reported early in the morning to Stone, which we will show by his testimony. Baker, of his own volition, reported at Stone's quarters between 10 and 11 a. m., and received his first order of the day, which he (Stone) varied somewhat in his first testimony,† i. e., "Colonel Baker came on the field in the morning; after I had made these dispositions (had sent Devens, Lee, Ward and cavalry scouts to the bluff), and I directed him to move to the right *and take control over there*, telling him all that had been done"—Stone having previously testified,‡ in answer to the question, "Were you in command there (Harrison's island) at the time of the fight at Ball's Buff? Answer: I was;

* Official Records, Series I, Vol. V, page 295.

† Report of Committee on Conduct of War, part 2, page 268.

‡ Report of Committee on Conduct of War, part 2, page 267.

yes, sir." Then we must conclude that Baker only had command on the Virginia shore, and that Stone was wholly responsible for the transportation and the crossing of troops, of which he has complained so bitterly and unjustly against Baker.

The means of transportation furnished by Stone, on the Maryland side, were two scows for crossing troops to the island, full capacity forty-five men each; on the Virginia side of the island, one scow, capacity about fifty men, one life-boat, capacity fifteen men, and two small skiffs, capacity four and five men each. The passage was necessarily very slow and tedious, under the most favorable circumstances, by the means above provided. The current was so strong that the flat-boats had to be poled up the Maryland shore quite a distance before being loaded, and then poled and floated diagonally across the stream until they touched the island shore, where they were again manœuvred in the same way and sent back by an opposite diagonal course. The crossing from the island to the Virginia shore, as well as that of returning the boats, was accomplished in the same manner. *Colonel*, afterward *General Wistar*, when before the Committee on the Conduct of the War,* was asked the question, "Were there means provided there to carry men over faster than one regiment on the other side could have killed off as they landed?" and, in answer, he described the boats as enumerated above, and in reply to the question, "How long did it take to cross from one side to the other, from the Maryland side to the Island, across the Island, and from the Island to the Virginia shore?"—he said,† "If you had gone right straight across, and found the boat ready on the Virginia side, I should say the trip would take about three-quarters of an hour." According to this estimate, which seems

* Report of Committee on Conduct of War, part 2, page 314.

† Report of Committee on Conduct of War, part 2, page 315.

to have been a very favorable one for General Stone, about 125 men could be crossed each hour to the Virginia shore. Other officers testified that an hour and a quarter was consumed in one round trip across one branch, and that it could not be made in less time on account of the swollen river, and imperfect means provided. Now we will find that General Stone had reported to General McClellan, first, that he could cross 250 men in ten minutes, and in a subsequent dispatch, he reduced this estimate to 125 men each ten minutes, and this latter estimate was the one which so grossly misled Colonel Baker; for we find that after Colonel Baker crossed to the Island, and saw what Colonel Wistar had accomplished by pushing the transportation to its utmost limit, he exclaimed, "*Is that all the men you have got across?*" Captain, afterwards Major Ritman, of the California Regiment, who, with Adjutant Newlin, of the same regiment, were ordered to take charge of the transportation on the Maryland side by Colonel Baker, "said that Colonel Baker told me that his orders stated that ample means of transportation had been provided, and were at hand, for shipping men and munitions of war, and that he was greatly surprised and annoyed when he arrived with orders to cross, and found little or no transportation at hand, and that he gave orders immediately to improve the means for crossing as speedily as possible."*

General Dana, who had been trained to a military life (who afterward served with marked distinction and success upon many a hard fought field), at the time of the affair at Ball's Bluff was Colonel of the 1st Minnesota Regiment, and in command of the troops on the Virginia side at Edward's ferry, testified† before the

* As related to the author, which agrees with Stone's testimony as to his opinion of the sufficiency of the means for crossing.

† Report of Committee on Conduct of War, 2, page 450.

committee, in reference to the different positions as follows: "Our position at Edward's ferry was far less dangerous than the position of our forces at Ball's Bluff, as
I have seen since. The enemy at Ball's Bluff, commanded our side of the river, at Edward's Ferry we commanded their side.

"Question. How? Answer. At Ball's Bluff the land
on the Virginia side is higher than on the Maryland
side, while at Edward's Ferry, the heights on the
Maryland side, with heavy artillery, commanded all of
the Virginia side of the river there."

General Dana had every opportunity of observing the
topography of the country at these points, while serving as Inspector-General of the Division, which duty devolved upon him immediately after the battle; but
before this testimony was given. Colonel Jenifer, a
Confederate officer in command at the Bluff remarked
to one of our officers (bearing a flag of truce after the
battle), *in reference to our troops having crossed at that
place,* "*What d—— fool sent you over here?*"

Now let us see what preparations General Stone had
made in anticipation of crossing the river. *He first
displayed engineering skill in building a fortification,
menacing an unguarded part of the enemy's line, a Gib-
raltar in itself.* This fortification was commanded by
Colonel Hinks on the day of the battle to which he referred in his report to General Stone, saying, "which
ditch and breastwork were made under your personal
direction," and concerning which he testified before
the committee,* in answer to the

"*Question.* How much higher than the island is
the bluff on the Virginia shore opposite to where you
were?

"*Answer.* I should say that it was from 100 to 125
feet; that would be my estimate. The island is very
flat, with no undulations upon its surface. It is very
remarkable for that.

* Report of Committee on Conduct of War, 2, page 441.

"*Question.* So you were fully exposed?

"*Answer.* Entirely exposed.

"*Question.* The crossing was effected by Baker's order, was it not?

"*Answer.* I think not; my impression is that it was not.

"*Question.* What was your condition, suppose the enemy had come on the Virginia side with artillery while you were on the island?

"*Answer.* It would have been very precarious, indeed, either with artillery or with rifles. It has always been a wonder to us all, why they suffered us to remain there, with less than 1,100 men, exposed as we were, for thirty-six hours. There was no position on the island they could not reach with rifles."

This opinion was concurred in by all the officers who were upon the island, and agrees with General Dana's opinion.

General Stone also prepared a flotilla for crossing troops over the Potomac, and reported that he had constructed five new flat-boats, four twenty-five feet long, twelve feet wide, and two feet deep; one twenty-seven feet long, twelve feet wide, and two feet deep. Three of these boats were used by General Gorman at Edward's ferry, and the remaining two by Colonels Devens, Lee and Baker at Harrison's island. In reference to these boats, Philip Hanger testified under oath, before the committee,* as follows:

"*Question.* Where do you reside?

"*Answer.* At Edward's Ferry.

"*Question.* Were you there at the time the battle took place, at Ball's Bluff?

"*Answer.* Yes sir, I was at Edward's Ferry.

"*Question.* Do you know anything of the boats that were provided for the transportation of our troops at the time of the battle of Ball's Bluff?

* Report of Committee on Conduct of War, 2, page 345.

"*Answer*. I know there were five scows built back of my warehouse, out of sight of the Rebels.

"*Question*. Are you familiar with boats, and boat building?

"*Answer*. I have had more or less to do with boats and their management for a great many years on the Susquehanna, and some on the Potomac at different times.

"*Question*. Will you describe the boats that were built there?

"*Answer*. The Lieutenant who had charge of the boats told me that they were to be twenty-five feet in length, and from eleven to twelve feet in width. They would vary a little from that, perhaps, from cutting the lumber to advantage. They were to be of flat bottoms, the sides from twenty-one to twenty-two inches in depth, with rather a steep rake at the ends, which would of course make them shorter on the bottom floor than at the top. *They were very flimsy affairs, as I thought, and I considered them unsafe for crossing troops in, as that is what I was told they were for.* I said to the same Lieutenant that the same quantity of lumber put in two boats eighty feet long, and just wide enough to pass out of the locks, *would be worth more than a dozen such as he was making.*

"*Question*. Was General Stone there looking at them, and directing their construction?

"*Answer*. I am positive that General Stone was there on three different occasions, and conversed with the Lieutenant in regard to them. There is not a shadow of a doubt that they were built under his eye and direction, from the fact that he was down there several times.

"*Question*. Were these same scows, that were built there used in crossing the troops there?

"*Answer*. One was used there at Edward's Ferry, and some of them up at Ball's Bluff, and some perhaps were down the river.

"*Question.* Were these scows not totally inadequate to the purpose for which they were constructed?

"*Answer.* I deemed at the time they were entirely inadequate, and that was the reason I gave my opinion to that effect, in advance of their going into the water.

"*Question.* You say you suppose these scows were used at Ball's Bluff?

"*Answer.* The men told me so, and I saw them up there."

The fact that not one of these boats had strong enough bottom to safely cross artillery in, is also in evidence, and Major Ritman also related "that he, under Colonel Baker's orders, launched from the canal into the river the only boat that was strong enough for shipping artillery and horses, while Colonel Baker was having a rope stretched across the river."

CHAPTER V.

GENERAL STONE reported to General McClellan, October 19, 1861,* giving him information obtained from a deserter of the 13th Mississippi, Colonel Barksdale's Regiment, as follows:

On Wednesday night there was an alarm that General Stone was crossing the river, and the trains were all brought from Leesburg to Goose creek, that he heard them say all the heavy baggage was in the trains, and that the troops would fight at Leesburg, and then if defeated fall back to Widow Carter's mill, below Goose creek, where they would make another stand, and if defeated there, they would fall back to Manassas; that the wagons were all kept ready to start for Manassas." * * "I believe the fellow's story. The evidences of the alarm he mentions were apparent, and it was probably induced by my strengthening my force on Harrison's Island, and making use of a large flat boat there ; the' place he mentions as the second for a stand (Widow Carter's mill) is a strong position, about one mile from Aldie, on the road from Leesburg to Gum Spring." * * "*I have prepared slight intrenchments on Harrison's Island, capable of covering several hundred men, sufficient to cover an advance of a considerable force to the Island, and to hold it for an hour or two, in spite of any artillery which might be placed on the commanding ground on the Virginia side.* CHARLES. P. STONE,
"*Brigadier-General, Commanding.*"

On the 19th, the same day that General McClellan received this report from General Stone, he ordered General McCall with his strong division to Dranesville,

* Official Records, Series I, Vol V, page 292.

(68)

where he promptly arrived, and threw out strong re-
connaissances to learn what he could of the enemy, and
to gain knowledge of the country.*

On the morning of the 20th (Sunday), General Mc-
Clellan received the following from General Banks'
headquarters.†

DARNESTOWN, October 20, 1861.

SIR: The signal station at Sugar Loaf telegraphs that the
enemy have moved away from Leesburg. All quiet here.

R. M. COPELAND,
Acting Assistant Adjutant-General.

On the 20th, the day General McClellan received this
dispatch from General Banks' headquarters, he ordered
General Smith with his division to act in concert with
General McCall, and to push "strong parties from his
division to Freedom Hill, Vienna, Flint Hill, Peacock
Hill, etc., to accomplish the same purpose in that part
of the front."‡

The following will explain this movement of the
Confederate forces. General Evans, in command at
Leesburg, learned on the evening of the 19th that
General McCall was advancing. Before daybreak on
the 20th, he drew his men up in line of battle and addressed them thus: "Gentlemen, the enemy are approaching by the Dranesville road, 16,000 strong, with
twenty pieces of artillery. They want to cut off our
retreat. Re-enforcements can't arrive in time, if they
were sent. We must fight." His command was at
once put in motion across Goose creek and along the
Dranesville road, anticipating a desperate engagement
with General McCall's column, reported to him to be
moving in that direction.

After McCall and Smith's divisions had marched,

* Official Records, Series I, Vol. V, page 32.
† Official Records, Series I, Vol. V, page 32.
‡ Official Records, Series I, Vol. V, page 32.

General McClellan sent to General Stone the following telegram:*

CAMP GRIFFIN, October 20, 1861.

General McClellan desires me to inform you that General McCall occupied Dranesville yesterday, and is still there. Will send out heavy reconnaissance, to-day, in all directions from that point. *The General desires that you will keep a good outlook upon Leesburg, to see if this movement has the effect to drive them away. Perhaps a slight demonstration on your part would have the effect to move them.*   A. V. COLBOURN,
Assistant Adjutant-General.

Comte de Paris, one of General McClellan's aides, writes: "McClellan had allowed too great a latitude to Stone by directing him to keep a watch over Leesburg, which could not have been done without crossing the Potomac."

When General McClellan had received General Banks' dispatch and had transmitted the above to General Stone, he asked of General Stone the probable number of the enemy before him and his means of transportation at hand for crossing the river. General Stone sent the following dispatch on Sunday night:†

POOLSVILLE, October 20, 1861.

MAJOR-GENERAL McCLELLAN: Made a feint of crossing at this place this afternoon, and at the same time started a reconnoitering party toward Leesburg from Harrison's island. Enemy's pickets retired to intrenchments. Report of reconnoitering party not yet received. Have means of crossing 125 men once in ten minutes at each of two points. River falling slowly.   CHAS. P. STONE,
Brigadier-General.

This correction of Stone's means of transportation seems to have been made after he had sent the reconnoitering party toward Leesburg, and was most probably the second dispatch upon the same subject,

* Official Records, Series I, Vol. V, page 32.

† Official Records, Series I, Vol. V, page 33.

for he testified under oath before the committee* in answer to the question, "Was General McClellan informed of your means of transportation for crossing troops" * * * "*I replied to him by telegraph, stating the number and character of the boats at each crossing, at Edward's Ferry and at Harrison's Landing.* In connection with that, I would say that from my dispatch of the previous evening (Sunday), *General McClellan might have supposed that those boats were of somewhat larger capacity than they really were.* In that dispatch, after reporting the demonstration I had made (on Sunday), *I reported that I had means of crossing 250 men in ten minutes at two points.* This estimate was made from a trial which I had made, on Sunday, at Edward's Ferry, of the boats there, which were of the same character as those used at Ball's Bluff."

No trial had been made on Sunday at Harrison's island, and, as afterward demonstrated, the difficulties were infinitely greater than at Edward's Ferry; hence after General Stone had sent his reconnoitering party across at Harrison's island, he reported to General McClellan, "I have means of crossing 125 men once in ten minutes at each of two points. River falling slowly."

When General Stone's means of transportation were fully tested on Monday, it was clearly demonstrated that he was again mistaken, that he could not under the most favorable circumstances, with no enemy to oppose him, cross to Ball's Bluff on an average more than 125 men each hour, and after another large boat (the only one in which artillery could be safely carried), had been added by Colonel Baker, and a cable stretched from the Maryland shore to the island, thus greatly improving the transportation.

Quartermaster Church Howe, of the 15th Massa-

* Report of Committee on Conduct of War, pages 489 and 490.

chusetts, who espoused General Stone's side of the case, testified before the Committee as follows:*

"*Question.* Of course you knew that a defeat would be disastrous, with the means of transportation you had?

"*Answer.* Yes sir, though our transportation was a great deal better than the management of it. * * There . was transportation, if rightly managed, to carry 200 men over in an hour."

In reference to this transportation, Captain Merritt, of the 19th Massachusetts, testified before the Committee as follows:†

"*Question.* Were you present at the battle of Ball's Bluff?

"*Answer.* My regiment did not cross the river; they crossed on to the island. My company was the first company that crossed to the island. I was there for three weeks before the fight, and my men were at work on the Island removing hay, under the superintendence of General Stone, and digging intrenchments, and assisting in getting the boats that General Stone brought there into the river from the canal.

"*Question.* What do you think of the means of transportation at the time of that battle?

"*Answer.* In my opinion, it was very poor: not sufficient.

"*Question.* Was not the transportation most manifestly insufficient?

"*Answer.* It was indeed. Another thing, there was no one there to take charge of them. General Stone was there several times in the night for days before the fight. And on the morning of the fight, after our folks had crossed, my men had to go and cut little trees there to get poles to push the boats across, what few poles they did have.

* Report of Committee on Conduct of War, 2, page 378.

† Report of Committee on Conduct of War, 2, page 421.

"*Question.* How were these boats manned ?

"*Answer.* They were very insufficiently manned, for the reason that we knew nothing about manning the boats until the time arrived for them to cross, and the men were then taken promiscuously from the companies, and consequently they took those that were unacquainted with boating. I think there might have been men picked out there who would have manned the boats very well. But our men were very green indeed, at that matter. In order to get poles long enough, the men had to cut down very sizable trees, and that made the poles so heavy as to make them almost unmanageable. *And until late in the afternoon, when Colonel Hinks had ropes stretched across there, no boat could make the passage from the Maryland shore to the island, across and back, in less than an hour and a quarter.*

"*Question.* What military reason could a man have for sending troops across there with only such means of transportation as you had? Was it not culpable neglect?

"*Answer.* It was criminal neglect, I call it. I thought so at the time. My first Lieutenant, on Sunday morning, remarked to me that if we undertook to cross there with the means for transportation we had, there would be a disaster. He remarked that there was no provision for a retreat, if we had to retreat.

"*Question.* Do you know anything about the swamping of the boat there?

"*Answer.* Some of my regiment were on the boat that was swamped, but not of my company. Company 'F' manned the boat on the Virginia side of the island. I was on the island at the time the boat was swamped. The way I understood and believed it to have been done was this: they had about thirty wounded persons in the boat to bring across, and Colonel Devens gave the order to his men to save themselves the best way they could.   A rush was made for the boat, and she careened and went down immediately.''

General McCall also testified before the committee, saying,* that *"General Stone had misstated unintentionally, no doubt, one or two things in his report.* It was proved afterward that he had not the means to cross at all; he could not have crossed in the face of the foe.''

The intent of this research being more particularly to direct attention to orders, incidents and circumstances immediately before and after the battle of Ball's Bluff (including that which may now be gleaned from the public records and the official Confederate reports) and to aid all who may be interested in judging for themselves who was most to blame for that disaster, we will refer to some of the incidents.

At first General Stone was roundly accused and charged through the public press not only with disloyalty, but most unjustly with the premeditated murder of Colonel Baker.   Although the carelessness and false generalship displayed by Stone, coupled with the expression made by Colonel Baker in a social chat with Major Robert Parish, of the California regiment, that "President Lincoln has given me the commission of a Major-General in the army,† to be announced and used by me at my discretion * * * but such are the jealousies against me entertained by the regular army officers,

* Report of Committee on Conduct of War, 2, page 261.

† Colonel Baker received the appointment of Brigadier-General U. S. volunteers, August 6, 1861, to rank from May 17, 1861. This he declined August 31, 1861. On September 21, 1861, he was appointed Major-General U. S. volunteers, but at the time of his death he had neither accepted nor declined the appointment. General McClellan was then the only other officer in the Army of the Potomac holding that rank.—*Editors "Battles and Leaders of the Civil War."*

that I do not expect to survive the first battle,"* were
well calculated to produce such an impression upon the
public. After a more thorough and careful investigation of the whole matter by cooler heads and under less
perturbed conditions, General Stone's loyalty was
found to be above suspicion, and the charge of premeditated murder likewise groundless. Would that after
light had cast so friendly a shade upon his character
for candor and fairness in dealing with his subordinates and for good generalship upon the field!

After General Stone had been held in close confinement for some time, without charges having been preferred or a trial granted him, a sympathetic reaction set
in, and, as is often the case, the tide of public opinion
surged too far the other way, covering up and over-
shadowing important facts in the case, to the detriment
of Colonel Baker. Some thought that Colonel Baker
was too willing a victim to the ill-devised plans and
movements of General Stone, whose plans and
directions a more wary officer would have questioned
before putting them into execution. No doubt Colonel
Baker felt that in a great measure the safety of the
troops which General Stone had crossed, and promised
to advance from Edward's Ferry, depended upon his cel-
erity, and close co-operation from the Bluff, and likewise
have an important bearing upon the movements of troops
under General McCall. It may be truthfully said of Colonel Baker that he was subordinate to General Stone,
and did his whole duty to his country, and most
loyally to his commander, without a question.

It has been reported that General Grant, in com-
mending the soldierly qualities of General Ord, said of
him, "He was one of the few who always did more
than was expected of him," and such would have been
the meed of praise bestowed upon Colonel Baker had
General Grant commanded in the place of General

* See statement in full, Post.

Stone; for a decided victory would have been achieved, beyond a doubt, by the close co-operation of the troops from Edward's Ferry, notwithstanding the meagre transportation. Instead of praise and merited commendation, we find that General Stone preferred charges against Colonel Baker.

Let us briefly consider these charges before going further into the history of the case, and thereafter see if the facts and testimony will support them, or whether it will appear that General Stone, upon second thought, intended to shield himself by casting upon a subordinate officer the odium of the disaster; if so, he had not decided upon that line of defence, when he wrote his despatch of 9:30 p. m., on the 21st, to his chief,* in which he said, "All was reported going well up to Baker's death, but in the confusion following that, the right wing was outflanked." *Neither in this despatch, nor in any of the four despatches sent by him to General McClellan that day, did he breathe the slightest suspicion of anything being done other than by his orders.* May we not take that as an assurance that there was then no thought in his mind that Colonel Baker had acted other than by his orders? Nor does it appear that he had such a thought for hours after the close of the battle. General Stone seems to have conveyed a wrong impression by his reports made previous to giving his testimony. He was no doubt in command of the forces at both crossings, on the Maryland side; one of his staff officers spent the whole day between his headquarters and Conrad's ferry, and his Chief-of-Staff was on the battlefield at the Bluff, and gave orders to Colonel Hinks on Harrison's Island in the name of General Stone.

General Dana and Major Bannister, of General Gorman's staff, have testified that General Stone was in command at both crossings, and the clinching testimony comes from Stone himself in answer to the

* Official Records, Series I, Vol. V, page 34.

"Question,* Were you in command there (Harrison's Island) at the time of the fight at Ball's Bluff?

"Answer, I was; yes sir."

This will surely set at rest all doubt upon that question,† therefore he should have directed all that was going on at both places, including transportation and re-enforcements. *No doubt both he and Colonel Baker thought they were acting strictly in accord with the wishes of McClellan, who had been informed of the crossing by Stone,* and of all the movements he was making, to which McClellan replied, "*I congratulate you and your command.*" General McClellan had dispatched Stone about 12 m., on Monday, the 21st, "*I may order you to take Leesburg to-day. Shall I push up one or two divisions from this side?*" to which Stone replied, declining assistance, "*I think I can take Leesburg,*" he thinking that McCall was near him, and that their forces "would be all-sufficient, and if that was not sufficient, then it was too late for any other division to come up." He also received a despatch in cipher, to which he replied, "I have received the box, but have no key."‡ General McClellan even telegraphed, "*Take Leesburg.*"||

He (McClellan) arrived at Edward's Ferry on the night of the 22d, and it must be observed that he uttered not one word of censure, and after conferring with Stone, telegraphed the President, "I have investigated this matter, and General Stone is without blame: had his orders been followed, there could or would have

---

* Report of Committee on Conduct of War, 2, page 267.

† Stone gave this testimony January 5, 1862, some time after all of his voluminous and varied official reports had been made, *i. e.*, October 29, November 2, December 2, 1861.

‡ Report of Committee on Conduct of War, pages 488-89.

|| Curiously enough this dispatch being in cipher, could not be read by General Stone, who replied, "I have the box, but not the key." At first it was supposed to refer to a box, and I

been no disaster." But some eighteen months thereafter, General McClellan testified, in relation to this
dispatch, "I think no formal investigation was ever
made," and he then evidently concluded that General
Stone was responsible, and almost the sole cause of the
disaster. After General McClellan had exonerated
General Stone, he (Stone) made his report of October
29, in which he stated that the disaster had been
caused by the bad management of the transportation,
that "at least 1000 more men should have been gotten
across"—enough, he claimed, "to have turned the
scale in our favor."* At the same time he had at least
three times that number standing at Edward's ferry,
on the Virginia shore, within two and one half miles of
the fight, idly listening to the engagement, and
anxiously awaiting orders to advance, and engage the
enemy.

In another report of November 2d, after reflecting
upon Colonel Baker's management upon the field,
General Stone takes stronger ground, and assumes
a much bolder front by reporting,† "*The plain truth is
that this brave and impetuous officer was determined, at
all hazards, to bring on an action, and made use of the
discretion allowed him to do it.*"

We will learn by the testimony and from General
Stone's subsequent statements under oath, how completely this charge is refuted—that the action was
brought on by Stone placing about nine hundred men
and two pieces of artillery on the Virginia bluff, *with-*

was sent to General Stone's family for the key, of course to
no purpose. General McClellan says he "thinks notice was
sent to General Stone of McCall's withdrawal from Dranesville.
He has a right to think, but the fact remains that no such notice was sent. I state this of my own knowledge."—*Colonel
Richard B. Irwin, "Battles and Leaders of Civil War."*

* Official Records, Series I, Vol. V, page 297.

† Official Records, Series I, Vol. V, page 302.

out the means for retreat, in the face of the enemy, which force he ordered to remain there after they had been attacked, and that he directed Colonel Baker to cross, and not yield the ground they held without resistance, and to occupy Leesburg if he could.

We will find that General Stone carefully designated the place at which the troops were to cross and the ground that Colonel Lee was to hold with one company, or 100 men, *i. e.,* "to occupy the heights on the Virginia shore after Colonel Devens' departure, to cover his return." We will also find that Colonel Devens is to decide whether to remain on the Virginia shore or return to the island; who testified, "I deemed it prudent to fall back to the bluff where Colonel Lee was;" who testified, "I concluded that he (Devens) intended to fight. I accordingly addressed a note to Major Revere, and sent it over to the island, saying: 'Colonel Devens has fallen back on my position; we are determined to fight.'" "Then a message came from General Stone, between 8 and 9 a. m., that I (Devens) was to remain where I was; that I would be re-enforced." Colonel Ward,* with the balance of the 15th Massachusetts, and Major Revere, with the balance of the 20th Massachusetts, crossed to his support, with two howitzers—all of which was reported to Stone. Then Colonel Devens reported to Stone, "that we were fully discovered, but that I was still in my old position," to which Stone replied, "Very well; Colonel Baker will come and take command." Baker himself so stated to Howe, and Stone told Howe that he had ordered Baker to cross. Stone testified, "I directed him (Baker) to hold on there (on the bluff), and of course not to yield ground we had taken possession of without resistance." Colonel Baker crossed to the bluff, between 1 and 2 p. m., just before Devens fell

---

* Who fell at Gettysburg, July 2, 1863, not far from the site where the 71st Pennsylvania erected their monument.

back on the bluff the second time, and he did "hold on
there," as directed by Stone, placing Colonel Devens
on the right, which was shortly thereafter heavily assailed, Wistar on the left, leaving Colonel Lee's troops
as he found them.   Devens testified, "He (Baker) said
that we must hold on there (Stone had so ordered); that
re-enforcements would come to us at the rate of about
so many hundred an hour," which Stone had fixed at
750 per hour.   This shows conclusively that the position held by Baker upon the bluff was selected by
Stone, and was held by Baker under Stone's orders.
Can we think Stone just in censuring Baker for bringing on the action at all hazards, and for posting the
troops or keeping them just where Stone had ordered
him to hold them, and for not yielding the ground
"we had taken possession of?"   The above shows that
Baker and Stone understood each other as to these orders before Baker's death; of whom Stone testified,*
"Colonel Baker came on the field in the morning after
I had made this disposition, and I directed him to
move to the right and take control over there, telling
him all that had been done."   We will see that Baker
left Stone's headquarters with orders, about 11 a. m.
Notwithstanding all this testimony of record, Stone
had previously reported, November 2, 1861,† "At
about 7 o'clock in the morning there were between
Harrison's island and Leesburg, on the Virginia side,
only seven companies of our troops (five of the 15th
and two of the 20th Massachusetts), which, under the
cover of two guns then on the island, of four guns on
the Maryland shore, and the large infantry force there,
might easily have been withdrawn, even in the face of
a largely superior force, and with the means of transportation which I knew to be there"   *   *   *   "and

* Report of Committee on Conduct of War, page 268.
† Official Records, Series I, Vol. V, page 300.

Colonel Baker left me at Edward's Ferry" * * *
"with full (discretionary) power to withdraw it."
This is in keeping with Stone's first report:* "Colonel
Baker, having arrived at Conrad's Ferry with the First
California regiment at an early hour in the morning,
reported in person to me." If Stone did not intend to
convey to his superiors by these reports the idea that he
had given Colonel Baker these orders very early in the
morning, what does he mean? It has and will be shown
beyond a doubt that Stone, after 7 a. m., ordered Devens
to remain upon the bluff, and there re-enforced him up to
11 a. m., when Baker left Stone's quarters for the bluff
with instructions from Stone, *i. e.*, "I directed him to
hold on there, and of course not to yield the ground we
had taken possession of without resistance."† Can
these two reports be frank and generous avowals of
facts without prejudice to the honored dead, or has the
General dissimulated with an intent to shield himself
beneath the bullet-pierced mantle of his brave subordinate? We will leave the reader to judge, after giving
the impression produced upon Colonel Van Allen,‡
who testified, in answer to the question, " Do you know
at what time General Baker was ordered to take command over there?

"*Answer.* I do not; I think it was five o'clock in
the morning."

General Stone further reported:|| " Had his eye for
advantage of ground in posting his troops equalled his
daring courage, he would have been, to-day, an honored, victorious general of the republic, instead of a
lamented statesman, lost too soon to the country."
When viewed by the light of the above facts and testimony, can these charges come with much force from a
general who directed the crossing at such a place with

---

* Official Records, Series I, Vol. V, page 295.

† Report of Committee on Conduct of War, 2, page 269.

‡ Report of Committee on Conduct of War, 2, page 461.

|| Official Records, Series I, Vol. V, page 302.

little or no transportation, and who had fortified Harrison's Island to hold the opposite bluff frowning upon
it from an altitude of 100 to 125 feet, and who did not
venture his person upon the bluff, or even upon the
island, during the action, for which he was censured
by the Committee on the Conduct of the War.

Colonel Lee testified* to the question, "What was
the conduct and bearing of Colonel Baker from the
time he came on the field until he fell?

"*Answer*. I think his bearing was that of a cool,
gallant and chivalric soldier.

"*Question*. He was cool and self-possessed?

"*Answer*. Perfectly so."

And Major Revere testified to the same effect, they
knowing whereof they spoke, having been with him
upon the field; and they further testified that the main
battle commenced very shortly after Colonel Baker arrived upon the field, that he did not have an opportunity to reconnoitre the ground, that the centre of the
line was well-placed, commanding a road, and that the
disaster resulted chiefly from the insufficiency of transportation; that the enemy far outnumbered our men,
in which latter all the officers upon the ground agreed
beyond a doubt, and Colonel Cogswell reported,†
"Colonel Baker welcomed me on the field, seemed in
good spirits, and very confident of a successful day."

Colonel Lee, of the 20th Massachusetts, with whom
Captain Bartlett served, has told us,‡ "I disposed of
my men in the best manner I could to cover the passage of the river, for that was still my duty, as I had
no further orders than to maintain my position there
on the bluff as a covering party for Colonel Devens."
* * * "I had reconnoitered it very carefully indeed. Colonel Baker left my command mainly as it

* Report of Committee on Conduct of War, 2, page 436.
† Official Records, Series I, Vol. V, page 321.
‡ Report of Committee on Conduct of War, 2, page 473.

was." * * * "'There was a little ridge just in front of us, a ridge which extended across the bluff." * * * "On our right we had been attacked very sharply." * * * "The firing was pretty heavy on our right." * * * "I moved my own line in advance to this ridge." * * "'The whole line delivered their fire." * * * "My men fell back steadily a short distance, perhaps ten feet; the ground there descending a little, where they loaded, and at the order, moved forward again very steadily." * * * "We had been obliged to move two companies of my own regiment from the line in the rear of us in order to take the place of companies in the front, which had been decimated or broken up by the fire." * * * "I think the centre line of battle was well placed. I think where I commanded myself was well placed, it was an open space that commanded the road.

"*Question.* Was there not a bluff on the left that protected the enemy from view until they got close to you?

"*Answer.* No sir; there was a ravine in the woods on our left."

This testimony was corroborated by Captain Bartlett's Major (Revere).* They also testified that the right of the 15th Massachusetts was well placed, and that the left (in support of the two howitzers), being on the lower ground, could not maintain a fire to assist Baker's extreme left while in that position.

We should not assume that Stone had received any early information from Colonel Cogswell, a prisoner of war, whose report was not made until nine months after Stone had finished his protracted reports, although Cogswell reported (September 22, 1862)† when he had crossed to the bluff after 2 p. m.: "At this time

* Report of Committee on Conduct of War, 2, page 486.
† Official Records, Series I, Vol. V, page 320.

the enemy was maintaining a fire of musketry on the boats from a wooded hill on our right, and to disperse them I ordered (my company C) to move to the right and front and brush them away, which was handsomely executed; thus the passage of the second branch was made secure from that quarter." * * * "I ascended the bluff." * * * "I found Colonel Baker near the bluff on the edge of an open field * * * the shortest parallel side near the edge of the bluff, and along this line was the 1st California regiment, while the 15th Massachusetts regiment was formed in line in the open woods forming the right hand boundary of the field, its line being nearly perpendicular to that of the California regiment. Two mountain howitzers * * * were posted in front of the angle formed by these two regiments. A deep ravine, having its mouth on the left of the point where we landed, extended along the left of the open field, and wound around in front of it, forming nearly a semicircle, bounded by wooded hills, commanding the whole open space." * * * "Some companies of the 20th Massachusetts were posted, in reserve, behind the line of the California regiment. I advised an immediate advance of the whole force to occupy the hills, which were not then occupied by the enemy." It should be observed that Cogswell had not been upon these hills to the left, and could not speak from experience. Therefore, let us see what the Confederate Colonel Jenifer reported:* "At 12 o'clock you sent the 8th Virginia regiment * * * to my support (which he lost sight of in the woods). At 1:30 o'clock I left my position on the left, and rode through the thick woods to where Colonel Hunton's regiment was stationed (just back of the edge of the hills), to the left of the Federal line.†

* Official Records, Series I, Vol. V, page 368.

† See Colonel Hunton's Report; Official Records, Series I, Vol. V, page 366.

I also suggested to him (Hunton) to make his men crawl on their hands and knees to the brow of the hill just in front, in order to make a more successful attack on the enemy" * * * "fifty or sixty yards distant," where Colonel Griffin, of the 18th Mississippi, found them, and* said they "'went into action between 1 and 2 p. m., and fought the enemy for more than an hour' * * * and that 'the Federalists were strongly posted * * * on an eminence, with the open field in front; their right protected by woods, and their left by woods and a deep ravine,'" when he came into action on the right of the 8th Virginia, at about 2:30 p. m.

We have learned that Colonel Baker was directed by Stone "to hold on there" on the bluff where he had placed Lee, and that he had no apparent authority to advance until Cogswell arrived on the field about 2:30 p. m., with the 11:50 a. m. order, *i. e.*, "If you can push them, you may do so, so far as to have a strong position near Leesburg, if you can keep them before you," which was Colonel Baker's first authority to move from that position, as indicated by the communication.

Cogswell reported, "I told him (Baker) that the whole action must be on our left, and that we must occupy those hills. No attention was apparently paid to this advice." Colonel Wistar, who had been put in command upon the left, has told us in his testimony,† "I took one company of my own skirmishers, and directed them to advance in open order to a hill, so as to see what they could ascertain of the enemy's position and strength. Just as they were about moving out, Colonel Baker and Cogswell came up to me (with 11:50 a. m. order, when Baker read it). Colonel

* Official Records, Series I, Vol. V, page 365.

† Report of Committee on Conduct of War, 2, page 308.

Baker said, "Colonel Wistar, I want you to send out two of your best skirmishing companies to the front and feel the enemy's position. * * * Make a thorough reconnaissance." * * * "They had (the first company), got about ten paces in the woods and I was about thirty paces behind with the second company, when the whole 8th Virginia Regiment rose up from the ground about thirty paces off, and ran right at them with the bayonet, without firing a shot." (Thus the main action commenced.) "*In the meantime, at the first fire, Colonel Baker moved up his reserve, and extended our left with it, so that we were then all in position.* The action then went on." This proves that Colonel Wistar found the 8th Virginia lying down where Colonel Jenifer said they were at 1:30 p. m., along the brow of the hill. Colonel Hunton placed them near the brow of the hill at a much earlier hour than 1:30 p. m., as shown by his report, so we must conclude that Cogswell was mistaken when he reported that at 2:30 p. m., "the hills * * * were not then occupied by the enemy,"* and that "No attention was apparently paid to his advice."

General Stone appended to his final report of December 2, 1861, seven concise statements, or declarations,† as follows:

"First. General Stone directed Colonel Baker to go the right, and in his discretion to recall the troops then over the river, or to cross more force. Colonel Baker made up his mind, and declared it before he

---

* Colonel E. V. White (Confederate), of whom we will have occasion to speak more than once, has informed the author: "The Confederate forces were not at Edward's ferry, but a mile or more up the river." * * * "I should suppose about 2 o'clock (p. m.) nearly all of our people were withdrawn from before Gorman," and that there was "nothing but the Confederate forces" between Baker and Gorman's forces, the distance between the two latter being about two and one-half miles.

† Official Records, Series I, Vol. V, page 307.

reached the crossing-place, to cross with his whole force."

Lieutenant Howe tells us General Stone informed him that he had given Colonel Baker orders to cross, which is corroborated by Colonels Lee and Devens, Major Revere, and others. We will learn that to have withdrawn the troops in the face of the enemy would have been disastrous, at the time Baker arrived opposite Harrison's Island with orders, not only to the troops on the bluff, but most probably to those across at Edward's Ferry, and the ground would have been yielded without the resistance which Colonel Baker was ordered by Stone to make,

Let us take what light we can get from General McClellan's headquarters, reflected by Comte de Paris, one of the chief's aides, who advanced to Dranesville with General McCall. Although, at the time he wrote, he did not know the true inwardness of the whole affair, but correctly wrote, "Stone, convinced that the enemy was not in force at Leesburg, thought he might make a demonstration in that direction, corresponding with those which McClellan had mentioned in his despatch, and thus take possession of that town without involving himself in a serious engagement." * * * "He advanced troops at Conrad's and Edward's Ferries. Stone thereby transcended the instructions of McClellan.* *His (Stone's) imprudence was aggravated by the evident insufficiency of his means for crossing the river.* The waters, which had risen very high during the last week, *rendered that operation extremely difficult.*" * * * "The reconnaisance was finished," * * * "and all the Federal detachments should immediately after have been brought back from the other side of the river. But at that moment (8 a.

---

* This relates to the movements early in the day. See Chapter XII, for Stone's testimony, for dispatches and McClellan's approval received later in the day.

m.—three hours before Baker took command) General
Stone, who had just witnessed the passage of a portion
of Gorman's Brigade at Edward's Ferry, full of confidence in the success of the manœuvre, sent the 20th
Massachusetts to Ball's Bluff (with two mountain howitzers), together with the detachments of the 15th which
had remained at Harrison's island. At the same time
he gave the fatal order to Devens to wait on the right
side of the river (at the bluff) for these re-enforcements. In his instructions, McClellan had allowed too
great a latitude to Stone, by directing him to keep a
watch over Leesburg, which could not have been done
without crossing the Potomac. He should, perhaps,
have more thoroughly impressed on his mind the isola-
tion in which any troops sent to operate on the right
borders of the river would find themselves. *The
errors committed by Stone were more serious;* putting
too much faith in the reports of his scouts, he persuaded
himself that a demonstration would be sufficient to
cause the evacuation of Leesburg, *and he combined all
movements of his troops as if he were sure of being able to
occupy that town.*"

"Second. General Stone directed five companies to
be thrown into Smart's Mill, on the right of Ball's
Bluff. Colonel Baker allowed these companies to be
directed to the front."

This charge will be completely refuted, and we will
find that Colonel Ward received his instructions at
least three hours before Colonel Baker took command,* and that Lieutenant Howe reported to General Stone, immediately after Colonel Baker left his
quarters and before he assumed active command (or
arrived opposite Harrison's Island with orders, say

* Colonel Devens reported (Official Records, Series I, Vol. V,
page 309): "I was rejoined at 8 a. m. by Quartermaster Howe,
who reported to me that I was to remain where I was, and
would be re-enforced by Colonel Ward and ten cavalrymen."

11:30 a. m.), that "our Colonel Ward, instead of proceeding to Smart's Mill, had re-enforced Colonel Devens;" to which General Stone made no objection, simply replying, that "Colonel Baker is at that place, and will arrange these things to suit himself." There is no evidence to specifically show that Colonel Baker knew anything of Colonel Ward's orders. A glance at the diagram of the battle-field will show that Smart's Mill was commanded by the bluff.

"Third. General Stone sent cavalry scouts to be thrown out in advance of the infantry on the right. Colonel Baker allowed this cavalry force to return without scouting, and did not replace it, although he had plenty at his disposition."

This charge seems glaringly false; these scouts were taken over and commanded by a member of General Stone's staff, who almost immediately returned with them to Stone's quarters, of which he very innocently testified: "The first thing I knew about that force they came back, having never been thrown to the front at all;"* and at the same time he had about four times as many cavalry scouts across at Edward's ferry, not more than two miles from Devens' position, ready for duty, but without orders. This staff officer with his scouts bore a message to General Stone, two or three hours before Colonel Baker took command, asking for re-enforcements, which Stone sent. Colonel Baker could find no transportation in which to cross his own cavalry when he arrived.

"Fourth. Colonel Baker assumed command on the right about 10 a. m., but never sent an order or message to the advance infantry until it was pressed back to the bluff about 2:15 p. m."

We will learn from the reports and testimony, beyond a doubt, that it was after 11 a. m. when Colonel Baker assumed command, most likely 12 m., and that

* Report of Committee on Conduct of War, 2, page 268.

he was upon the bluff between 1 and 2 p. m., having made good use of the time in the interim. It must be borne in mind that it took some time to ride up from Stone's quarters, and considerable time to cross the two branches of the swollen river, to reconnoitre the island, to improve the transportation, as herein mentioned, and to prepare for a retreat, in case it should be necessary.

"Fifth. Colonel Baker spent more than an hour in personally superintending the lifting of a boat from the canal to the river (which Stone made one and a half hours in his testimony), when a junior officer or sergeant would have done as well, in the meantime neglecting to visit or give orders to the advanced force in the face of the enemy."

Colonel Wistar tells us[*] that he himself had this boat lifted from the canal into the river, i, e., "These were all the facilities I know of when I commenced to cross; but about half an hour afterward (say 12 m.) I had another boat, which I had noticed in the canal about a mile above when I marched down. I sent a detachment of my men after it, had it brought down the canal, and then by force of muscle lifted it out of the canal and run it into the river."[†] It would seem that Colonel Baker did spend a little time before crossing, but no more than was necessary in giving orders for the assembling of troops to advance to his support, if needed, and in trying to improve the means of transportation by having a cable stretched across the river.[‡]

---

[*] Report of Committee on Conduct of War, 2, page 314.

[†] See Major Ritman's statement concerning transportation and this boat, *ante.*

[‡] Colonel Wistar testified (Report of Committee on Conduct of War, 2, page 308), "I had crossed six companies on to the island, and had got one company across from the island to the Virginia side. Then Colonel Baker himself arrived on the island, having been engaged in futile attempts to stretch a rope

A more needed and important work could not have been performed (had a whole hour been consumed in the work), as shown by subsequent events. After allowing Colonel Baker time to cross to the bluff, it would seem that he had moved quite rapidly, although he did stop a few minutes to encourage the men while getting a boat into the river—the only one in which artillery could be safely crossed—by telling them "the harder they worked and the greater the transportation the less fighting would they have to do."

"Sixth. No order of passage was arranged for the boats; no guards were established at the landings,* no boat crews were detailed."

We have learned that when Stone was under oath before the committee, he answered the question "Were you in command there (Harrison's Island) at the time of the fight at Ball's Bluff? *Answer.* I was; yes, sir;" which of itself should be an all-sufficient answer.

But the testimony proves that boat crews had been detailed from Colonel Hinks' regiment, before the Massachusetts men had commenced to cross, early in the morning, and that they were composed of the men whom Stone had previously placed upon the island in charge of the boats. Colonel Wistar will tell us that

across from the Maryland side to the island, which up to that time had failed. Afterward that was successful."

* Colonel Lee and Major Revere testified, as to guards (Report of Committee on Conduct of War, 2, pages 484 and 486), as follows:

"*Question.* Could any guards have been placed over the boats to have afforded any reasonable chance for the escape of the men when they were obliged to fall back to the river?

"*Answer.* I think not. The boats were liable to be destroyed by the fire of the enemy; one was sunk. We supposed the bottom had been riddled by bullets. The metallic boat floated down the river, the man who was bringing it over having been shot, and every man who undertook to swim was exposed to a heavy fire."

"There was no guard necessary, for there were troops in them (the boats) all the time." Each regimental commander guarded and controlled the transportation as his command passed over; first Devens, then Lee, then Captain Candy and his scouts, followed by Ward and Major Revere; then came Wistar, Cogswell, and finally Hinks. This seems to have been Stone's arrangement, with which he afterward became dissatisfied, as shown above. Major Bowe, of Cogswell's regiment, was in command on the Island and controlled the boats running to the Virginia shore when they were lost (See Colonel Hinks' report), the enemy having again opened fire upon the boats and the troops then crossing. We will learn that this miserable transportation furnished by Stone was used to its utmost capacity, although with great difficulty, in a swollen and rapid river, aggregating five hundred yards in width, until the enemy opened fire on the boats at the crossing, thus proving that General McCall was right in testifying that General Stone had misstated, and that he had not the means to cross at all in the face of the enemy, in which General Banks fully concurred. Colonel Lee and Major Revere testified,* as follows, to the question, "If there had been sufficient means of transportation across the river, were there not sufficient troops in the vicinity to have re-enforced you so as to have enabled you to win the day?

"*Answer.* Undoubtedly. There might have been 3,000 to 4,000 troops passed over.

"*Question.* So that the whole disaster resulted from insufficiency of transportation? * * *

"*Answer.* Yes, sir; there is no question about that."

A small corps, 1,600 strong, was obliged to fight a force of 3,200 (that being the enemy's force, as stated to me, while a prisoner, by a rebel officer), and fight them under great disadvantage; while Comte de Paris

* Report of Committee on Conduct of War, 2, pages 484, 485.

wrote, "His (Stone's) imprudence was aggravated by the evident insufficiency of his means for crossing the river."

When General Stone came up in person, about 5 p. m. (after Colonel Baker fell), and showed some disposition to move out of his quarters, our men were still fighting on the other side. Was it not a crying shame that he did not make the slightest effort to extricate or re-enforce them by his troops at hand, or make use of the artillery on the Maryland side, if practicable, which he reported should have been used, and, under its fire, send boats to their rescue?

"Seventh. The troops were so arranged on the field as to expose them all to fire, while but few could fire on the enemy. His troops occupied all the clear ground in the neighborhood, while the enemy had the woods and the commanding wooded height, which last he might easily have occupied before the enemy came up."

This is manifestly untrue. Stone, not having risked his person near the field, was correctly informed by nearly all the official reports,* which it would seem he had not read carefully, or, to serve his purpose, utterly disregarded. Colonel Devens had his command in an open field at first, but as soon as the enemy approached in force he fell back to the edge of the woods, and Colonel Baker there formed his line of battle, with the artillery on the rising ground in front, but as near the edge of the woods as it could be served, while he occupied the highest wooded grounds (selected by Colonel Lee), with the infantry force at hand, the ground from which he could best retreat or cover his crossing-place for re-enforcements. He placed the 15th Massachusetts in the woods on the right skirting the open field, and Wistar with his battalion on the left along the edge of the woods, his left protected by a deep ravine, with three

---

* Cogswell's report, referred to, was not made until eleven months after the engagement.

companies of the 20th Massachusetts as a reserve in the rear of the centre, covering the break between the two regiments, but protected from the direct fire by the bluff until they went into action. The fourth company of the 20th was thrown out to the rear of the right flank, and the fifth company to rear of the left flank as skirmishers, which is corroborated by nearly all the National and Confederate official reports and the testimony taken. Colonel Devens' and other reports, as well as Colonel Lee's and Major Revere's testimony, show that the reserve companies of the 20th Massachusetts were engaged, and that Colonel Baker some time thereafter ordered Devens to detach two companies from the right to the support of the left, and to draw in his right proportionately, which he did; while Colonel Wistar has told us that "Colonel Baker moved up his reserve and extended our left with it."

It would tire the reader's patience beyond endurance, to consider all the conflicting statements and contradictory reports, made by Stone from time to time with evident dissimulation, perhaps to divert attention from his false generalship at Edward's Ferry, as well as at the bluff, and from his very apparent worthless transportation;* therefore, we will omit much that might be written, with the remark that when an officer is forced to grasp at straws and indulge in innuendoes, it shows to what a desperate strait he has been driven, and how easily his cause could be shattered and felled in pieces, were it to go before a court of inquiry, through which Colonel Baker's name would have passed scathless, his record brightened by the contrast, his light burning clearly and steadily to the close of his brilliant career.

---

* See Opinion delivered by Committee on Conduct of War, Chapters X and XII.

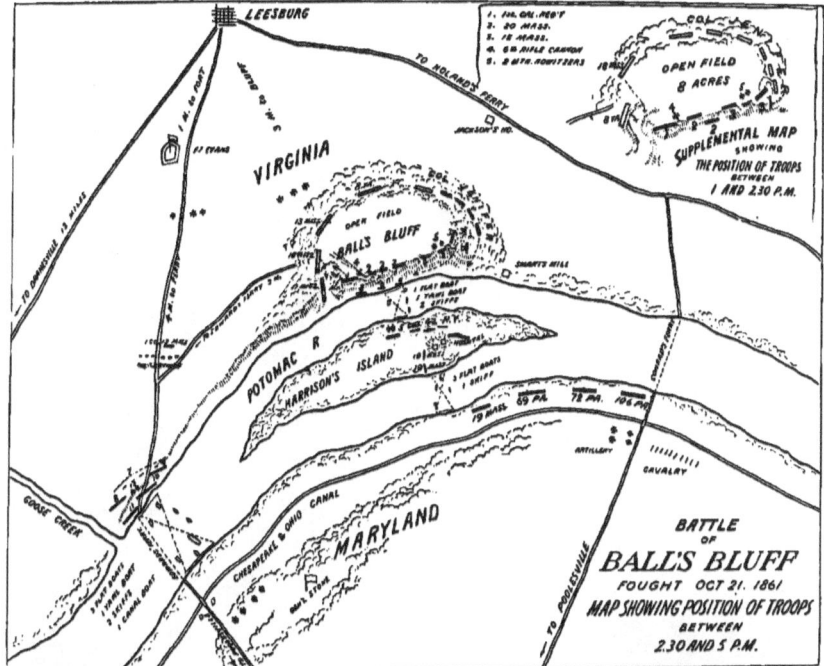

BATTLE
OF
BALL'S BLUFF
FOUGHT OCT. 21. 1861
MAP SHOWING POSITION OF TROOPS
BETWEEN
2.30 AND 5 P.M.

STONE'S TROOPS AT EDWARD'S FERRY.

No. 7. Cavalry—Skirmishers—Sharpshooters.
" 8. 1st Minnesota Regiment.
" 9. 2d New York Regiment.
" 10. 34th New York Regiment.
" 11. 7th Michigan Regiment.
" 12. Two 12 lb. howitzers.

TROOPS NEAR HARRISON'S ISLAND.

No. 1. 8 Co's 1st California Regiment, 520 men.
" 2. 5 Co's 20th Massachusetts, 318 men.
" 3. 15th Massachusetts Regiment, 625 men.

1463 men.

" 4. 6 lb. rifle cannon.
" 5. 2 Mountain Howitzers.
" 6. 5 Co's 42d N. Y. Regiment, 300 men.

1763 men.

* One on the right, two coming in on the left, and two moving from boat landing, about 300 men, when retreat was ordered by Col. Cogswell. (See page 169.)

CHAPTER VI.

OFFICIAL ORDERS AND INSTRUCTIONS FOR THE FIRST ADVANCE.

HAVING now given an outline of the incipient stages of this movement and of the charges preferred, we will turn to some of the early orders issued by General Stone, under which nine hundred or more men with two mountain howitzers were placed on the bluff opposite Harrison's island.

HEADQUARTERS
CORPS OF OBSERVATION,
POOLESVILLE, October 20, 1861.

COLONEL: You will please send orders to the canal to have the two new flatboats now there, opposite the island, transferred to the river, and will at 3 o'clock p. m. have the island re-enforced by all of your regiment now on duty on the canal and at the New York battery. The pickets will be replaced by the companies of the 19th Massachusetts there.

Very respectfully, your obedient servant,

CHAS. P. STONE,
Brigadier-General,

*Colonel Charles Devens, commanding 15th Regiment Massachusetts Volunteers.**

COLONEL DEVENS testified before the committee† as follows:

"The next order I received was a verbal one, about night, received through Captain Stewart, General Stone's Adjutant-General. It directed me to send Captain Philbrick over with a small party. He took ten or fifteen men, and crossed opposite the bluff in the place where the men had before been across, where Captain

---

* Official Records, Series I, Vol. V, page 299.

† Report of Committee on Conduct of War, 2, page 404.

Philbrick himself had been across, as General Stone knew. *He crossed one day, when General Stone and myself were both present,* with two or three of his men, had gone up the bluff to the crest of the bluff, and satisfied himself that that portion of the river was not picketed. Captain Philbrick, as soon as it was dark, was to cross the river with ten or fifteen men, push out to within a mile of Leesburg, if he could do so without being discovered, and then return and report. * * * They went out, as they supposed, somewhere about a mile in the direction of Leesburg, and then returned and reported that they had come upon a camp of the enemy * * * less than half a regiment. I directed the quartermaster (Church Howe) to immediately report the facts to General Stone. I directed him to go, because he had been across with Captain Philbrick. I remained on the island, waiting for General Stone's directions, and I received from General Stone, somewhere about 12 o'clock, this order:

"HEADQUARTERS
CORPS OF OBSERVATION,
POOLESVILLE, October 20, 1861, 10:30 P. M.

[*Special Orders, No. —*]

"Colonel Devens will land opposite Harrison's island with five companies of his regiment, and proceed to surprise the camp of the enemy, discovered by Captain Philbrick in the direction of Leesburg. The landing and march will be effected with silence and rapidity. Colonel Lee, 20th Massachusetts volunteers, will immediately after Colonel Devens' departure occupy Harrison's island with four companies of his regiment, and will cause the four-oared boat to be taken across the island to the point of departure of Colonel Devens. One company will be thrown across to occupy the heights on the Virginia shore after Colonel Devens' departure, to cover his return. Two mountain howitzers will be taken silently up the tow-path and carried to the opposite side of the island, under the orders of Colonel Lee.

"Colonel Devens will attack the camp of the enemy at daybreak, and, having routed them, will pursue them as far as he deems prudent, and will destroy the camp, if practicable, before returning. He will make all the observations possible on the country, will, under all circumstances, keep his command well in hand, and not sacrifice them to any supposed advantage of rapid pursuit. Having accomplished this duty, Colonel Devens will return to his present position, unless he shall see one on the Virginia side, near the river, which he can undoubtedly hold until re-enforced, and one which can be successfully held against largely superior numbers. In such a case he will hold on and report. CHAS. P. STONE,

Brigadier-General."*

Colonel Devens further testified, "Somewhere between 12 and 1 o'clock I commenced crossing the river, which was done with great care, great anxiety not to make a noise and disturb any pickets above or below. The men were put into the boat very silently, and ferried across. Somewhere about 4 o'clock we had crossed five companies of my regiment. * * * Colonel Lee ranked me. He said he would go across with that company himself, and sent across about 100 men, and came with them. * * * I went across to the Virginia side. I then waited with the men until daybreak—until the first glimmer of light. In the meantime I had sent my scouts out to the right and left, to see if they could find anything in our immediate vicinity in the woods. They reported all quiet. As the light began to appear * * * I set my column in motion, leaving Colonel Lee and his company of men on the bluff * * * we passed across this field, which was afterward the field of the main action of the day, into the woods, and crossed one or two more open spaces before reaching the front of the woods, which was toward Leesburg. On arriving there, as it had grown lighter, I saw what had caused the mistake of the scouts, and in a moment or two satisfied myself that there had been a mistake, and in the uncertain light, even in the first light of the morning, it

* Official Records, Series I, Vol. V, page 300.

did not look unlike a row of tents. * * * We then
halted the force. Captain Philbrick and myself, with
three or four men, pushed over the slope. It had then
begun to get so light that the high valley in which
Leesburg lay was in full sight, and we were apparently
three-quarters of a mile from the town. I then fell back
again into the woods. At that time I deemed it my duty
to report, as my force had not been discovered, and as I
was in a position well protected. * * * Accordingly
I directed the quartermaster of the regiment (Church
Howe) to return to General Stone as rapidly as possible,
and report that the camp was all a mistake, and that I
was well protected in the woods, and concealed, and I
waited his further orders. After the quartermaster
left, possibly an hour—it might be perhaps at 8 o'clock,
a body of riflemen, afterward found to be Mississippi
riflemen, were observed to be going up on our right,
which was in the direction of Conrad's Ferry above.
* * * We pursued them over this slope a little way,
they falling back until they got into the cover of a
ditch or trench, and then the firing commenced—they
firing first. We returned the fire; they were driven
out of this trench, and then forced into a field, which
afforded them very good ground indeed, because it was
a cornfield in which the corn had been cut, and stood
in stacks. In the meantime I sent back for another
company, intending to throw it over between the
enemy and the woods; but before they came, a body of
Rebel cavalry was reported to be on our left, coming
from the direction of the town of Leesburg. I thought
there was no advantage to be gained by being so far
from my covering force as I then was, and I ordered
Captain Philbrick to fall back to the woods, which he
did. I then waited there half an hour perhaps * * *
My messenger not having returned, and our presence
having been fully discovered, I deemed it prudent to
fall back to the bluff, where Colonel Lee was, which

we did in perfect order. In that skirmish we lost about 3 men killed, and some 7 or 8 wounded. I then scouted the woods again in every direction to the right and left, and no sign of the enemy appearing, I determined to return to the former position, which I did. Somewhere between 8 and 9 o'clock, the quartermaster (Church Howe) returned, *with a message from General Stone that I was to remain where I was; that I would be re-enforced;* that Lieutenant-Colonel Ward, who had part of my regiment on the tow path, would proceed up the river to Smart's mill, and that some cavalry would be sent over to me for the purpose of scouting in front. I then directed the quartermaster to immediately return to General Stone, and report that we had had a skirmish between one of our companies and a company of the enemy, in which the loss was probably about the same on either side, and that we were fully discovered, but that I was still in my old position. At about 10 o'clock the quastermaster returned with the answer (must have been much later, as will be seen hereafter), ' *Very well; Colonel Baker will come and take command.*' "

First-Lieutenant Church Howe, quartermaster of the 15th Massachusetts regiment, testified before the Committee* as follows :

"We crossed over at daybreak, and found that we had been mistaken, that there was no camp there. Colonel Devens, Captain Philbrick, and myself, proceeded a long way farther than we went the night before, and looked all around, and saw nothing except some two or three camps on the hill near Leesburg. There was not a man to be seen, I then returned to General Stone, and reported that we had been deceived, that there was no camp there, and that Colonel Devens saw nothing that indicated any enemy of any amount there. In the meantime he (Stone) had ordered that the rest

* Report of Committee on Conduct of War, 2, page 375.

of our regiment up at camp the night before should
come down to the river, and he ordered me to say to
Colonel Ward as I went back to cross with the rest of
our regiment (the other five companies), to proceed
to Smart's mill, which is at the right, where Colonel
Devens then was with his men. He also directed one
of the captains (Assistant Adjutant-General Candy,
serving upon Stone's staff), to take ten cavalry, and
report to Colonel Devens, and make a reconnaissance.
I went back and gave Colonel Ward the order. He
commenced crossing his men, and had them partly
across when Captain Candy arrived with his cavalry.
After our men were partly over, Captain Candy took
the boats and took his horses and men over. I re-·
ported to Colonel Devens that ten cavalry would shortly
be there, and that Colonel Ward was going to take a
position at Smart's mill (fixed by Devens between 8
and 9 a. m.). I found when we got there that we had
had a skirmish with a rifle company of Mississippians.
Colonel Devens then ordered me to report this to General Stone, that we had had a skirmish. As I was
going, I met Captain Candy; he had got his cavalry
over, and had gone up the bluff as far as where Colonel
Lee of the 20th Massachusetts was. Colonel Lee was
having a conversation with him. I immediately
crossed down, and made the report to General Stone
that our regiment had had a skirmish, and as I went
down *I met Captain Candy returning with his cavalry.
He did not go then and report to Colonel Devens at all;*
he merely crossed and reported to Colonel Lee, of the
20th Massachusetts, *then brought his cavalry all back
again to this side.* I met Colonel Lee, and he told me
to say to General Stone that if he wished to open a
campaign into Virginia, now was the time; he believed that there was a good chance. And as I was
going back to report this, I met Colonel Baker on the
tow-path coming up from General Stone's quarters,

Colonel Baker asked me 'if I was from across the river,' I said 'I was.' He asked me 'if I had messages for General Stone,' I said, 'I had.' He asked 'what they were.' I told him 'that the regiment had had a skirmish with the enemy, and that we still maintained our position where we had been,' and then I told him 'that Colonel Lee had sent a message to General Stone that if he wished to open the campaign into Virginia, now was the time.' Colonel Baker remarked, 'I am going over immediately with my whole force to take command.' He then struck spurs to his horse, and went off rapidly. I went down and reported this to General Stone, who told me that Colonel Baker would probably be over in a very few minutes, as Colonel Baker had got his orders, and was going to take charge of the division on the right, while General Gorman was to cross at Edward's ferry.''

"*Question.* You understood General Stone to say that he had given orders to General Baker to cross above?

"*Answer.* Yes, sir; *given orders to Baker to cross.* In reporting to him, I told him that in this encounter our Colonel Ward, instead of proceeding to Smart's Mill, *had re-enforced Colonel Devens.* General Stone replied, 'Colonel Baker is at that place, and will arrange these things to suit himself.' I went back and reported to Colonel Devens that General Baker was coming right across, as he had told me, with his whole force. We waited some time, but General Baker did not come; and the skirmish took place, and we drove the enemy back, maintaining our ground. Colonel Devens then sent me back to the river to see where Colonel Baker was. I did so three different times.''

COLONEL WILLIAM R. LEE, of the 20th Massachusetts, who was a keen observer of all that transpired on the bluff, gave his testimony before the committee* as

* Report of Committee on Conduct of War, 2, page 473.

follows (which was corroborated in full by his Major, Paul J. Revere, who was sworn to that effect):

"I ordered Major Revere to remain on the island, in command of the residue of my battalion on the island, while I took command of the one hundred men who were to cross over into Virginia. I felt it my duty to go with them. I found there a small row-boat, a metallic boat and two small skiffs. I think I found I could carry 28 men in the metallic boat and two skiffs. When I arrived at the top of the bluff it was quite dark, but I could distinguish men moving. I sought out Colonel Devens and stated to him that I was there with my command and that he was at liberty to move in advance. He immediately marched his battalion forward. I proceeded to make the best disposition of my force which I could without any knowledge of the ground and in the dark. This was about 5:20 o'clock on Monday morning. At 7:30 o'clock there was firing on our right, the right of the bluff, in and about a ravine where a party of my scouts, a sergeant and two men, had been sent to reconnoitre. Just before that I had also sent my adjutant and two officers out to reconnoitre. The adjutant came back and said that the sergeant of that scouting party had been shot, and immediately after that the sergeant himself came in; I found that he had been shot in the arm. After that there was some little firing of pickets; the pickets of the enemy seemed to have come down, and were apparently firing across to the island. At about 8 o'clock we heard a heavy volley in advance, and after that an irregular firing, which seemed to be a return fire. I judged from the sound, that the firing was perhaps a half mile from where my command was then posted on the bluff. Soon after this firing became irregular, as between skirmishers apparently; the wounded men began to appear, man followed after man wounded, until I think there were eleven or thirteen had come back.

"The firing in front ceased, and, perhaps, in the course of three-quarters of an hour, Colonel Devens' battalion appeared on this road, coming out of the woods on the open space of the bluff when they reached the position where I stood. I went forward a little to meet them. I found Colonel Devens and his command perfectly cool. I asked Colonel Devens what had happened. Colonel Devens did not say much to me; he seemed very much vexed; in fact, he seemed angry at the result of the operation. I finally said to him, "If you are going to stay here, Colonel, you had better form your line of battle across the road, instead of leaving your battalion in column and halted in the road." To that he made no reply. I wanted to see whether he would retire and take the boats, or not. After remaining there twenty minutes, or perhaps a half hour, Colonel Devens put his battalion in motion again and moved them in advance once more, and moved again up this road without saying to me what he intended to do; as he had not retired, I concluded that he intended to fight. I accordingly addressed a note to Major Revere and sent it over to the island, saying: "Colonel Devens has fallen back on my position; *we are determined to fight.*"* We remained there a considerable time before the firing was resumed in the advance in front of me. By and by it commenced again; it was irregular, evidently the firing of skirmishers. It was not a heavy firing, but still it was pretty active. The quartermaster (Howe) of the 15th regiment had gone over with Colonel Devens early in the morning, but had left before the first firing. He now returned and said that General Stone desired to know what our opinion was. I told him that we were on the Virginia shore; that if the Government designed to open a campaign at that

---

* After Major Revere got this note he crossed his three companies to the bluff with the two howitzers, he having previously brought around to that side of the island a large flat-boat.

time and on that field, we had made a lodgment, but we should want re-enforcements; that the means of transportation were small, and that we also required subsistence. He then went forward and consulted with Colonel Devens, and then returned and crossed over to the island. Captain Candy, of General Stone's staff, followed. He came over with a small force of cavalry, two fours, as we call it, of cavalry, eight cavalrymen, I think. Captain Candy rode up on the bluff and asked me what the condition of things was. I told him to sit down and take his pencil and write what I told him. I stated to him precisely what had occurred, and what I had stated to the quartermaster. I reported that to him, and he put it in writing. That is the memorandum related to what had happened to our condition, and *what it would be necessary to do if we were expected to maintain our position.* After this interview he retired with his horse—went back to the island, I supposed. He went down the bluff to the landing. A battalion of the 15th Massachusetts came across between 11 and 11:30 o'clock and passed to the front and re-enforced Colonel Devens. At about 12 o'clock—I will not be sure about the time—Major Revere appeared on the field with the residue of my battalion, which had been left on the island under his command. This increased my force to 317 men. I disposed of my men in the best manner I could to cover the passage of the river, for that was still my duty, as *I had no further orders than to maintain my position there on the bluff* as a covering party for Colonel Devens. After having disposed of my men in the best manner to carry out these orders, I left the bluff to go to the river to cross over to the island to see Colonel Baker, with a view of explaining to him not only the condition of things so far as the troops were concerned, but also the nature of the ground upon which we stood and were to operate, for I had reconnoitered it very carefully indeed. After proceeding toward the river for that purpose for perhaps one hundred feet, the firing in front opened again very heavily. I immediately returned to my command, judging that to be the proper place for me if there was going to be an action.''

In compliance with General McClellan's desire, General Stone made a demonstration, late on Sunday afternoon, at Edward's Ferry, after which he put his whole division under marching orders, some to report at the ferries the next morning at daybreak, and others to be ready to march at a moment's notice—all to be prepared with ammunition and rations.* That night he sent the scouting party out toward Leesburg to see if the enemy had actually left.

We have learned that his scouts first reported an unguarded camp of the enemy near the river on the Virginia side. Then Stone ordered Colonel Devens to cross and destroy it at daylight, supported by Colonel Lee. He advanced at daylight until Leesburg was in full view, and reported no enemy on his front or in sight. Then Stone ordered him to hold on there, that he would be re-enforced; and he was re-enforced by Colonel Ward, while Major Revere re-enforced Colonel Lee, with his reserve on the island, and two pieces of artillery.

In the meantime, at day-break of the 21st, General Stone had thrown across at Edward's Ferry some cavalry and the 1st Minnesota regiment, which were immediately thereafter followed by the 2d and 34th New York regiments and two pieces of artillery, having given Colonel Wistar orders, then at Conrad's Ferry, to cross to the support of Colonels Lee and Devens, should they become heavily engaged.

After matters had assumed this magnitude, Colonel Baker arrived at Stone's headquarters, between 10 and

* No litters were provided for the wounded, and it took three and four persons to handle one man without a litter.

11 a. m., to learn what was going on—of which he really knew nothing—and in a lengthy conversation Stone explained everything to him, and then directed him to go to the right and take command of the troops on the Virginia side at Ball's Bluff, with authority to call for and order across certain other troops and artillery at his discretion.

After receiving his instructions (see page 155) and when about leaving, he asked for some written authority, when General Stone hastily gave him a somewhat general order; of which Stone testified: " I then took out my pencil, and, on my knee, wrote that order, which has been referred to, giving him authority to take command of Cogswell's regiment and the other troops there, to retire those already over the river, or to advance the California regiment and Cogswell's regiment in his discretion. That is the first order which he received during the day," which is as follows:

HEADQUARTERS
CORPS OF ———, (Torn off.)
EDWARD'S FERRY, October 21, 1861.

COLONEL E. D. BAKER, *Commanding Brigade:*
Colonel: In case of heavy firing in front of Harrison's island, you will advance the California Regiment of your Brigade, or retire the regiments under Colonels Lee and Devens upon the (almost illegible by blood stains) Virginia side of the river at your discretion, assuming command on arrival.

Very respectfully, Colonel, your most obedient servant,
CHAS. P. STONE,
*Brigadier-General commanding.**

After Baker had left Stone on the field, between 11 a. m. and 12 m., with this order, and his instructions under it, he met Lieutenant Howe, carrying a despatch to Stone from the bluff, and he inquired of Howe the condition of affairs over there. Howe replied that the advance had been attacked, but was still holding its position, and "that Colonel Lee had sent a message to

* Official Records, Series I, Vol. V, page 303.

General Stone *that if he wished to open the campaign into Virginia, now was the time,*" to which Baker replied, "I am going over immediately with my whole force to take command."

Baker then ordered Chaplain Kellen, of his staff, to ride rapidly forward, and order Colonel Wistar to cross the California Regiment to the support of Lee and Devens, and Wistar commenced crossing his regiment. Lieutenant Howe proceeded to General Stone's headquarters, and made his report, in reply to which, he said, "General Stone *told me that Colonel Baker would probably be over in a very few minutes*, as Colonel Baker had got his orders, and was going to take charge of the division on the right, while General Gorman was to cross at Edward's Ferry," and that he had given orders to Baker to cross, which Howe reported to Lee and Devens as soon as he could recross.

We have learned from Colonels Lee and Devens that there had been heavy firing on the advance, and also from Lieutenant Howe of the contents of his report, and that he had been down to the river, to ask Colonel Baker to hurry his troops over; therefore, it became his duty under his written order and instructions, to cross at least the battalion of the California Regiment, the greater part of which he then had upon the island, and Cogswell's Regiment from the Maryland shore to the island.

QUARTERMASTER YOUNG, of the California regiment, then acting as brigade quartermaster and aid to Colonel Baker (whose testimony and reports seem to be somewhat confused), who, after coming up from Stone's quarters with orders for Colonel Wistar early in the morning (about 9:30 a. m.), to cross in case of heavy firing on his front, testified before the Committee :*

" I then went back to camp and met Colonel Baker his brother, son and chaplain, coming down from

* Report of Committee on Conduct of War, 2, page 318.

camp; and found the brigade turned out under arms. I changed my horse and returned to Harrison's Island. On the way I met Captain Harvey, the adjutant-general of our brigade, and he informed me that Colonel Baker had had an interview with General Stone since I had left him, and had been put in command of the Federal forces in Virginia—not on this side—those that had crossed and those that were going over. Captain Harvey was with Colonel Cogswell, and we had some talk about it. Colonel Cogswell and I got on our horses and went to Harrison's Island, and Captain Harvey went after the brigade and brought it up. * * * There were on the island at the time some 400 or 500 of our men waiting transportation. I galloped back to the crossing on the Maryland side of the island. General Baker had arrived on the island, and was on horseback. He said, 'Well, how is it getting on?' I told him. He said, '*Is there only one boat there?*' I said, "Only one boat." He went over and looked at it. He turned and was looking at me, not saying anything at the moment, when an officer of the Massachusetts regiment on the Virginia side ran down the hill to the water's edge and shouted out, 'Hurry over! We can see three regiments of infantry coming down from Leesburg.' *Colonel Baker paused for a moment, and then seemed to make up his mind and shouted back, 'Then there will be the more for us to whip.'** * * * He

* "In reference to those orders, the first one in writing that came up directed that Colonel Baker should cross and re-enforce Devens in case of heavy firing, or to retire him in his discretion. Now there was no way to retire him—no way to get them back. But I do not think that Colonel Baker would have crossed into Virginia if it had not been for this officer I spoke of, about running down the hill to the edge of the river, and shouting out, 'Hurry over, we can see three regiments coming from Leesburg.' I think that decided Colonel Baker to go over and throw in his lot with the rest. He was talking with me about the boat, apparently hesitating about going over."

then said to me, 'Go right back for Cogswell and the artillery, and I will go over. You come back as soon as you can.' * * * I went over to the Maryland side of the island, and shouted over to Cogswell, who was on the Maryland shore, and asked him if he could hear me. He replied, that 'he could.' I then said, 'Leave your regiment, and bring over your artillery.' He held up a paper, saying it was an order from General Stone to Colonel Baker, just received. I told him to open and read it. He did so, and said it was 'to go ahead.'"*

This was General Stone's second written order to Colonel Baker, of the 21st, marked 11:50 a. m., issued after Lieutenant Howe had reported the attack upon the advance (page 101), and was delivered to Colonel

---

* Major Ritman also related "that before all of the California battalion had crossed, Colonel Cogswell arrived; so did a mounted orderly from General Stone's headquarters with a dispatch for Colonel Baker. I handed the dispatch to Colonel Cogswell; he opened it and read it, saying, 'I will communicate it.' He then went over. Just at this time Captain Young shouted across from the island to hurry up the troops, that the enemy were coming down on Colonel Baker in force. I turned to the orderly, who was waiting, and asked him if he heard what that officer had shouted across to me, he said that 'he had,' and he repeated it to me verbatim. I directed him to return, and report that to General Stone; and with my permission, the chaplain of a Massachusetts regiment rode down to Stone's quarters after the orderly to see that this message was correctly reported. Upon the chaplain's return, he reported to me that he arrived there just as the orderly was leaving Stone's presence, who, with his staff, were standing around a fire in a field, and when he reported the object of his mission to General Stone, he was asked in a rude manner, 'who he was,' and then ordered back to his command," as related to the author.

It will be seen that this statement points to the 11:50 a. m. communication, concerning which Colonels Devens and Wistar testified that Colonel Baker read a dispatch to the officers upon the field when Colonel Cogswell arrived upon the bluff.

Baker on the battle-field by the hand of Colonel Cogswell after he had crossed the river about 2 p. m.
Thus we have seen that Colonel Baker was on the
island before 1 p. m., and that Colonel Lee was correct
when he testified:* "Some time after 1 o'clock, between 1 and 2 o'clock, I heard a voice behind me in-
quiring for Colonel Lee, and Major Revere, I think,
said, pointing to me, 'There he stands.' I turned
around, and a military officer on horseback presented
himself, and bowed very politely and said, 'I congratulate you on the prospect of a battle.' I bowed and
said, 'I suppose you assume command.' I knew it
was Colonel Baker; I had seen him once before at
Poolesville. He said 'he would assume command.'
Colonel Baker was followed by a battalion of the California regiment."†

Knowing how easily we may be mistaken as to the
hours of the day, when the mind is preoccupied with
an exciting scene like a battle, and the importance of
keeping the occurrences of each hour correctly, so as to
preserve intact the thread of our research, we had
better stop, and take our reckoning. We find that
Colonel Devens tells us that he was fired into at 8 a. m.
(which agrees with Captain Bartlett's report and Colonel Lee's testimony, who were on reserve and made
careful note of time). Lee tells us that about three-

* Report of Committee on Conduct of War, 2, page 478.

† In confirmation of heavy firing in front, making it necessary
for Baker to cross under his orders, General Evans will tell us
(Official Records, S. I., Vol. 5, page 349,) that at 10 o'clock "I
directed Colonel Hunton to form line of battle immediately in
the rear of Colonel Jenifer's command, and drive the enemy to
the river. *That I would support his right with artillery.* About
12:20 o'clock p. m., Colonel Hunton united his command with
that of Colonel Jenifer, and both commands soon became hotly
engaged with the enemy in their strong position in the woods."
This has been corroborated by Colonels Griffin, Hunton, and
Jenifer's reports given above.

quarters of an hour thereafter Devens fell back upon him,* and after remaining about half an hour advanced again,† and after some considerable time had elapsed, Lee heard irregular firing of skirmishers. Then Lieutenant Howe returned from Stone to the bluff for information from the field, and after interviewing Lee he went forward to consult Devens,‡ and then returned across the river to report to Stone and for orders.|| Lieutenant Howe says, " As I was going back to report, I met Colonel Baker on the tow-path coming up from General Stone's quarters," with whom he conversed about matters over the river, and that Colonel Baker remarked, "I am going over immediately with my whole force to take command," and that he (Howe) made his report from Lee and Devens (asking to be either re-enforced or withdrawn), and that he also reported to Stone what Baker had said about crossing. Then Stone told Howe that he had given Baker orders to cross and take command. Howe so reported to Devens and Lee, both of whom testified to having received such word by Howe from Stone, and Howe reported to Stone at this time that Colonel Ward's force had gone to the front and re-enforced Colonel Devens, which Colonel Lee fixed at 11 or 11:30 a. m., and Bartlett at 11 a. m., all of which strongly indicates that Howe and Baker had met near Stone's quarters between 11 a m. and 12 m., and Stone testified while under examination as to movements at Edward's Ferry that he had received a report about 11 a. m. that Colonel Baker was crossing with his whole force—no doubt the report from Howe. At the same time it would

* Say 8:45 a. m., Bartlett's report makes it 10 a. m.

† Say 9:15 a. m., while Bartlett's report says 11 a. m.

‡ Who had advanced the second time, fixed by Bartlett in his report at 11 a. m.

|| All of which must have consumed more than an hour, say between 11 a. m. and 12 m.

seem that Stone knew perfectly well before Baker left his quarters that he would cross, for Stone told Howe that he had given Baker orders to cross, which he reported, as above, to Lee and Devens shortly thereafter. Therefore it must have been about 12 m. when Baker arrived opposite Harrison's Island and assumed command, notwithstanding Stone reported that Baker assumed command upon the right about 10 a. m.,* being one of Stone's many misstatements. We also find many other inaccuracies as to time and occurrences by carefully comparing Stone's reports, a number of which he subsequently corrected when testifying before the Committee, when he acknowledged that he was in command at Harrison's Island, and after his release from prison he supplied other important omissions. How far there may have been a motive for these misstatements, how far "the wish was father to the thought" we will leave the reader to judge. Captain Young also testified that he was at General Stone's headquarters about 9 a. m., and while awaiting orders for Colonel Wistar fed his horse, and that he left shortly thereafter, and after he had ridden back at least five miles and delivered his orders to Colonel Wistar and had started up the tow-path toward camp, he met General Baker and his staff and told him of the orders. Colonel Wistar says about a half hour after receiving the order from Captain Young,† Colonel Baker and his staff came down from camp, and after talking with him about his orders, he, with his staff, galloped down to Stone's quarters; and about a half hour after that the chaplain of the regiment returned with orders, and said, "General Baker directs you, sir, to cross at once." Allowing an hour for the ride of ten miles back and forth, and sufficient time for a conference with General

---

* While Baker did not arrive at Stone's quarters so early as 10 a. m.

† Say 10 a. m.

Stone, who says in his first report, "I decided to send him (Baker) to Harrison's Island to assume command, and in a full conversation with him explained the position of things as they then stood according to reports received. I told him that General McCall had advanced his troops to Drasnesville and that I was extremely desirous of ascertaining the exact position and force of the enemy in our front, and exploring as far as it was safe on the right to Leesburg, and on the left toward the Leesburg and Gum Spring road, that I should continue to re-enforce the troops under General Gorman opposite Edward's Ferry and try to push them carefully forward, to discover the best line from that ferry to the Leesburg and Gum Spring road already mentioned," with various other details—it is quite probable that more time than an hour had elapsed during this interview, and ride back and forth, thus corroborating the time fixed above. No doubt it was about 11:30 a. m., when the chaplain delivered the order to Wistar to cross.

Colonel Wistar, in compliance with Stone's order,* had marched his first battalion (the second battalion being then on picket duty under Major Robert Parrish) promptly, about 4 a. m. on the 21st, concerning which he testified before the committee:†

"I marched in the morning (Monday), and arrived at Conrad's Ferry about sun-rise (say 7 a. m.), with 570 men, officers included. I sent the quartermaster (Captain Young), who was the only mounted officer I had along, down to Edward's Ferry, where I understood General Stone to be in person, to report my arrival at Conrad's Ferry, and ask for orders. He returned, perhaps, by 8 o'clock, during the forenoon—I can only give an approximation to the hour—with an order to me from General Stone 'to wait further orders where I

---

* See page 43.
† Report of Committee on Conduct of War, 2, page 307.

8

was, unless I should hear heavy firing across the river, in which case I was to cross and support Colonel Devens.' About an hour before receiving these orders through my quartermaster, there had been a scattering fire of skirmishers over the river,* which I took to be the enemy driving in our pickets. But about the time the quartermaster returned with the orders, they commenced bringing over the wounded;† but for some time after receiving this order, there was no firing, either heavy or light. I moved my regiment down a little way, so that in case I should have to cross I should be nearer the place of crossing where Colonel Devens had gone over. About a half hour after receiving this order,‡ and I had taken my new position, Colonel Baker and his staff came down from the camp and asked me what my orders were. I told him. He said, 'I had better go down to Stone, had I not?' I said, 'I don't know; these are my orders.'|| He started off

* Fixed by Lee, Devens, and Bartlett at 8 a. m., which, if correct, would indicate that Colonel Wistar had received his first order at about 9 a. m., instead of 8 a. m.

† For which more than an hour's time should be allowed, which would indicate a later hour than 9 a. m. for Colonel Wistar's first order, fixed above at 10 a. m.

‡ 9:30 a. m., fixed above at 10 a. m.

|| Captain Young has also testified, "I waited for some further order (when at Stone's quarters), and then asked, 'General, have you any further order?' He spoke very imperiously and curt, as he always does, and said, 'You have your orders, sir.' The reason for my waiting for further orders, was that on coming down the tow-path I had passed the crossing where the Massachusetts boys had gone over in the night, and I had been very much surprised when they told me they had gone over in the two flat-boats that were there; and there had been some jesting between myself and the men who were there on the tow-path, about going over in that manner. That was the reason of my asking General Stone if he had any further orders. But he spoke so imperiously that I got on my horse, and went back and delivered my orders to Colonel Wistar, * * * who

on a gallop down there. About half an hour afterward,* the chaplain of my regiment returned in great
haste, and directed me from General Baker to cross.
His words were, 'General Baker directs you, sir, to
cross at once.' I immediately marched my regiment
down to the boats and commenced crossing.† I had
scarcely commenced—I had sent over one boat load—
when General Baker himself arrived ‡ and hurried me as
fast as he could, directing me to press everything into the
service, and get across as quickly as I could. I did so.
I went over there to the island with the second boat load,
directing my senior captain (Ritman) to attend to transporting the troops over. I remained on the island, in
order to superintend the transportation on both sides
of it, as the most central place." Before leaving the
Maryland shore Colonel Wistar had sent for another
boat, of which he said, "About a half hour afterward
I had another boat, which I had noticed in the canal
about a mile above when I marched down. I sent a
detachment of men after it, had it brought down the
canal, and then the men by force of muscle lifted it out
of the canal and run it into the river, so that after that
we had three scows on the Maryland side of the island."
Colonel Wistar further says, "By about 2 p. m.‖ I
asked me 'if I was sure I was right.' I then proceeded up the
tow-path and met General Baker. * * * I reported what
General Stone had said to me. General Baker said, 'that can't
be.' I told him that those were the orders, and I repeated them
again—to cross. He said, 'In what?' I told him 'the orders
were to cross.'" Report of Committee on Conduct of War, 2,
page 319. And when Colonel Baker came back, he told Captain Ritman that General Stone had informed him 'that ample
means of transportation had been provided, and were at hand
for shipping men and munitions of war.'" See page 63.

* Most likely an hour or more, say 11 or 11:30 a. m

† Most likely at 11:30 a. m.

‡ Most likely 12 m.

‖ Approximately.

had crossed six companies on the island, and had got one company across from the island to the Virginia side; then Colonel Baker himself arrived on the island."*

We also find that Colonel Wistar said, when the large boat, the third one, had been added, *he could cross about 220 men at once*, and that if they went straight across the trip would consume about three-quarters of an hour, and that he tells us, by expediting matters, he had crossed six companies to the island† and one company to the Virginia shore.

If Colonel Wistar commenced crossing at 11 a. m., it is fair to assume that he had his six companies on the island before 1 p. m.; for if six companies of 70 men each, 420 men, consumed three hours in crossing—that would be 210 to the hour—five-sixths of them, about half-way across, should not consume nearly so much time. This would also seem to fix the hour when Colonel Wistar received the order from his chaplain at 11 a. m., or later, and when Baker arrived upon the island perhaps earlier than 1 p. m. Then Colonel Wistar testified that he had begun the main action of the day with his skirmishers at 2:30 p. m.,‡ previously having accounted for the lapse of considerable time after Baker had arrived upon the island.

Colonel Lee testified that between 1 and 2 p. m. Colonel Baker came upon the field at the bluff and took command, that the 15th Massachusetts were engaged heavily with the enemy, but had not yet fallen back; and in the meantime, *while he and Baker were reconnoitering and examining the bluff* and consulting,

* Which proves that all the Massachusetts men had crossed some time before Baker arrived upon the island, say at 11:30 a. m.

† Rather more than half-way across.

‡ After Colonel Cogswell had arrived with orders.

the 15th Massachusetts were driven in.* Colonel Baker formed his line of battle where Lee had his men, simply extending the line right and left to hold the ground and cover his transportation, the troops then coming over being directed to the left.

The facts and circumstances given above prove almost conclusively that Wistar commenced crossing about 11:30 a. m., and that Baker arrived from Stone's quarters about 12 m. and was upon the island before 1 p. m. and upon the Virginia shore shortly thereafter, having spent some little time in issuing orders for his cavalry, infantry and artillery, to report at Conrad's Ferry in readiness to cross if needed, examining the transportation and the island for defense in case of a retreat, and in doing every thing in his power, even to having a cable † stretched across the river, to improve the means of transportation which Stone had so grossly neglected and misrepresented to him, about which Baker seemed very much worried and exercised before leaving the Maryland shore, although he then did not fully realize how meagre was the transportation on the other side.‡ Thus he was hurried into action in response to orders and urgent appeals, to which he was too brave to turn a deaf ear.

Let us again glance at the force on the Virginia shore, placed there by Stone's orders before Baker arrived. Colonel Devens, of the 15th Massachusetts, said, "Between 9 and 11 o'clock I was joined by Lieutenant-Colonel Ward with the remainder of my regiment, making in all a force of 625 men with 28 officers;" and Colonel Lee, of the 20th Massachusetts,

---

* Followed by Jenifer's command, while the 8th Virginia had taken possession of the knoll across the ravine on the left of the battle-field of the day before 1:30 p. m.

† Which he could not wait to see completed.

‡ Of this time about three quarters of an hour should be allowed for crossing from the Maryland shore to the bluff.

testified, "At about 12 o'clock Major Revere appeared on the field with the residue of my battalion, which had been left upon the island. This increased my force to 317 men," who took with them two six-pound howitzers, which they were supporting on the island. In all, with the men attached to the battery, about 900 men, and two mountain howitzers being fully two-thirds of all the troops and artillery that were in the action. The first troops crossed by Baker's orders were the first battalion of his old regiment. Stone had informed his chief of his own movements previously.

"EDWARD'S FERRY, October 21, 11:10 a. m.
MAJOR-GENERAL MCCLELLAN.
The enemy have been engaged opposite Harrison's island, our men behaving admirably.   CHAS. P. STONE,
                                          Brigadier-General."*

It will be observed that no mention of Colonel Baker's name is made in this dispatch. In relation to the position our troops were placed in across the river, Colonel Lee testified, in reply to the

"*Question.* Was not the placing you on that bluff to protect the retreat of Colonel Devens' forces placing you in rather a hazardous position, liable to be cut off?

"*Answer.* If we did our duty I suppose we should have been destroyed. I knew that perfectly well when I went there."

We have also learned that Captain Candy, of Stone's staff, returned with his cavalry scouts to Stone before Baker arrived, bearing a written message from Colonel Lee, not having made the scout as directed by Stone. No doubt he found his force too small to scout against the enemy's squadron of cavalry hovering around Devens, and too large to lose. After Candy and Howe had returned to Stone, each bearing a message from Colonel Lee, *i. e.*, "That, if the Government designed

---

* Official Records, Series I, Vol. V, page 33.

to open a campaign at that time and on that field, we had made a lodgment (or, if he (Stone) wished to open the campaign into Virginia, now was the time), but we should want re-enforcements; that the means of transportation were small, and that we also required subsistence." Stone then issued the following order (evidently in response to Lee's message and Howe's report), about the time Baker arrived opposite Harrison's island, and before he had placed any of his men on the Virginia shore, excepting one company of his old regiment in transit: .

"EDWARD'S FERRY, October 21, 11:50.

COLONEL E. D. BAKER, *Commanding Brigade.*

Colonel: I am informed that the force of the enemy is about 4000 all told. If you can push them, you may do so, as far as to have a strong position near Leesburg. If you can keep them before you, avoiding their batteries—if they pass Leesburg, and take the Gum Spring road, you will not follow far, but seize the first good position to cover that road. Their design is to draw us on—if they are obliged to retreat as far as Goose creek, where they can be re-enforced from Manassas, and have a strong position. Report frequently, so that when they are pushed, Gorman can come in on their flank.

Yours respectfully and truly,

CHAS. P. STONE,

Brigadier-General commanding."*

It is very evident, from the tenor of this order, that Stone thought Baker was about crossing the river in force and had received his orders to that effect, which would agree with his reply to Lieutenant Howe, that he had ordered Baker to cross and had arranged all the details with him during their interview about 11 a. m., having previously ordered Devens to remain where he was, that he would be re-enforced, and with his testimony, "I directed him (Baker) to hold on there, and, of course, not yield ground we had taken possession of without resistance."

*Official Records, Series I, Vol. V, page 303.

Comte de Paris, in commenting upon this order, writes, "On being informed that there were nearly 4,000 Confederates between Leesburg and Baker's (1,400) men, he gave himself no uneasiness on account of the latter, but merely pointed out to them the means of pursuing the enemy. Instead of guarding against his attack as he should have done" * * * "he persuaded himself that a demonstration would be sufficient to cause the evacuation of Leesburg, and he combined all the movements of his troops as if he were sure of being able to occupy that town."

CHAPTER VII.

LET us now turn our attention to Edward's Ferry, and see what General Stone has been doing there in the meantime.

MAJOR JOHN MIX testified before the committee as follows*:

"I am Major of the Third New York cavalry and Second Lieutenant of the Second Regular cavalry. I took coffee in the course of the evening (Sunday, October 20th) with General Stone, and he said that he thought probably I might have an opportunity of crossing the river and having a dash at the enemy if things went the way he expected them to do. In the morning (Monday) I took my force of cavalry (five officers and thirty men) across the river, and either one or two companies of the First Minnesota were sent over to cover me. I went out, and drove in the enemy's pickets until I met a regiment of the enemy's infantry, the 18th Mississippi, and, after drawing their fire, I returned to the river, and found that more troops were coming over, which rather surprised me (thinking it only a reconnaisance), but finding that I did not consider that it was advisable for me to recross the river, although such were my instructions, until I received orders, I sent to General Stone, and he sent me word to stop where I was. I scattered my party out as videttes, and occupied the ground as well as I could. We heard firing on our right.

"*Question.* Up at Ball's Bluff?

* Report of Committee on Conduct of War, 2, page 462.

(121)

"*Answer.* Yes, sir; and some one informed me that our people were engaged up there and were having a pretty serious time of it.

"*Question.* What time in the day was that?

"*Answer.* I should say it was about 11 or 12 o'clock. I paid but little attention to the time. Colonel Tompkins was then in command (of 1st Minnesota, 2d New York, and some other troops). I went to him, and said, 'Our men are engaged up above here, and I guess we can get up the river bank and get at the enemy's right flank and rear, and we may get up in time to do some good. If our people are beating them we will share the victory, if they are being beaten we can help them; and, if it is doubtful, we can decide the matter. He said, 'He was ordered to hold his position where he was,' and I could not persuade him to take the responsibility and go up.

"*Question.* You stated that you heard firing above, and endeavored to get permission to go up there?

"*Answer.* Yes, sir.

"*Question.* What was there that you know of, any obstacle, in the way of your going up there?

"*Answer.* In a conversation that I have had with General Stone since, I said it was a mistake—our not going up there; he told me that General Evans, with three guns and a thousand men, were in position waiting for us, and we could not have got up there.

"*Question.* Was not Evans at Ball's Bluff?

"*Answer.* General Stone said that Evans was not at Ball's Bluff, but that he was below watching for our advance, and I have understood that the 18th Mississippi was not up there.

"*Question.* Was there any fortification between the two places that would have obstructed you?

"*Answer.* Yes, sir; there was an earthwork on a hill—some three and a half foot wall—which did not amount to much. If I had not met that regiment, it was my intention to gallop through that work.

"*Question.* Were there any guns in it?

"*Answer.* I was informed by General Stone that there were not. He said 'the guns had been moved out a day or two before.' I asked him if I could go through it, and he said I might if not held too strongly. I took a prisoner who said if I had gone three hundred yards further, I would have run right on to those guns. I suppose that was what General Stone referred to, and this regiment I met was going up there to take position.

"*Question.* General Stone did not apprehend anything from that earthwork?

"*Answer.* No, sir; they could not hurt us while we held that position.

"*Question.* Would it have impeded your going up there?—did he think it would?

"*Answer.* No, sir; I do not think he did.

"*Question.* He thought there were a thousand men with three guns in the way?

"*Answer.* I only heard that statement about the regiment and three guns about three or four weeks ago. In a conversation with General Stone I was regretting that we had not moved up, and he said, 'We could not have got there,' for that reason.

"*Question.* Did you know at the time of any obstruction to your going up there?

"*Answer.* No, sir.

"*Question.* And General Stone never said anything about it until you said to him what you have stated?

"*Answer.* I was regretting that I had not been permitted to go up, and he said, 'I could not have got up there.'

"*Question.* He said that this one thousand men and three guns were there?

"*Answer.* Yes, sir; and Evans in person was commanding there, and he was not at Ball's Bluff.

"*Question.* How many men had you over there at the time you wanted to go up to Ball's Bluff?

"*Answer*. I think not over fourteen hundred men.

"*Question*. Suppose you had gone up with what men you had at the time you wanted to go up, what, in your judgment, would have been the effect?

"*Answer*. If we had got there we would have struck the enemy on the right wing and rear, and that would have very soon decided the matter in our favor, for the men were in very good condition.

"*Question*. Did you on Monday night after the disaster at Ball's Bluff remain on the Virginia side of Edward's Ferry?

"*Answer*. Yes, sir.

"*Question*. How many men were there?

"*Answer*. I think there were about 4,500 men there at the time we commenced sending them back that night—Monday night."

GENERAL DANA testified before the Committee* as follows:

"About one o'clock that night (Sunday, 20th), I received another order directing me to take my regiment at daybreak (then commanding the First Minnesota), to Edward's Ferry and to cross. I sent two companies forward to begin the embarkation, and took the balance of my regiment down there. I formed my regiment on the bank. The first two companies went over in three boats, and, I suppose, in about two hours' time, perhaps in an hour and a half, my whole regiment was crossed over. We occupied a position there at the mouth of Goose creek, which we continued to occupy until we returned to this side. I never received an order while I was on that side of the river, except one on Monday night—to return to the Maryland side, and shortly after an order countermanding that, so that I put no part of it into execution.

"*Question*. What was the feeling in the army in regard to the movement at that time?

"*Answer.* On the Virginia side of the river where we were, the opinion was freely expressed among persons whom I knew in military affairs that we had not transportation enough, and there was a great deal of talk about going over to remonstrate about the matter. I was consulted about it, and my reply was that 'I could not pass any opinion upon an order that my superior officer had given.'

"*Question.* With whom did they propose to remonstrate?

"*Answer.* Well, sir, it was a conversation that took place among several persons, who proposed to go back to the Maryland side and see General Gorman or General Stone, or whoever might be on that side at the landing, and see what plan was to be adopted, and to make suggestions.

"*Question.* How far from the shore did you go?

"*Answer.* My regiment was the first one to go over, and we took up a position at the mouth of Goose creek, right at the landing, and I do not suppose we went one hundred yards from there at any time. I received no orders excepting about returning, the first of which was countermanded.

"*Question.* With your limited means of transportation, were not your troops put in great jeopardy by being taken over there and left on that bank of the river?

"*Answer.* If we had been attacked by a superior force we would have been. I do not think we would have been in danger of being captured, however, for our position was such that it could have been protected somewhat by artillery on this side of the river. Our position at Edward's Ferry was far less dangerous than the position of our forces at Ball's Bluff, as I have seen since. The enemy at Ball's Bluff commanded our side of the river; at Edward's Ferry we commanded their side.

"*Question.* Was there anything in the way of your

being moved from Edward's Ferry up to re-enforce our forces at Ball's Bluff at the time of the battle there?

"*Answer.* There was an earthwork there, which was there when I arrived in the middle of October. I do not know whether it was armed or not. It was understood that there was a covered battery in the woods somewhere, which we would have to come in contact with in going from Edward's Ferry to Leesburg.

"*Question.* My question was in relation to moving up to Ball's Bluff?

"*Answer.* You would have had to advance toward Leesburg, as I understand the topography of the country—the roads run in toward Leesburg.

"*Question.* You never saw anything of that battery?

"*Answer.* I saw the earthwork, but there was another battery reported, which it was said we would come against immediately before we could see it.

"*Question.* Where did you get that information from?

"*Answer.* Merely from the general talk in camp.

"*Question.* Did you see anybody who had seen it?

"*Answer.* No, sir; I was a stranger when I first came there, but it appears to me that there was a talk in camp at that time that some refugee had come over from Leesburg and told of this battery, which was a dangerous point; that we would come right on it before we could see it.

"*Question.* Do you know anything about a couple of cannon being on the Virginia side of Edward's Ferry at the time of the skirmish there, with no officer there to command them?

"*Answer.* I was told, to my astonishment, that there was only a sergeant in command of two twelve-pound howitzers there.

"*Question.* How much time was General Stone on the Virginia side?

"*Answer.* I think he came over in the morning of the third day.

"*Question.* For the first time?

"*Answer.* I think so; I do not think he came over before that. General Stone was sent over immediately on the arrival of General McClellan, I understood.

"*Question.* Was it not a very unusual thing to send cannon into a skirmish or engagement without an officer to command or manage them?

"*Answer.* I should think it an impropriety decidedly not to have a commissioned officer in command, or of even a single piece of artillery if it was isolated.

"*Question.* Was General Gorman in command of the troops on the Virginia side of Edward's Ferry at the time of the battle of Ball's Bluff?

"*Answer.* General Gorman was most of the time on the Maryland side. He was over for a few minutes at a time several times the second and third days.

"*Question.* Was his brigade on the Virginia side?

"*Answer.* His entire brigade was on the Virginia side. I am ashamed to say that for a long time I was the only colonel on the ground. The colonels would go back to the Maryland side and sleep. I never saw such a state of things in my life.

"*Question.* What duties would General Gorman naturally have on the Maryland side, if his whole brigade was on the Virginia side?

"*Answer.* He was ordered to superintend the passage of the troops and the artillery across the river; but, if I had received such an order as that, and my brigade had been on the Maryland side, I should have superintended at that end of the ferry. I could not see the necessity of his staying on the Maryland side, except that there were some houses there, which were comfortable to stay in. It was a bad state of things—*we wanted a commanding officer over there very much*—there was nobody there to give orders.

"*Question.* Then General Stone or General Gorman should have been in command on the Virginia side?

"*Answer.* There should have been some one there, I do not know who. It was certainly not General Stone's place. General Stone certainly ought not to have been there, as he saw the thing then. *He was crossing troops in two places* (Edward's Ferry and Conrad's Ferry) five miles apart, *and his business was to be with his reserve and control the two crossings.* A man came to me asking for orders. I had been there but two weeks and was the junior colonel, but I received messages from this side of the river and assumed command.

"*Question.* From whom did you receive them?

"*Answer.* From every Tom, Dick and Harry who came across the river, and said that General Gorman had told them 'I would command.' There were three colonels senior to me at the time. * * * I would have been rejoiced to have got an order myself to do something."

GENERAL LANDER,* who arrived at Edward's Ferry at daylight on Tuesday the 22d, crossed to the Virginia side and was there seriously wounded, later in the day, while reconnoitering and resisting an attack, testified before the Committee as follows:

"I went down to the river, crossed, and went to the front. On my way I met General Gorman, who urged upon me to go back and press upon General Banks the propriety of withdrawing all our troops then and there. I replied that I had already advised carrying out the orders of the general-in-chief and holding the position at all hazards, as I had a regiment there without arms. *Having lost one regiment, the 20th Massachusetts,* I believed it was about time to save another. He said the position could be enfiladed by the enemy's fire, that he knew the country, and that it was a very risky matter. I did not reply, but went to the front. He asked if I had come to take command, saying, ' if so,

* Report of Committee on Conduct of War, 2, page 253.

he was glad of it.' I said I would not take it then; if
there was fighting, however, I would take it. At four
o'clock in the afternoon the enemy attacked us on our
extreme left. I was the only general officer then at
the front, and was confident that no general officer was
near enough to make any report.

"*Question.* What distance were they (our troops)
from Ball's Bluff?

"*Answer.* There is a bend in the river, and reported
to be three and a half miles around.

"*Question.* I mean to go round in their rear?

"*Answer.* The captain of the sharp-shooters told me
it was only three and a half* miles, and when they
heard the firing they wanted to join their friends.

"*Question.* Was there any insuperable obstacle in the
way of throwing a body of men in their rear and capturing the attacking force?

"*Answer.* That was the arrangement of General
Stone.

"*Question.* Why was not that move made?

"*Answer.* That I cannot tell. From the checking
of the first advance, I suppose (the scouts).

"*Question.* Suppose these men had advanced at
double-quick, and attacked the enemy in the rear?

"*Answer.* It is said there was a masked battery between, but that could not interfere with skirmishers
and sharp-shooters—they could not lose over one hundred men in passing them. I think the junction could
have been made.

"*Question.* You do not consider the obstacle insuperable?

"*Answer.* Not at all; not by any means. It appears
strange to me that either General Stone or General
Gorman did not order up men to relieve the men engaged when they heard the firing that (Monday) afternoon.

* Two and a half miles is the correct distance.

9

" *Question.* Did you see any batteries there that were an obstacle to moving up to relieve Baker?

" *Answer.* I told my lieutenant-colonel I was of a great mind to steal three thousand men and take the town of Leesburg. It is true that as there were two generals there who outranked me, I should have been broken. I could have done it, I think,—at least that shows I did not think much of their batteries. Batteries are pretty bad things for columns of troops, but not for riflemen and skirmishers."*

COLONEL TOMPKINS, of the 2d New York, testified before the Committee† as follows:

---

*The above would not seem to be an idle or empty boast. The gallant and accomplished General Lander, while still suffering from the wound received at Edward's Ferry, took command of a force to protect the Baltimore and Ohio R. R. He had a wily and energetic opponent in " Stonewall Jackson," who was endeavoring to gain what Floyd, Wise and Lee had lost, and to hold possession of the Shenandoah Valley. General Lander, with a force of about four thousand men, made a series of rapid movements against " Stonewall Jackson," and with only four hundred horsemen he dashed upon him in the night at Blooming Gap, in the middle of February, captured seventeen of his commissioned officers and nearly sixty of his rank and file, and compelled him to retire. General Lander's career as an independent commander was short. His wound became painful from constant exertion, and this, with anxiety and exposure, brought on disease which assumed the form of a fatal congestion of the brain. He died on the 2d of March, when his country lost one of its ablest defenders. General Shields, another brave officer who had done good service in Mexico, succeeded Lander in command of his troops. We have learned that General Shields had commanded the brigade in Mexico where Colonel Baker gained his first experience as a soldier, while in command of the Fourth Illinois Regiment. At Cerro Gordo, when Shields was wounded, Baker, as senior colonel, took command of his brigade, " and led it successfully against the Mexican position," thereby winning renown.

† Report of Committee on Conduct of War, 2, page 289.

"*Question.* Where were you at the time of the disaster at Ball's Bluff?

"*Answer.* I was in command of the forces on the
Virginia side at Edward's Ferry. The evening before
(Sunday, 20th), I received orders to have two days'
rations cooked and my regiment marched as still as
possible to Edward's Ferry, and be there by daylight
or before. In accordance with that order, I was there
with my regiment. The 1st Minnesota regiment then
commenced crossing over in three scows, which would
hold fifty men each, and two small row-boats and a
boat which had been used as a ferry-boat before. There
were no planks there and no ropes, and the boats had
to be shoved across with poles.

"*Question.* What was the condition of the current
there?

"*Answer.* The current was running, I should judge,
at the rate of three to four miles an hour.

"*Question.* How far would it carry a boat down the
stream before you landed?

"*Answer.* One of my companies was carried down
two or three hundred yards below Goose creek, and
they were a long while poling up against the current,
and after a great deal of effort they succeeded in landing. *The whole two regiments were landed, I think,
in the neighborhood of 11 o'clock.* We had previously
sent over thirty cavalry under Major Mix. Having no
knowledge of the country or of the ground, *and no orders or information in regard to what was to be done,* I
simply threw out two companies of the Minnesota
regiment and of my own men as skirmishers and
picketed them on a little hill, and put the two regiments in line of battle.

"*Question.* What was your force then?

"*Answer.* Some 1,400 or 1,500 men. Immediately
after we got over there, two twelve-pound howitzers
were sent over, but without any orders, in charge of a

corporal and with no commissioned officer with them. I took the two howitzers and posted them upon a hill.

"*Question.* Were you over there while the battle of Ball's Bluff was going on?

"*Answer.* Yes, sir.

"*Question.* At what time did you begin to cross?

"*Answer.* The cavalry had crossed just before we got there, and the Minnesota men were then crossing. We crossed as fast as we could in the scows, and *I suppose we got our regiment all across in the neighborhood of nine or ten o'clock*—could not tell within an hour.

"*Question.* Did you hear firing?

"*Answer.* Yes, sir; we did. The fore part of the morning.

"*Question.* Where was General Stone?

"*Answer.* He was on the Maryland side of the river, I think, part of the time up on a hill, and part of the time in his own quarters—he was circulating around. He was not on the Virginia side at all at that time.

"*Question.* Were there any obstacles in the way of your going up to Ball's Bluff?

"*Answer.* None at all. No doubt we would have had to fight a little on our way up, but I think by going up that way on that side we could have drawn their attention toward us and engaged them so that Colonel Baker's forces would have had an opportunity to have got a better foothold than they had. He had a horribly bad place to cross there.

"*Question.* Now, in your judgment as a military man, knowing that a fight was going on at Ball's Bluff, what object could you have had in remaining where you were and not going up to assist them?

"*Answer.* I do not know about that. I cannot say. I could not have any object in particular.

"*Question.* What purpose was there to be effected by your remaining across there at Edward's Ferry?

"*Answer.* I do not know, because I was but a subordinate in command there. I did not know the general's plans; *I had no orders given me.* I acted on the defensive on my responsibility.

"*Question.* Who ordered you to cross there?

"*Answer.* I was ordered across by General Gorman, who was a Brigadier-General.

"*Question.* Had you any further orders what to do, after you had got across?

"*Answer.* No, sir, except one that General Gorman gave me, that if I was attacked—my men were posted about 150 feet from the river—to fall back to the banks of the river and maintain that position at any sacrifice, as that was all that was left to be done. I thought at the time that it was a good joke, and told him so.

"*Question.* You would have had the choice between being shot and being drowned?

"*Answer.* Yes, sir; there was a high bank there, and we must have maintained our position on that or have been driven into the river.

"*Question.* Where was General Gorman?

"*Answer.* On the Maryland side.

"*Question.* Do you know of any obstacle having been in the way to have prevented you from going from Edward's Ferry to the relief of Colonel Baker at Ball's Bluff?

"*Answer.* I think a force could have been got up there. I know of no impediment except it be the nature of the ground. I do not know how the ground is above where we were.

"*Question.* Did you see any batteries, or any thing of that kind, that would have prevented you going to Ball's Bluff?

"*Answer.* No, sir, I did not. We did not receive any fire from any batteries.

"*Question.* How many men did you have over there?

"*Answer.* About 2,500 men.

"*Question.* What purpose was to be effected by your

remaining over there all that night with such a force as that?

"*Answer.* I do not know what the purpose was. I had had 1,513 men over there in the afternoon, as I reported, and then some more men came over that afternoon, making about 2,500 men in all.

"*Question.* Was there any chance for you to be re-enforced?

"*Answer.* There were men enough on the Maryland side, if we would have got them over.

"*Question.* Suppose you had been attacked, would you have got re-enforcements across there?

"*Answer.* No, sir; not very well. We might have got a few across.

"*Question.* What would have been your condition had you been attacked by the force that had just been victorious at Ball's Bluff?

"*Answer.* We should either have been taken prisoners, killed, or driven into the river."

MAJOR BANNISTER testified before the Committee[*] as follows, he having served as General Gorman's volunteer aid, and after explaining the movements of troops on Sunday, 20th, at Edward's Ferry. He said:

"The next morning news came that the troops had passed down to the river again, and, as I had promised General Gorman the night before, I went back and acted as his aid. He had already sent over the First Minnesota with a company of cavalry under Major Mix. I then went back to General Stone for some orders to take over hard bread and rations. We continued to cross our troops more or less during the day. I could hear the firing at Ball's Bluff; I remained at Edward's Ferry all the while; we were posting our troops advantageously on the Virginia side, and I could hear the firing all the while. General Gorman was occupied in passing over troops, and from great exertion brought

---

* Report of Committee on Conduct of War, 2, page 283.

on a chill. This was about sun-down or dark. He went into a house near there, and ordered me to remain with his other aid and see that the provisions were sent over. We had nearly all the troops over there at that time.

"*Question.* How many troops did you pass over?

"*Answer.* We had 3,740 men. I went back to General Gorman to report progress. Just before this, however, Captain Candy, General Lander's Adjutant-General, who had been carrying despatches to Harrison's island or to Colonel Lee, came down about six o'clock in the evening, and stated that Colonel Baker was killed and they were bringing down his body. I stated this to General Gorman while I was reporting progress, and General Stone sent in word that he had passed up to the right of his column, that is, up to Harrison's island. He was gone about an hour, and when he came back he called out General Gorman and consulted with him. In a little while General Gorman sent for me to come out, and told me to go over on the opposite side of the river, strengthen the pickets, put out the lights there, and have Colonel Dana bring off the troops as quietly as possible without attracting attention, and to be very careful and make no noise in transporting the artillery. I understood this to be by General Stone's order, who had just come back from Ball's Bluff, where he had learned the full extent of the disaster. I went over and reported, and we had got across all but one regiment and the pickets when General Gorman sent word over to me by his aid to state to Colonel Dana that General Banks was coming up on the other side with 5,000 men, and that we would probably have re-enforcements from Dranesville, and to immediately recross the troops and have them take their original positions on the Virginia side. This was done, and completed about four o'clock on Tuesday morning.

"*Question.* Did you see any batteries in the way, or any obstacles to throwing a force up toward Ball's Bluff, on Monday afternoon?

"*Answer.* I saw nothing but a sand battery, I should think about forty rods from the river, between us and Ball's Bluff; but we could not understand from our prisoner that it had any guns.

"*Question.* Probably it had none?

"*Answer.* I could not say as to that; but from the conversation with the prisoner we could not understand that there were any guns there, and we could not see any with our glasses.

"*Question.* You could hear the firing at Ball's Bluff?

"*Answer.* Yes, sir.

"*Question.* You could see no insurmountable obstacle to throwing a force around from Edward's Ferry to the assistance of those at Ball's Bluff?

"*Answer.* Not at all. On Monday evening General Gorman came to me as we were crossing provisions, and said, "My boy, we will sleep at Leesburg to-night.' It seemed to be the understanding of all that we were to make a move immediately on Leesburg, but we had not then heard the extent of the disaster at Ball's Bluff. This prisoner told us there was this battery, which he supposed had no guns in it, and another battery near Gum Springs, which I understood was to the left of Leesburg as we approached from this side, but that back of Leesburg there was a formidable battery commanding the whole town, and that any force going into Leesburg from the river would be in danger of being cut all to pieces.

"*Question.* Then you saw nothing and heard of nothing, except this sand battery, where you understood there were no guns, to prevent moving the troops that had crossed at Edward's Ferry up to Ball's Bluff to assist the men then engaged?

"*Answer.* No, sir; I saw nothing, and, in fact, it

was my impression during the whole day, that as soon
as we got our provisions over we should move right up
to the support of our forces at Ball's Bluff.

"*Question.* How early in the day could you have
moved a force up to Ball's Bluff?

"*Answer. We could have moved two regiments by 10
o'clock in the morning.*

"*Question.* What time did the action at Ball's Bluff
commence?

"*Answer.* The heavy firing we heard seemed to
commence about half-past nine o'clock.

"*Question.* And, in an hour and a half after 10
o'clock, you could have been there?

"*Answer.* Yes, sir.

"*Question.* And you know of no obstacle in the
way?

"*Answer.* No, sir; and, further than that, I believe
now and I believed then, that the enemy's whole force
was engaged at Ball's Bluff, except this skeleton regiment.

"*Question.* There was no force opposed to you at
Edward's Ferry?

"*Answer.* No, sir.

"*Question.* General Stone was there?

"*Answer.* Yes, sir; on a hill on the Maryland side,
directing everything. General Gorman could not do
anything without General Stone's orders.

"*Question.* Do you know whether General Stone
took any steps to learn what was going on at Ball's
Bluff?

"*Answer.* He had Captain Candy carrying despatches up to Colonel Lee. I have statements from
Captain Candy of the orders that he carried back and
forward. I have not them with me, but can furnish
them to you. Colonel Lee told the captain to tell
General Stone 'that, if he wanted to make a campaign
into Virginia, now was the time, and to send up re-

enforcements; but that if he did not intend to make a campaign into Virginia, he had better withdraw the troops at once.' Captain Candy made this report to General Stone.

"*Question.* Then, if I understand you, during the whole day of Monday, after half-past nine o'clock, you heard heavy firing at Ball's Bluff?

"*Answer.* Yes, sir.

"*Question.* And General Stone was engaged merely in crossing troops at Edward's Ferry?

"*Answer.* He was not; he himself was on a high bluff or hill, up about half a mile from the Ferry, *directing generally at both places—Edward's Ferry and Ball's Bluff.* General Gorman was in command at Edward's Ferry.

"*Question.* General Stone did not go up to Ball's Bluff?

"*Answer.* Not until Captain Candy came down and reported to General Stone that Colonel Baker was killed.

"*Question.* How many men were thrown over there at 12 o'clock that day?

"*Answer.* I do not think there were many over two and a half regiments.

"*Question.* About 2,500 men?

"*Answer.* Yes, sir. I say there was no obstacle to moving up. There was none but this sand battery, which I understand had no guns. We were so near that if they had guns they could have impeded our landing at Edward's Ferry.

"*Question.* Suppose the battery had guns mounted, could not the troops have gone around it?

"*Answer.* We could have flanked the battery very easily, at least it seemed so to us. We did not go up to it.

"*Question.* If there had been guns there, they would have fired on you, would they not?

"*Answer.* I suppose they would. They were in full sight of us.

"*Question.* Did you hear any complaint at that time of the management of Colonel Baker in crossing the troops and landing them—any criticisms as to his action in battle?

"*Answer.* No, sir; I only heard this fault ascribed to him. Colonel Baker stood out in the open ground about ten feet in advance of his men, when he might have stepped back in the bushes. His only fault was being too brave."

MAJOR DIMMICK, who arrived on the morning of the 22d, testified before the Committee* as follows:

"There is no question that there has been a want of confidence in General Stone since the Ball's Bluff affair.

"*Question.* In his loyalty?

"*Answer.* Well, in his generalship. There are two parties there; of course Stone's friends throw the blame upon Baker, and Baker's friends throw the blame upon Stone. There is a great question about the orders received, whether they were transmitted to General Baker or not.

"*Question.* Did you satisfy yourself that there were no guns there (Edward's Ferry), at the time of the Ball's Bluff disaster?

"*Answer.* Yes, sir; on the day after.

"*Question.* How near did you go to it?

"*Answer.* Within 300 yards. There might have been a dozen men behind it then (Tuesday), but they kept themselves out of the way of our skirmishers, who protected us.

"*Question.* It is your opinion that that fort was not garrisoned at that time?

"*Answer.* It was only a breastwork thrown across the road, about breast high.

"*Question.*† Could you see any reason why our

troops should not have gone up from Edward's Ferry to Ball's Bluff to the assistance of General Baker?

"*Answer.* I could see none at all. I think we could have done it and turned them on their flank, and captured them all. * * * They (our troops) expected us to come up there to assist them, and that was the reason they made such a desperate resistance there. One of our men made his way up there from Edward's Ferry; how he got up there I do not know, but so anxious was he to get into the fight that he left his regiment and made his way up there, and went with the Tammany regiment.

PHILIP HANGER, who resided near Edward's Ferry, further testified before the committee* as follows:

"*Question.* How long have you lived there at Edward's Ferry and in that neighborhood?

"*Answer.* For six years.

"*Question.* Are you acquainted with the ground on the Virginia side between Edward's Ferry and Ball's Bluff?

"*Answer.* I certainly think I ought to be. I have been up and down a great many times.

"*Question.* Is there any difficulty in the way of men passing from Edward's Ferry to Ball's Bluff on the the Virginia side?

"*Answer.* I should think not.   ·

"*Question.* Are there any fortifications there that you know of?

"*Answer.* It was reported that there was a little embankment there, but the men would not be required to go within a half mile of that to go to Ball's Bluff.

"*Question.* Were there any guns mounted there?

"*Answer.* I never heard of any.

"*Question.* What is the distance from Edward's Ferry to Ball's Bluff?

---

* Report of Committee on Conduct of War, 2, page 345.

"*Answer.* About three miles, I should think, in a direct line.

"*Question.* There was no obstacle to infantry marching right up?

"*Answer.* None at all, except right on the bluff by the river. The land is rolling there, as it is about Chain Bridge; but, after you get from the river about an eighth of a mile, it is perfectly accessible for infantry.

"*Question.* How long would it have taken to have thrown a rope across at Edward's Ferry, so that these boats could have been taken across in that way by pulling on the rope?

"*Answer.* A very little time.

"*Question.* Would it have taken more than an hour?

"*Answer.* An hour or two at the outside."*

It seems useless to tire the reader by a further recital of the whole volume of damaging evidence as to Stone's peculiarities and inefficiency as a commander. Perhaps too much has already been given for pleasant reading, while less might not satisfy a "doubting Thomas." Therefore, all who may wish additional testimony, can find it by referring to the Report of the Joint Committee on the Conduct of the War, part 2.

This testimony relates directly to a commander who testified as to the management at Ball's Bluff. "I do not think a careful commander would have attempted that crossing so heedlessly. I think any careful commander would have himself gone to the field, and attempted to look before him before he attempted to cross 2000 men in the face of the enemy. One of the chief faults is that he commenced crossing the troops, remaining himself on this side." We have learned that

---

* We have noticed that Stone censured Baker for wasting time on the transportation while trying to have a rope stretched across from the Maryland shore to Harrison's island while crossing his troops.

of the 1500 men and 3 pieces of artillery that crossed
there, Stone had crossed 900 men and 2 pieces of artillery, and that Baker simply went to their rescue, and
was on the battle-field before 100 of his men had
crossed to the Virginia shore, and that he got but 500
or 600 men and 1 piece of artillery across in all, *that
Stone never went upon the field himself* on the day of the
fight, but gave the orders to cross, not only there, but
also at Edward's Ferry, *where he did not go upon the field
until sent across by General McClellan*, nor did he even
go upon Harrison's island, although he has told us he
was in command there during the fight at Ball's Bluff.
As to Edward's Ferry he testified:

"I sent over 31 cavalry with four officers, at daybreak, or shortly after, with two companies of Minnesota skirmishers. * * * There were very few troops
sent over there, for we did not try to increase our force
largely over there until I got information from Colonel
Baker.*   I should say that about 11 o'clock, perhaps,†
I will not be positive about the hour, but about that
time I received a report from Colonel Baker that he
was crossing his whole force.   I then commenced
crossing over Gorman's brigade, pushing them over
much more rapidly than I had been doing before.   The
number that was over there at the time this action was
going on on the right, was about 1500 or 1600 infantry,
30 cavalry, and a section of howitzers with their
horses and equipments."

We have learned how completely Stone has been
contradicted as to the time of crossing, and the number
of troops crossed, by the testimony of General Dana,
Colonel Tompkins, Majors Bannister and Mix, which
will be corroborated in part or in whole by Henry R.
Foot, quartermaster,‡ in charge of transportation, and

---

* Howe's report to Stone of Baker's conversation, page 101.

† If not later.

‡ Report of Committee on Conduct of War, 2, page 364.

Major Dimmick. Also by Stone's own testimony previously given in parenthesis* *i. e.*, "One of the last words that I said to Colonel Baker when he left me (THERE WAS ANOTHER LARGE OPERATION AND RECONNAISSANCE GOING ON DOWN AT GOOSE CREEK, WHICH I WAS WATCHING)—one of the last things I said was, 'If you use artillery there (Ball's Bluff), if you move artillery, please see that it is well guarded.'"

This large operation *was moving long before Baker received his orders to cross.* Stone had then crossed two regiments, and was about crossing the third, while in his direct testimony he would lead us to believe that he had only crossed two companies of skirmishers at the time Baker left him. And in later testimony he admitted that he had 2500 troops across during the action, and we have learned that he had about 4000 troops across before Colonel Baker fell.

We find, by referring to General Stone's first report, that he had told Colonel Baker "that I should continue to re-enforce the troops under General Gorman opposite Edward's Ferry, and try to push them carefully forward."† Meaningless, cold and Stone-like words! The much-disgusted officers who were upon the field at Edward's Ferry have told us of the exasperating state of affairs there as to means of transportation and management of troops, of which General Evans exclaimed: "*If the enemy won't come to us, we must go to them,*" and he left Stone's front and threw his whole strength upon Baker, all of which

---

* Report of Committee on Conduct of War, 2, page 269.

† Major Ritman stated that "Lieutenant Wade of my company (D) was in the advance on the left when he discovered the Confederates moving through the ravine there, which he reported to Colonel Baker (who was then posting his men as they arrived), to whom Colonel Baker replied, 'No doubt they are General Gorman's men coming up from Edward's Ferry,' showing that he expected support from that quarter." As related to the author.

most unquestionably reflected Stone's criminal neglect and inefficiency as a soldier. His representations to Colonel Baker when he sent him to the right to take command, were mere snares and delusions; he did not even make the slightest diversion in Colonel Baker's favor, or by force of arms try to ascertain the position and strength of the enemy confronting his own forces, while Colonel Baker, *relying upon his promise and co-operation*, had gone to the bluff to save the imperilled troops placed there by Stone, almost hopelessly surrounded by the enemy, with no adequate means of retreat across the river, and against whom the Confederate troops were being constantly detached from Stone's front, the effect of which General Wistar accurately described in his address referred to: "As the hostile regiments arrived in position, the weight and effect of their fire increased, and the action soon became close and severe. The enemy's superior numbers enabled them to detach constantly against our exposed left without slackening their overpowering fire in front. While much occupied with the difficult situation of our left, Baker came up with a dispatch just received from General Stone to the effect that 'four regiments have been seen by our scouts crossing an open place and marching towards you.'

"As the despatch had traveled five miles and twice crossed the river, it was considered that those regiments must already be in our front, and we were feeling their maximum effect. With our left enfiladed and in close contact with the enemy during the overpowering front fire, it was dangerous either to manœuver or withdraw, even had means existed to recross the river. But the command, though pinned fast, was firm, and it was thought that if the gun could be got into action (again) and the enemy shaken in our front, our people might be able to clear away the enemy's flanking force and get forward through the woods on the left," but soon "the scanty ammunition in the limber-box was exhausted, by which time the piece was disabled by having the spokes shot out of the wheel."

10

CHAPTER VIII.

A GLIMPSE AT THE CONFEDERATE FORCES AND THEIR MOVEMENTS FROM FORT EVANS AND EDWARD'S FERRY TO BALL'S BLUFF.

LET us now glance at the official Confederate reports to ascertain, if possible, the position and strength of the enemy's forces that confronted General Stone on that eventful Monday of the 21st.

General Evans* reported, in "observing the movements of the enemy from Fort Evans (three miles from Edward's Ferry), at six o'clock a. m., I found he had effected a crossing both at Edward's Ferry and at Ball's Bluff, and I made preparations to meet him in both positions, and immediately ordered four companies of infantry" * * * "and a cavalry force to relieve Captain Duff—the whole force under the immediate command of Lieutenant-Colonel W. H. Jenifer, who was directed to hold his position till the enemy made further demonstration of his design of attack. This force soon became warmly engaged with the enemy, and drove them back some distance into the woods. At about 10 o'clock I became convinced that the main point of attack would be at Ball's Bluff, and ordered Colonel Hunton with his regiment, the 8th Virginia volunteers, to repair immediately to the support of Colonel Jenifer. I directed Colonel Hunton to form line of battle immediately in the rear of Colonel Jenifer's command and drive the enemy to the river, *that I would support his right with artillery.* About 12:20 o'clock p. m. Colonel Hunton united his command with that of Colonel Jenifer, and both commands

* Official Records, Series I, Vol. V, page 348.

soon *became hotly engaged with the enemy in their strong position in the woods.* Watching carefully the action, I saw the enemy was constantly being re-enforced, *and, at 2 o'clock p. m.,* ordered Colonel Burt to march his regiment, the 18th Mississippi, *and attack the left flank of the enemy while Colonels Hunton and Jenifer attacked him in front.* On arriving in his position, Colonel Burt was received with a tremendous fire from the enemy concealed in a ravine,* and was compelled to divide his regiment to stop the flank movement of the enemy. At this time, about 3 o'clock, finding the enemy were in large force, I ordered Colonel Featherstone with his regiment, the 17th Mississippi, to repair at double-quick to the support of Colonel Burt, where he arrived in twenty minutes, and the *action became general along my whole line, and was very hot and brisk for more than two hours, the enemy keeping up a constant fire."* * * * "At about 6 o'clock p. m. I saw that my command had driven the enemy near the banks of the Potomac. *I ordered my entire force to charge, and to drive him into the river.* The charge was immediately made by the whole command, and the forces of the enemy were completely routed " * * * "along his whole line. *In this charge the enemy were driven back at the point of the bayonet, and many killed and wounded* by this formidable weapon. In the precipate retreat of the enemy on the bluffs of the river, many of his troops rushed into the river and were drowned, while many others, in overloading the boats, sunk them and shared the same fate. The rout now, about 7 o'clock, became complete, and the enemy commenced throwing his arms into the river. During this action I held Colonel William Barksdale, with nine companies of his regiment, the 13th Mississippi, and six pieces of artillery, as a reserve, as well as to keep up a demon-

* Colonel Wistar's battalion of the California regiment, where Colonel Burt fell.

stration against the force of the enemy at Edward's
Ferry. *At 8 o'clock p. m., the enemy surrendered* his
forces at Ball's Bluff, and the prisoners were marched
to Leesburg. I then ordered my brigade* to retire to
the town of Leesburg and rest for the night. * * *

"The engagement on our side was fought entirely
with the musket. *The artillery was in position to do
effective service, should the enemy (at Ball's Bluff) have
advanced from their cover.*"

Now we understand that General Evans concluded as early as 10 o'clock a. m., that he had
not much to fear from Edward's Ferry and that he
could throw his whole strength upon Colonel Baker's
forces ; and why he should so conclude would seem
a mystery to us, if we had not been informed by
our officers in command at Edward's Ferry that they
had no orders, and simply lay at their ease doing
nothing, with a force outnumbering Colonel Baker's at
Ball's Bluff, almost three to one. The First Minnesota,
Second New York, one skirmishing company of the
Nineteenth Massachusetts, and a company of telescopic
sharp-shooters under Major Howe, and cavalry under
Major Mix, making a force of at least two thousand
men, were across between 10 and 11 o'clock a. m., who
were re-enforced by the 34th New York and two
twelve-pound howitzers of a Rhode Island battery before one o'clock p. m., and during the early part of the
afternoon, before 4 o'clock p. m., by the 7th Michigan
regiment, making a total of 3,740 men in addition to
officers on the Virginia side at Edward's Ferry, so reported by Major Bannister, General Gorman's aid, who
assisted him in superintending the crossing of these
troops. This force was confronted by the 13th Mississippi regiment, the 17th and 18th Mississippi regiments
lying farther up the river in the rear, with six pieces of

* Excepting the 13th Mississippi Regiment, which was sent
back toward Edward's Ferry.

artillery posted for the protection of Leesburg in the early part of the day. We have now learned that the 8th Virginia regiment was ordered to Ball's Bluff at 10 a. m., which General Evans then thought would be the main point of attack, and placed his artillery to resist an advance on Leesburg from that point, which was held in reserve for Colonel Baker's forces should they advance through the woods. At 2:30 p. m. the 18th Mississippi was engaged at Ball's Bluff, and at 3 p. m. the 17th Mississippi arrived on the double-quick, followed shortly thereafter by the 13th Mississippi, the Colonel of which regiment, Barksdale, reported :*

"At this moment I was ordered by you to hasten to the support of the 8th Virginia, the 17th and 18th Missisippi regiments, which were engaged with the enemy *two miles from Edward's Ferry* and near Conrad's Ferry : I at once, and in double-quick time, started to their relief, *leaving Captain Worthington's company to observe the movement of the enemy at Edward's Ferry."* * * * "I am satisfied that the presence of my command in position at Edward's Ferry prevented the advance of a large column of the enemy which was intended to re-enforce General Baker's command near Conrad's Ferry, then engaged in battle with our forces."

General Evans has told us that he withdrew his forces at 8 p. m. We will find hereafter that they were considerably shattered and required rest and reorganization, having made every preparation to retreat to Leesburg just before Colonel Baker fell.†

* Official Records, Series I, Vol. V, page 354.

†After the close of the war a staff officer, late of the Confederate army, related that he had been sent to General Evans with orders and reached him on the morning of October 21st, and requested permission to remain and witness the action which then seemed imminent. He did remain, and saw many things that happened on their side. He said just before General Baker's death they had made every preparation for a retreat, that the people of Leesburg were fleeing from the town,

The 13th Mississippi came up toward the close of the engagement, apparently to cover the retreat; it not having suffered much, was ordered back toward Edward's Ferry, while all the other troops fell back to the artillery on Leesburg. Colonel Barksdale* reported† that he had returned "to the vicinity of Fort Evans" (3 miles from Edward's Ferry, and 1 mile from Leesburg), having directed the "companies of Captain Randall, McIntosh, and Worthington to remain in the rear to prevent the advance of the enemy that night from Edward's ferry." Lieutenant-Colonel John Mc-Quirk, of the 17th Mississippi, tells us in his report‡ to General Evans, how matters stood at Ball's Bluff when he went upon the field at 4 p. m.: he found "that the

and that they had no expectation of holding the place; but when General Baker fell they saw that his death caused a demoralization among the Nationals, and they renewed the attack with more vigor. *Thus turned the tide of battle upon the death of one man;* so are battles lost and won. In the camps of the Nationalists in the neighborhood of the battlefield on that gloomy night, there was darkness and woe, so suggestively expressed in the old camp song—

> " We're tenting to-night on the old camp ground,
>   Give us a song to cheer
>   Our weary hearts ; a song of home
>   And friends we love so dear.

> " We've been fighting to-day on the old camp ground,
>   Many are lying near ;
>   Some are dead and some are dying,
>   Many are in tears."

—while the little panic-stricken village of Leesburg near by " was brilliantly illuminated, and the Confederates there were wild with joy"—as they marched many of the sorely tried and battered Nationalists to Libby. Thus by the neglect and inefficiency of our general commanders, fright and sadness at Leesburg had been turned into joy and gladness.

* Afterward General Barksdale, who fell at Gettysburg, July, 1863.

† Ante.

‡ Official Records, Series I, Vol. V, page 361.

brave 8th Virginia Regiment * * * had been
forced to retire from exhaustion and the want of ammunition," and that "upon the surrender to him of
Colonel Cogswell" (about 7 p. m.), "I was left with
two companies of the 18th Mississippi to secure and
bring forward the balance of the prisoners. On leaving
the field with a strong detatchment of prisoners" (officers and men who had surrendered with Cogswell or
Lee), "I was met by Colonel Hunton of the 8th Virginia,
who requested me to return with 15 men to act as picket
guards. I went forward, reported the prisoners to you,
and by you was ordered back to the battle-field, and
to remain until relieved. I took from my regiment a
detachment of ninety men. When I reached the field,
I found a small picket under the charge of a Lieutenant. Shortly after I arrived, Mr. E. White entered the
field with two companies of the 8th Virginia.* I
joined my forces to his, and leaving a small detachment above to fire on the enemy if they attempted to
escape by boats across to the island, with the remainder of the detachment we went forward under the
cliffs, and took many prisoners—in fact, the greatest
number taken at any one time. To do this, we were
compelled from the red shale cliffs to fire upon them as
they attempted to cross in the scows to Harrison's
island. Many who had reached half-way across turned
back."

*Colonel Elijah V. White, of Ashby's cavalry, bore upon his
person, at the close of the war, a dozen wounds, among them a
bullet still remaining in the head—whose perfect familiarity
with the ground and country over which the contest at Ball's
Bluff was being waged, in addition to his reckless bravery,
made him peculiarly useful to the Confederates during the day,
and after they had retired rather hastily to Leesburg without
securing the howitzers or the bulk of the officers and men on
the bluff, he, by personal exertion, raised volunteers, whom
he brought back, and with them gathered up our scattered
forces on the bluff, and along the shore, as well as the artillery,
long after night-fall.

Now it has been made plain that during the heat of the battle and while the enemy were on the eve of a retreat, our forces at Edward's Ferry were held in check by one company of the 13th Mississippi, perhaps less than one hundred men. Colonel White,* an undoubted authority, has informed the writer as to the distance between Gorman and Baker's men: "I do not think over two and a half miles," and that there was nothing between the two commands "but the Confederate forces," while in General Stone's vivid imagination are seen concealed fortifications and masked batteries in the woods; therefore, his four thousand troops and artillery could not advance until Colonel Baker's fourteen hundred men cleared the country of all such obstacles, and made the way perfectly safe, in which case he will fall upon the enemy's right flank and capture them. But, unfortunately, Stone's strategy did not work well; while he was so patiently waiting to hear from Colonel Baker that the road was clear, the whole of the enemy's forces, about four thousand strong, swooped down upon the brave Baker and his devoted band of fourteen hundred men, and, after a hard struggle of from four to five hours, killed, wounded and captured almost his entire force. Notwithstanding the enemy had been badly crippled and retired from the hard-fought field hastily, without going over the ground held by their enemy, to gather up the prisoners and spoils of war, General Stone, with great secrecy and unseemly haste, ordered his force to retreat; and, while he was making this masterly retreat of four thousand troops and two pieces of artillery

*"On the 21st of October Mr. White was riding along the road to Leesburg with a lady, when he heard the firing at Ball's Bluff. He entered the field as a volunteer aide to General Evans (and thereafter served in the war as related). He is now an esteemed Old School Baptist minister, residing at Leesburg, and is held in high estimation in Loudon county by Unionists, his comrades and neighbors alike."—*Colonel Banes.*

in the face of about two hundred of the enemy's pickets, he received an order from General McClellan to recross the troops, and hold the Virginia shore at all hazards.

We will now leave General Stone reposing upon his laurels at Edward's Ferry, busily engaged in explaining his movements so as to relieve himself from all blame, hence his first report contained many straws which subsequently sank beneath him. We will notice here but one of the many statements in that report, "one thousand men (would have been) enough to have turned the scale in our favor," which must have been a consoling thought to Stone, when mindful of the fact that he had about four thousand men and two pieces of artillery within two and a half miles of the battle-field, idly listening to the whole engagement, to whom he gave no orders to advance and engage the enemy, although they were in good condition and eager for the fray.

CHAPTER IX.

COLONEL BAKER AND LIEUTENANT-COLONEL WISTAR ON THE BLUFF.

Now Colonel Baker has arrived at Harrison's island, amid a scene of strife, having in his possession his first order of the day (*i. e.*, "In case of heavy firing in front of Harrison's island, you will advance the California Regiment," etc.), without much time for reflection or consultation; while from the information given him by General Stone, he is led to believe that the transportation is adequate, and that the enemy's force in his front is but a small one. The second order from General Stone, given above, containing the following, "I am informed that the force of the enemy is about 4000 all told. If you can push them you may do so," was received by Colonel Baker upon the field, while hopelessly surrounded, and just before being heavily engaged in battle by the enemy. Let us now understand what General Stone meant by this first order of so general a character. He tells us in his official report that he had fully explained his wishes and intentions to Colonel Baker before giving him this order. Not being able to get from Colonel Baker his version of their interview, we must content ourselves with Stone's while testifying in his own defense.*

"*Question.* You did not give Colonel Baker an order to cross?

"*Answer.* No sir, I did not. Fortunately there was a written order found in his hat, in which I gave him discretionary orders.

---

* Report of Committee on Conduct of War, 2, page 270.

"*Question.* (page 269) Did you intend that he (Baker) should cross?

"*Answer.* I intended and instructed him to use his discretion about crossing, or withdrawing the troops already over there. If we found that Leesburg had been abandoned by the enemy, we had nothing to do but to occupy it. I directed him to hold on there, and of course not yield ground we had taken possession of without resistance. But if this party found that there was not a strong force there—if it was a force he could easily drive before him, he should drive it off; if it was of such a size that he could not drive it off easily, then he was to fall back. But he was to use his discretion as to whether he had the means to drive off any force which might be there. After this reconnoitering party had advanced so far, it was not an unreasonable supposition that they were in small force there. Still it was a thing to be guarded against, that there might be a force there, and a strong one. * * * I then told him (page 275) to go up and take entire command, entire control* of the right, four miles from from where I stood. He said 'Then I am to have entire command.' 'Yes,' said I. 'Please put that in writing,' he said. I then took out my pencil, and on my knee wrote that order"—Baker's first order of the day, given above.

Thus General Stone, the regular army officer, who had been trained in all the arts of war at the expense of the government, would make us believe that he had turned over to Colonel Baker, a brave and ardent patriot (whose experience in military affairs was slight, when compared with that of the regular army officers),

---

* We must bear in mind that Stone has previously told us under oath (page 267), in answer to the "*Question*, Were you in command there (Harrison's island) at the time of the fight at Ball's Bluff?

"*Answer.* I was ; yes sir."

two-thirds of his whole division, 6000 to 7000 men, and
8 pieces of artillery, to carry out Stone's plan of occupying Leesburg if abandoned, in holding the ground we
had possession of across the river, and in driving off
any force of the enemy there if possible, with transportation estimated by him sufficient to carry over 750
men an hour, which, when put in use, would not carry
over, under the most favorable circumstances, 200 men
each hour, without artillery, for which latter purpose it
was almost useless.

General Stone thereby considered himself relieved of
all responsibility on the right, and passed the day
without apparent concern at his headquarters (and in
utter disregard of his promise to push Gorman forward), not even assuming the responsibility of allowing the troops at Edward's Ferry to make a diversion
in Colonel Baker's favor.

Now Colonel Baker has assumed the duties of a general in command of the advance. He finds 900 of his
men upon the Virginia shore, and has been instructed
to occupy and hold Leesburg, if abandoned, "and of
course not to yield ground we had taken possession of
(on the Virginia shore) without resistance," and, if possible, to drive any force of the enemy there before him.
Can any one reasonably say that Colonel Baker would
not have to cross the river to carry these orders into
effect? If not, then Colonel Baker was verbally ordered to cross, and we have Stone's testimony for it,
and Stone designated the ground he was to hold, the
bluff on which Stone had placed his troops. Lieutenant Howe has said that Stone told him that he had
given orders to Baker to cross, and Colonels Lee and
Devens testified that they were confident that they received word from Stone that Colonel Baker would come
over and take command. Chaplain Robert Kellen, of
Baker's staff, testified that he saw an order, and that it
was most unquestionably a pre-emptory order to cross.

CLIFF AT BALL'S BLUFF OPPOSITE HARRISON'S ISLAND.

Is not General Stone's word enough, without this additional evidence, that he intended that Baker should
cross and hold the bluff where Stone had placed his
troops? Baker so understood Stone, and if he had not
crossed and held that position, he would not have carried out Stone's orders and instructions. Did Baker
exercise a sound discretion in obeying Stone's instructions, when he had given him little or no means of
transportation, or did his patriotic zeal and ardor out-
run discretion? When he arrived opposite Harrison's
island, he found that the means of transportation was
not one-quarter as great as Stone had represented it to
be; so he did all in his power to improve and supple-
ment it by adding a boat before leaving the Maryland
shore and by stretching a cable across the river* (which
was not completed when he left, but was shortly thereafter) to avoid the slow and tedious process of poling
the boats across, thus shortening the course and time
at least one-half, from the Maryland shore to the island,
(a more needed and important work could not have
been performed), and when he crossed to the island he
found the means of transportation to the Virginia shore
much worse, with no possible way of improving it in a
short space of time, while upon the bluff were troops
placed there by Stone's orders, heavily skirmishing
with the enemy and calling loudly and repeatedly for
help. Could Baker withdraw them safely to the island,
with the means of transportation at hand?

COLONEL DEVENS testified† in answer to the question, "Was the means of transportation used by you
in the morning when you crossed provided by General
Stone?

"*Answer.* It was then.

"*Question.* General Stone knew the means you had
to make the crossing?

---

* Not in wasting time while his men were lifting a boat from
the canal, as Stone charges in his report of December 2, 1861.

† Report of Committee on Conduct of War, 2. page 412.

"*Answer.* I take for granted that the general who directs me to cross knows what I am to cross in.

"*Question.* What did you cross in?

"*Answer.* I crossed my regiment with a life-boat and two skiffs. The life-boat would hold something like 25 men. The two skiffs would hold 7 or 8 each. I did not take so many as that in crossing."

It took him about four hours to cross 300 men in the night. Captain Bartlett reported that the large boat would hold 16 men, and the other two boats 4 and 5 each; and Colonel Lee testified that the three boats would hold 28 men in all. This transportation had been increased by another boat, before Baker arrived, that would hold about 40 men. These were the means at hand for a rapid retreat of 900 men and two pieces of artillery, if it became necessary, which would carry back about 200 men per hour, under favorable conditions, requiring from four to five hours to recross the force that Stone had placed on the Virginia shore.

It was evident if Baker attempted to withdraw, and the enemy got possession of the bluff (the key to the position), the retreating troops, the transportation, and the whole island, would be swept by a murderous fire. Stone had placed his troops in a perilous position, where they could not retreat for want of means to re-cross the river, and for the same reason they could not be successfully re-enforced in the face of the enemy, and he instructed Baker to hold on there and not to yield the ground without resistance. Was ever a general placed in a more perplexing position? *Was not his position as hopeless as that of the brave Uriah the Hittite of old?* General Stone afterward claimed that through kindness he had given Colonel Baker the opportunity of earning his commission to the rank of major-general, which had been bestowed upon him by President Lincoln and only awaited his own acceptance. If in kindness, it seemed against great odds—most cruelly so. We

know that Baker hesitated, and was greatly annoyed
upon viewing the inadequate means for crossing from
the Maryland shore, *which Stone deemed all-sufficient.*
When he had crossed the island he again hesitated,
and at the second crossing exclaimed: "Is there only
one boat there?" Then came the urgent appeal for
help, from the overhanging bluff, sharpened by the
unmistakable sound of the approaching conflict, when
hesitation gave place to stubborn valor, born of necessity, and he boldly faced the inevitable.

Perhaps in that one supreme moment his great heart
echoed the sentiments, so feelingly quoted by General
Wolfe, on that beautiful starlit night, when he scaled
the Heights of Abraham:

"The boast of heraldry, the pomp of power,
    And all that beauty, all that wealth e'er gave,
Await alike the inevitable hour ;
    The paths of glory lead but to the grave."

The bluff, the key to the whole position, must be
held at all hazards, and the transportation covered, or
the troops there or in retreat would be destroyed if they
could not successfully hold out, and repulse the onset
of the foe. Colonel Baker could not think of abandon-
ing them to their fate; every impulse of his noble
nature rebelled at such a thought, he climbed to the
post of danger, and ordered the balance of the troops
and artillery to cross to their support, but unfortunately
not more than 500 or 600 additional troops were able to
cross.

GENERAL N. P. BANKS testified, "I do not think myself that Colonel Baker could have done otherwise
than he did. Being across, it was necessary for him to
fight. *I should have done the same thing.*"[*]

COLONEL JAMES H. VAN ALLAN testified,[†] in answer

* Report of Committee on Conduct of War, 2, page 420.

† Report of Committee on Conduct of War, part 2, page 461.

to the "*Question.* Do you know at what time General Baker was ordered to take command over there (Ball's Bluff)?

"*Answer.* I do not; I think it was at 5 o'clock in the morning.*

"*Question.* They were in the enemy's territory, limited in numbers, and threatened by a force the strength of which they did not know?

"*Answer.* Exactly.

"*Question.* Under those circumstances, would you not have used such transportation as you had to have re-enforced those men?

"*Answer.* I think I would."

GENERAL LANDER whose testimony we have read, said, in answer to the "*Question.* Whose duty was it to have provided sufficient transportation for that passage before it was made?

"*Answer.* It is regarded as the duty of a good commanding general *especially when he has inexperienced men, to see that all these things are provided.* * * * I think there was an error there. Perhaps from want of information they did not make preparations beforehand. If we had orders to cross that river, we should have had them a week beforehand."

We have learned from Stone's statements and reports that he had been making some preparations to cross for more than a week before the battle, which Lander evidently thought were of little or no use when made, thereby agreeing substantially with General McCall that Stone had not transportation enough to cross at all, while Stone thought it adequate.

GENERAL McCLELLAN† testified, "I only know what I learned from General Stone. My recollection is that

---

* This shows the impression produced by Stone's reports. No doubt they were generally understood as he had intended they should be.

† Report of Committee on Conduct of War, 2, page 506.

General Stone gave discretionary orders to Colonel Baker to cross if certain conditions could be fulfilled. *I think that General Stone was responsible to the extent that he ought to have informed himself whether it was possible to fulfil those conditions or not.* * * * *What I allude to as the "conditions" is the means of transportation for ferrying the troops across the river.*"

"*Question.* Why did you, after you arrived at Edward's Ferry cross over troops to hold the position at Edward's Ferry, instead of recalling the troops already on the Virginia side?

"*Answer.* Reports came that the enemy were about to attack the troops on the Virginia side. I regarded it as unsafe, if not impossible, to withdraw the troops then over during the day-time, and I sent over others to support them merely as a precautionary measure for their safety."

If General McClellan displayed good generalship in not withdrawing the troops at Edward's Ferry, in daylight, while the enemy showed no disposition to press them, where our men could be withdrawn, under cover of our guns on the Maryland side, by transportation ten times greater than Baker had at Harrison's island, on the Virginia side. What a strong endorsement of the generalship displayed by Colonel Baker in re-enforcing Stone's men, instead of withdrawing them from the bluff,* from which the enemy could have commanded his whole line of retreat, across both branches of the river, the island, and even on the Maryland shore. It would seem, from the testimony of some of our best generals, that no officer having the courage to face the danger, would have entertained for a moment, under such circumstances, the thought of a retreat, notwithstanding Stone officially blamed Baker

---

* Baker knew that Stone was able at least, to hold the enemy at Edward's Ferry, and possibly come to his assistance, which he looked for throughout the whole afternoon.

11

for not ordering a retreat, which would have been followed by wholesale murder, without giving his troops an opportunity to strike a blow in self-defense. Baker's reputation would have been blasted, and his name blazed not only as an incompetent officer, but as wanting in courage, had he ordered a retreat.

Then we must conclude that Baker, with great courage and forethought, grandly and nobly did his whole duty as long as life lasted; and when he remarked, just before his death, "The officer who dies with his men men will never be harshly judged," he surely did not realize, that the accomplished " Chesterfield" would so quickly assume, the rôle of the distorter of truth and destroyer of evidence.

After Colonel Baker had crossed, General Stone sent the following despatch:

> EDWARD'S FERRY, October 21, 1861, 2 P. M.
>
> MAJOR-GENERAL McCLELLAN: There has been sharp firing on the right of our line, and our troops appear to be advancing there under Baker. The left under Gorman has advanced its skirmishers nearly one mile, and, if the movement continues successful, will turn the enemy's right.   C. P. STONE,
> Brigadier-General.*

We here notice one of Stone's peculiarities; while he was thus moving his troops on the left upon paper to turn the enemy's right, *he failed to give the order to move upon the field.* It is evident from this despatch that he intended his right as well as his left should advance, and, at the writing of this despatch, he did not complain of hidden batteries in his way; that seems to have been an after-thought, with little or no foundation, although it became the rock of his defense.

Let us hear from Colonel Wistar, what he saw upon the left of Colonel Baker's line, that was being crowded by the enemy from Stone's front. He further testified before the committee† as follows:

* Official Records, Series I, Vol. V, pages 33 and 34.
† Report of Committee on Conduct of War, 2, page 307.

"I continued crossing my six companies over into Virginia. But, when I had crossed four of them, I became anxious lest their disposition on the other side might not be such as I desired, and I went over myself. As soon as I got upon the field, Colonel Baker came up to me, and said in a hurried manner, 'Come, and go round with me, and look at my disposition and plans, and say what you think of them.' There was then a slight spitting fire from the tree-tops around, but no enemy in sight. They were firing at the officers. The officers and men of the line were all lying down, by Colonel Baker's orders, to avoid this fire. He explained to me very fully, and asked what I thought of it. I expressed no opinion, but said I would ask permission to extend the skirmishers of my regiment on the left, they being within a few paces of the left of our line, He said, 'I throw the entire responsibility of the left wing upon you.' I then went to the left wing and sent Captain Crowningshield away, directed him to re-join his regiment (the 20th Massachusetts), and took one company of skirmishers of my own, and directed them to advance in open order to a hill, so as to see what they could ascertain of the enemy's position and strength. Just as they were moving out, Colonel Baker and Colonel Cogswell came up to me; Colonel Baker said, '*Colonel Wistar, I want you to send out two of your best skirmishing companies to the front, and feel the enemy's position*, and see what is on our flank; make a thorough reconnaissance.' I have omitted to state that just before this he read me a dispatch which he said he had just received from General Stone (of 11:50 a. m., brought over by Cogswell, given above). It was something like this, 'Sir, 4000 of the enemy are marching from Leesburg to attack you.' I at once re-marked to him, that considering the time it must have taken this dispatch to pass through to us, those 4000 men must then be in front of us. Said I, 'We are greatly

out-numbered in front.' ' *Yes,*' *said he,* ' *that is a bad
condition of things.*' I was about advancing these skirmishers when I received his directions to push out two
companies to the front. I said, 'The enemy cannot be
less than 5000 men, and probably 7000 in front, and
around this field, and to send out two companies of
skirmishers will be to sacrifice them.' He said, 'I
cannot help it, *I must know what is there.*' 'Well,'
said I, turning to the captain of the company I was
about advancing, 'you hear what my orders are: do
you understand them?' 'Yes, sir;' said he. Captain
Markoe had a good company which I could trust, an
excellent company, and I sent it out: I then took a
company out myself in support. While advancing toward the enemy, they had to pass across an open
field; they had no time to go around. The enemy however did not fire on them, until the first company entered
the woods. They had got about ten paces in the
woods—I was about thirty paces behind with the second company—when the whole of the 8th Virginia
regiment rose up from the ground about thirty paces
off* and ran right at them with the bayonet, without
firing a shot. Captain Markoe held his men steady.
I ran up with my company, and a very hot fire immediately commenced on our part. Our men, being in
open order, had that advantage, and a great many of
the Virginians broke and ran away. The rest of them
had to stop their charge, and fire lying down and from
behind trees, etc. The enemy over here (along the
front and toward our right), hearing pretty sharp
firing where we were, supposed we had attacked their
right flank in force, and immediately threw in a heavy

---

* We have learned that Cogswell incorrectly reported that
"the hills were not then occupied by the enemy," and this is
an additional confirmation of that mistake, the enemy having
been found within sixty paces on the ground and concealed by
the wood.

volley upon our main body, and our men returned it. I put these two companies in the charge of Captain Markoe, and ran back as hard as I could to take command of my regiment. Captain (afterward Colonel) Markoe with his two companies held this position there for about fifteen minutes, during which time they lost all their officers, all their sergeants but two (one of them wounded), all their corporals but three, and two-thirds of their privates; when the rest of them, under the command of the only remaining sergeant unwounded, fell back in pretty good order, bringing with them *a first lieutenant and fourteen men of the 8th Virginia regiment prisoners* under the fire of their whole regiment. They fell back, and I posted them in a point of woods as skirmishers to cover the open place there and prevent our being outflanked. In the meantime, *at the first fire, Colonel Baker moved up his reserve, and extended our left with it*, so that we were then all in position. The action then went on. The first fire brought on by these skirmishers advancing commenced at half-past two. About half an hour afterward, the 8th Virginia, having got rid of our skirmishers, attempted to charge our left. They moved across the open place in column, came around behind the hill, which concealed them from us, and under shelter of the hill*deployed into line. Fortunately, I had seen them; I had feared that, and having no skirmishers to watch them, I kept a pretty sharp lookout, and detected their movement in time to prepare for it. I at once changed front of three or four companies to meet them. I knew of course they would deploy behind the hill. From the top of the hill to our left, was about sixty yards.† About fifteen

*Should have been the 18th Mississippi, which came in on the left of the 8th Virginia at 2:30 p. m., and moved to their right.

† Which agrees with Colonel Jenifer's report as to the position held by the 8th Virginia at 1:30 p. m.

yards from there ran a gully. The ground sloped
down gently to the bottom of the gully, and then rose
quickly to the top of the hill. I changed front of three
or four companies, and held their fire until the Virginia regiment had got to this gully, and when they
had accumulated their men there, I delivered them a volley, which threw them into entire confusion. They broke
and ran. They cleared out, and no more was seen or
heard of them. They never rallied afterward. About
twenty minutes after that, the 18th Mississippi Regiment tried the same thing. They came up, deployed
suddenly, delivered their volley, and charged upon us.
We repeated the same tactics, let them come within
fifteen yards of us, when we fired a volley, and they
broke and ran.* This was repeated at least seven or
eight times between then and dark (by the 17th and
18th, and possibly by the 13th Mississippi.)† * * *
When the battle did begin, the men (regulars) who
manned those two howitzers (on our right) disappeared
(their lieutenant commanding having been disabled by
a wound), and I never saw any more of them. The
guns were not again fired. The six-pound gun was a
rifle gun, and had a crew of nine men; five of whom
were shot at the first fire, and the other four disappeared, except the lieutenant of the gun, who remained with it, and acted bravely during the action.
Seeing this gun idle, and knowing how much execution it might do, and being pressed so severely by
this constant necessity of changing our front, I went
over there and asked Colonel Cogswell‡ if he could

---

* It was here that their Colonel Burt fell.

† It would seem from this testimony as well as from the Confederate reports, that Wistar held a strong position on the left.

‡ Colonel Cogswell reported (Official Records, Series I, Vol.
V, page 321), "Colonel Baker ordered me to take charge of the
artillery, but without any definite instructions as to its service,"
and he seems to have done nothing with the artillery, although

load the gun. He said 'he could.' We took that
gun and moved it out to command this open space, and
with the aid of Mr. Bramhall (and some volunteers
from the California Regiment), kept up a fire on their
front. Occasionally we got an opportunity to annoy
their columns, that came from behind this hill upon us.
Once we destroyed one entirely—opened a hole straight
through them, so that we could see right through.
That gun in that way was of great service. Even
when the columns managed to get across the field and
close up, they were so shattered and disorganized by
this gun, that we had less difficulty in repelling
them. In that way the battle continued until about
dark—just beginning to be dusk—when they charged
with a very large column indeed. I should say
there were at least 2000 men in it, from the glimpse
I got of them, from 2000 to 2500, which we did not get
a shot at with the gun. I instantly attempted to change
front with my whole command, knowing that there was
no joke about that. I had only about 400 men alive
there at that time. I was doing it as fast as I could,
they being concealed in the woods and behind
these hills, when I stepped out to see if there was a
support coming up. Just as I stepped out I got my
third wound, which disabled me entirely, and was carried off. But the moment after I received the wound,
and while I was still sensible, I staggered against Colonel Baker. He asked, 'where I was hit,' and I told
him. I said, 'There is not an instant to lose; there is
a heavy column deployed behind that hill. You must
see if you can repel that attack, for it is serious.' He
left me, and had not gone more than ten or fifteen steps
before the enemy appeared upon the top of the hill,
their right wing closed in column and their left wing

it was silent until Colonel Wistar called upon him to help with
one gun, while the other two still remained silent, although
well supported by infantry.

deployed in line. The left wing delivered their volley, and the right wing charged with a yell down the hill. At that moment a captain of one of the regiments, I suppose it was, called out in a very loud voice, 'Company A, 20th Massachusetts, retreat to the ferry.' His men immediately broke. Somebody repeated the same order for Company 'B,' which followed their example. They ran against the Tammany regiment (two companies just coming up) and threw it into confusion, and that confused our whole line. At that moment the column of the enemy struck them, and away they went. The column of the enemy up to that time had been partially held back by the recovery of Colonel Baker's body (who had fallen a little in advance of his men). There was a desperate charge of about thirty or forty of my men upon the enemy to recover Colonel Baker's body, and that checked the whole column for about three minutes, and it was during that delay, which was a bayonet fight, that this order to retreat was given (which Colonel Devens has told us Cogswell ordered), and we were pressed back to the bluff. The bluff was exceedingly steep, about as steep as a man could climb up and carry his musket. You could not preserve any line on it. It was covered with rocks and trees and bushes. It was very dark down there, and when the enemy came up to the brink of the bluff they had a dark place to fire into, while our men had them against the sky in pretty close order. As our men were going down the bluff Captain Harvey (Baker's assistant adjutant-general) rallied the men of my regiment on that bluff. They were all broken and confused, but the men at his command fell down on the ground and opened a spitting fire up the bluff at the enemy, and in that way with the aid of other companies of the other regiments they held the bluff until 10 o'clock that night. At that time the enemy, having entirely surrounded us, found their way down to the

river bank and took prisoners all who were left. In
the meantime a number had swam the river, but they
captured all who were left."

After the retreat* Colonel Devens swam the river.
Colonels Cogswell, Lee and other officers were either
captured, or, with some of the men, seeing that the
day was lost, ascended the bluff and surrendered.
Captain Harvey, who had been wounded, was killed
by the enemy's fire later in the evening, while trying
to re-form and keep the balance of the men together as
skirmishers against the enemy. Thereafter they broke
up in small parties, without a commander, and tried to
make their way across the river, most of whom were
captured by small Confederate forces, as related by their
reports given above.

Let us see further what General Stone was doing
during this action. Quartermaster Henry Foote, who
had charge of the transportation at Edward's Ferry,†
testified:

"On Monday morning we crossed over in force.
General Gorman, our brigadier-general, had his orders
to take the troops over at that point. He ordered me
to seize the canal-boats as they came up and put them
into the river, so that, on Monday, besides these three
scows and skiffs, we had one canal-boat, which I had
put into the river, and by that means I was enabled to
cross our entire brigade between Monday morning and
Monday evening;" and in confirmation of this statement we have Stone's despatch:

* "Colonel Cogswell reluctantly gave the order to retreat to
the river bank. * * * As I descended upon this plateau, in
company with Colonel Cogswell, I saw the large boat, upon
which we depended as the means of crossing the river, swamped
by the number of men who rushed upon it."—Devens' report,
Official Records, Series I, Vol V, page 311—which is very fully
corroborated by Devens' testimony, Report of Committee on
Conduct of War, 2, page 410.

† Report of Committee on Conduct of War, 2, page 364.

"EDWARD'S FERRY, October 21, 1861, 4 P. M.

GENERAL MCCLELLAN: Nearly all my force is across the river. Baker on the right. Gorman on the left. Right sharply engaged.   C. P. STONE,
                                        Brigadier-General."*

We have been told by General Dana and General Gorman's aid that General Stone was busy commanding on the Maryland side at both crossings, and, therefore, was not expected to be upon the Virginia side, where either Gorman or Baker was in command, and we have learned from Stone's testimony that he was in command at Harrison's island. We also know that Captain Candy and an orderly passed the day between Stone's headquarters and Harrison's island, bearing orders and carrying information back and forth; and Colonel Hinks further testified:† "I may remark here that just previous to my crossing myself from the Maryland shore to Harrison's island, when the extremity was very pressing and there was a vague report that our men on the other side were being worsted, Captain Stewart, General Stone's adjutant-general, came (from the battle-field) across the river in a light boat that had been used to convey troops across. I stopped him for a moment upon the shore and asked him how things were going on. He made the remark, 'Indifferently well.' He did not give me any idea exactly how things were going. I said to him, with considerable vehemence, perhaps, 'that it was a very great shame that there were no more boats there,' and asked him why there had not been boats sent up from Edward's Ferry. There were canal-boats there that would carry from 200 to 300 troops each. He did not tell me, but said, 'Can those boats be got up here?' I replied, 'They could have been gotten up this forenoon.' He then said, 'I authorize you now, in the

* Official Records, Series I, Vol. V, page 34.
† Report of Committee on Conduct of War, 2, page 439.

name of General Stone, to get one of those boats up.'
I told him 'it would take four hours to do it then.'"

It seems that after Stewart returned to Stone, his aid,
Candy, was sent up to Harrison's island again, and
General Stone testified:*

"I think it was about 5 o'clock in the evening that
a staff officer whom I had sent to Colonel Baker returned to me * * * at Edward's Ferry, and said,
'I found the body of Colonel Baker being brought off
the field as I went to report to him. He has been
killed.' I immediately asked, '*in what condition did
that leave the troops?*' He replied, '*They are enraged
at the loss of their leader, and are fighting even better
than before.*'† I immediately mounted my horse, rode
down to the tow-path, sent directions to General Gorman, commanding at Edward's Ferry, 'that I was going to the right, to take command there, as I had
heard that Colonel Baker had fallen.' I then rode
rapidly up the tow-path, not dreaming of any greater
disaster than the serious one of the loss of Colonel
Baker, when I met the body of Colonel Baker being
brought down. * * * I stopped for a moment, out
of respect to the brave man we had lost, and then
galloped up the tow-path to the crossing. Just as I
reached there, I saw some men who appeared to be
wet, without arms, and only partially clothed, coming
along in small squads on the tow-path. I said, 'Men!
How did you get across the river?' They replied, 'We
swam the river.' I was so anxious to get up there
that I did not stop to question the men more closely,
but giving them one word of sharp reproof for deserting
their comrades, I rode on. I met more of the men, and
began to fear we had had a disaster. I again stopped,

---

* Report of Committee on Conduct of War, 2, page 487.

† After Baker fell, his men recovered his body, and the troops
upon the field tried to cut their way through to Edward's Ferry,
in which they were repulsed.

and enquired of the men. They said to me, 'We have been beaten on the other side, we swam the river, and those left behind are either all killed or captured. The enemy came down on us 10,000 strong.' *This was the wild talk of the fugitives.* I passed on until I got opposite to the crossing, where I found great confusion. I looked around for a cool man of whom I could learn something, and found a chaplain of the 15th Massachusetts, who was taking care of the wounded. I asked him what had happened. He said the best information he could get from those who were fleeing across the river was, that the entire command on the Virginia side was either killed or captured. I at once saw the danger to both our right and left, the left at Edward's Ferry, and at least what remained of the right—those under General Gorman, and those still left on Harrison's island.* I immediately sent orders over to Colonel Hinks, of the 19th Massachusetts, who was on the island, to secure all the wounded and fugitives as rapidly as possible, and to maintain the island at all hazards until he had removed the wounded to the Maryland shore, watching carefully that the enemy made no crossing to the island; and then, knowing that I could go quicker myself than anybody I could send, I turned my horse and galloped down to withdraw my troops at Edward's Ferry back to the Maryland shore.†

Baker is dead and Wistar insensible, suffering with wounds almost fatal. Colonel Lee, Captain Harvey,

---

* The site where Stone had built his intrenchments to cover a retreat.

† Stone did not stop to give an order to the several thousand men of all arms standing along the tow-path, who, weary from idleness, and at receiving no orders (not being able to cross), returned to their camps during the night. Nor did he think of using the artillery on the Maryland shore, which he afterward blamed Baker for not using.

and other brave officers, are holding the enemy at bay, with the men that had survived the action, anxiously expecting the arrival of the delayed succor from the left or the means to recross to the island; but neither re-enforcements nor means of transportation arrived. General Stone was on the Maryland shore at the critical moment when strength of will and daring would have proved the pivotal point upon which he could have recovered from his inattention and blunders; *but he did not so much as cross to the island, nor did he wait to interview any officer who had come from the scene of conflict* to ascertain the true state of affairs at the bluff. He simply took counsel of the early fugitives, and galloped off to his quarters, to consummate his folly by withdrawing, in the face of a mere picket guard of the enemy, the only supporting column in reach. No more was seen or heard of him at Harrison's island that night. He folded his tent "like the Arabs" (with whom he afterward took shelter), and as silently "stole away."

Of Stone's boasted transportation, not more than one boat had been sunk, and perhaps not any at the time when he arrived, while a much larger one had been added by Baker and a cable stretched across the river, thus placing the transportation, even with the loss of one boat, in better condition than when he sent Baker up to cross. When Stone arrived opposite Harrison's island and concluded to order a general retreat, why did he not stop and order some of the regiments standing idly along the canal, to the island, if his entrenchments there would protect them in covering a retreat —the purpose for which they were built—and why did he not use the artillery, which he said should have been used from the Maryland shore, where he was in command, and blamed Baker for not using, and under its fire send the boats over to bring off the men, then wearied, without ammunition and sorely pressed, left

to shiver along the Virginia shore, at the mercy of
the enemy, for hours after Stone had deserted them?
*The only explanation we have is that the fugitives,
whom he sharply rebuked for leaving their comrades*
across the river, told him that the enemy were 10,000
strong, and that all but they had perished or were captured. *He believed them, and swelled the throng in unseemly haste.*

Colonel Wistar further testified*:

"*Question.* When you were holding them in check
that day, from 3 o'clock until dark, with the force you
had, would not, in your judgment, a re-enforcement of
1500 men, coming up the river on the Virginia side,
have turned the battle?

"*Answer.* It might have turned the victory.

"*Question.* Would not, in your judgment, 1500
fresh troops, coming in their rear while they were on
the bluff, have turned the day?

"*Answer.* I think 1500 good troops would have
done it. It is hard to say: they would certainly have
been a great assistance.

"*Question.* (page 318) Did you know the condition
of the enemy?

"*Answer.* I supposed we had shattered them very
considerably. I know the gully on our left was piled
full of their dead over the top.

"*Question.* Did you know anything about their
forces there?

"*Answer.* Only what I have stated. I was not in a
condition that night to tell anybody about the enemy.
I was insensible and fainting, and supposed I was to
die in the course of the night.

"*Question.* Did you yourself know the actual condition of the enemy?

"*Answer.* I knew this much, that if I had had 2000
men, I should have felt confident of successfully carry-

---

* Report of Committee on Conduct of War, 2, page 312.

ing that position. Whether I could have made my way to Leesburg or not, I could not tell. I considered them very much shattered.

"*Question.* I mean as you judged them to be from what you saw?

"*Answer.* I judged them to be very much shattered, so that a good officer with good troops, I think, could have carried the position. In the first place, they must have been nearly out of ammunition. We were entirely out of it. For the last half hour all the ammunition we fired, we took from the enemy in the gutter, where the enemy's killed were piled up. Our men would run out there and cut a cartridge box from some of the enemy, and then come back and go to firing again. We went into action with forty rounds of ammunition. I was only a regimental officer, and could not tell about the plans and arrangements at the two points, Edward's Ferry and Ball's Bluff.

"*Question.* (page 313) Suppose you had meditated an attack on Leesburg, would it not have been easy to have thrown a pontoon bridge across the Potomac, and brought Stone and Banks' divisions over, and made a demonstration?

"*Answer.* That, I suppose, would have been the proper course, if it had been intended to take Leesburg.

"*Question.* Now, if it was not the object to take Leesburg, what in God's name was this fragment of a force sent over on those miserable scows for?

"*Answer.* I do not know. I do not know whether the object was to take Leesburg or not. I do not know anything about it at all. I was ordered over there, and I went. I would have gone if there had been a million men there."*

---

* This last sentence recalls an incident of a more recent date, interesting to Colonel Wistar's men, showing the counterpart of the soldier. Having a strong desire to refer to it, I hope the reader will pardon the digression. At the dedication of the

Some hours after General Stone had reached his
headquarters and given orders for the withdrawal of

Monument of the 71st Pennsylvania Volunteers (late California
Regiment), at Gettysburg, July 3d, 1887, General Wistar rose to
deliver the shaft to the care of the "Monumental Association."
The young soldier of stern will and iron nerve had given place
to the citizen fast growing gray. The voice of the young leader
that had been heard above the din of battle was then broken
and subdued with emotion, while with moistened eyes, and a
heart overflowing with sympathy, he looked upon the few survivors of his old regiment. He had hardly begun with his well-
chosen words when he became unnerved and spellbound by the
thoughts and feelings of the occasion. He paused to keep down
the choking sensation fast getting the mastery of his voice. Old
scenes and associations crowded in review, and an overwhelming
tide of feeling came surging up in his bosom, far too much for the
speaker, with which he struggled manfully, and by an effort almost superhuman, with choked and tremulous accents, he said,
    "You must give me a moment to recover myself. I cannot
look on your small array, pitiful indeed in numbers though in
nothing else, when contrasting it with the numerous and gallant
body I once led: the feeling is too much for me." This incident
affected all present, and moved many to tears, presenting a
touching scene, in which were the few survivors who, not unlike their torn and tattered flags, were torn and tattered by
battles, disease, and the ravages of many years in life's storms.
Continuing, he gave a slight history of the three years' service
of the regiment, and very feelingly concluded, "I cannot
speak to you with calmness. If you think I can, or ought to,
look on the scanty and battered remnant of your once splendid
array unmoved, you are wrong. I cannot do it. Enough, however, has been said here by far better orators, though one
hundred times as much would not be inadequate to express the
reminiscences and solemn thoughts which this historic spot,
and our dwindled ranks of scarred and battered survivors, send
surging through our breasts, and welling from our eyes. I cannot look into your faces and speak with steady voice. I can
say no more now, but will express one single sentiment, which
I believe will reach all of our hearts—that while life remains
for this small remnant, we may, every one of us, till our last
breath, conntinue to cherish for our friends and comrades,
affection, love, and personal friendship, and to share with our

the troops at Edward's Ferry, he sent the following despatch:

"EDWARD'S FERRY, October 21, 1861, 9:30 P. M.

"MAJOR-GENERAL McCLELLAN: I am occupied in preventing further disaster and trying to get into a position to redeem. *We have lost some of our best commanders. Baker is d ad; Cogswell a prisoner or secreted.* The wounded are being carefully and rapidly removed, and Gorman's wing is being cautiously withdrawn. Any advance from Dranesville must be made cautiously.

"*All was reported going well up to Baker's death*, but in the confusion following that the right wing was outflanked. In a few hours I shall, unless a night attack is made, be in the same position as last night, save the loss of many good men.

C. P. STONE,

Brigadier-General."*

We learn from this despatch that General Stone classed Colonel Baker among *our best commanders*, and says, "All was reported going well, up to Baker's death." He does not breathe a suspicion of any thing having been done other than in accord with his plans, and simply regarded the defeat following Baker's death as the fate of war, and so reported to his chief. But that was not satisfactory to the public, who held Stone responsible for the disaster resulting from the movements which he had planned and directed throughout the day with McClellan's approval; therefore, he suggested to General McClellan, who had arrived during the night of the 22d, that he desired an expression from him. Then McClellan telegraphed to President Lincoln, "I have investigated this matter, and General Stone is without blame. Had his orders been followed, there could (or would) have been no disaster;" and he also had the following despatch filed:

gallant enemies of long ago—enemies, thank God! no longer, peace, concord, and fellowship, under one common flag for evermore."

*Official Records, Series I, Vol. V, page 34.

ARLINGTON, October 24, 1861.

GENERAL McDOWELL, *Eighteenth and Q streets:* The following just received from General McClellan:

"The affair in front of Leesburg, on Monday last, resulted in serious loss to us, but was a most gallant fight on the part of our men, who displayed the utmost coolness and courage. It has given me the utmost confidence in them. The disaster was caused by errors committed by the immediate commander, not General Stone.

"I have withdrawn the troops from the other side, since they went without my orders, and nothing was to be gained by retaining them there.   JAMES B. FRY,
Assistant Adjutant-General."*

Now let us see what General McClellan said, eighteen months later, when under oath before the Committee on Conduct of War :†

"*Question.* Can you tell us who was responsible for making the crossing at Harrison's island (Ball's Bluff)? Was it General Stone or was it Colonel Baker?

"*Answer.* I only know what I learned from General Stone. My recollection is that General Stone gave discretionary orders to Colonel Baker to cross if certain conditions could be fulfilled. I think that General Stone was responsible to the extent that he ought to have informed himself whether it was possible to fulfil those conditions or not. * * * What I alluded to as the 'conditions' is the means of transportation for ferrying the troops across the river.

"*Question.* Whom do you consider responsible for the disaster at Ball's Bluff?

"*Answer.* I have no means of knowing except from the report of General Stone, which makes Colonel Baker directly responsible for the result.

"*Question.* Did you make any investigation, or come to any conclusion at the time you were there, as to who was responsible for that disaster?

* Official Records, Series I, Vol. V, page 626.

† Report of Committee on Conduct of War, 2, pages 506, 507.

"*Answer.* When I was at Edward's Ferry I conversed with several officers who were concerned in the affair. My recollection is that they regarded Colonel Baker as mainly responsible for the result.

"*Question.* Can you give us the names of the officers with whom you conversed, or who expressed that opinion?

"*Answer.* I conversed mainly with the officers of the staff of General Banks and General Stone. I think I was thrown almost exclusively in contact with them. But I cannot, at this late day, pretend to particularize.

"*Question.* The officers of General Banks' staff could have had no knowledge in relation to the matter except from hearsay, could they?

"*Answer.* I think not: I do not think that any of them were present at the time the affair occurred.

"*Question.* Do you remember now what officers composed General Stone's staff at that time?

"*Answer.* I do not, except one, the assistant adjutant-general of General Stone, named Stewart. I do not remember who were his aids, or others of his staff.

"*Question.* Do you know why the troops that had crossed at Edward's Ferry on Monday did not go up to the relief of Colonel Baker?

"*Answer.* I do not know. I only remember what was said to me at the time. The reason given, as far as my recollection serves, was that in a wood which intervened between Edward's Ferry and Ball's Bluff, there was a fortification of the enemy.

"*Question.* If there were 1500 men, or about that number across the river at Edward's Ferry, as early in the day as 12 or 1 o'clock, would the fortification which they referred to as being between them and Ball's Bluff, have been a sufficient excuse for not sending that force to the relief of Colonel Baker?

"*Answer. My belief is that there was no serious obstacle to a communication between Edward's Ferry and*

Ball's Bluff. I do not think that the enemy had any large force, or any strong works, between those two points near the river, that would have interfered with that communication.

" *Question.* You mean by that, in your opinion, those troops should have been sent to the relief of Colonel Baker?

"*Answer.* No; because I do not remember well enough what occupation they had in front of them. I merely mean to say that I do not think there was any serious obstacle to their going on that path, independently of what might have occupied their attention in front, unless the enemy were too strong in force in front of them. *I think they should have either been thrown upon Leesburg, or sent to assist Colonel Baker.**

" *Question.* Was there any investigation or inquiry whatever, into the conduct of General Stone and the battle of Ball's Bluff?

"*Answer. I think no formal investigation was ever made. I have no recollection of any specific formal inquiry into the affair.*

"*Question.* Do you remember whether or not you communicated or expressed, to the President, or the Secretary of War, your satisfaction with the conduct of General Stone on that occasion?

"*Answer.* I think I did, the night that I arrived there, after hearing General Stone's explanation. But I have not seen the telegraphic despatches since."

Thus General McClellan admitted that his telegram to the President, and his official despatch, were based mainly upon Stone's statements and hearsay evidence. If they had been intended to forestall and prevent all investigation, they did not have that effect. Stone's vindication, couched in the strongest possible terms, coming from his chief, virtually settled the military in-

---

* We have learned that one company of the 13th Mississippi confronted Stone during the main action of the day.

vestigation, and relieved Stone from all responsibility for the time being.

By some persons the following testimony, given by General Stone,* would be considered significant, in view of subsequent events, partaking perhaps, more of devotion to his chief than duty and candor would indicate.

"*Question*. Did this reconnaissance originate with yourself, or had you orders from the general-in-chief to make it?

"*Answer*. It originated from myself, the reconnaissance.

"*Question*. The order did not proceed from General McClellan?

"*Answer*. I was directed the day before to make a demonstration, as is seen in General McClellan's printed orders. That demonstration was made the day previous.

"*Question*. Was that demonstration or the reconnaissance made for the purpose of ascertaining whether the right wing of our army could be thrown across the Potamac? Did it look to that?

"*Answer*. I am not at liberty to state, if I know, what the commanding general's views were. But all the information that I had previously, is given in a telegraphic despatch from General McClellan to myself, which is published.†

"*Question*. Did you receive an order from the general-in-chief to make this reconnaissance?

"*Answer*. No, sir.

"*Question*. You received the order to make the demonstration?

"*Answer*. Yes, sir."

After Stone had been arrested and incarcerated by McClellan, he did not continue a like devotion and reticence as to messages from his chief. We will here-

---

* Report of Committee on Conduct of War, 2, page 272.

† See McClellan's dispatch to Stone of the 20th of October, to "keep a good lookout upon Leesburg." Page 70.

after learn from General Stone's testimony, given some time after his many futile efforts to satisfy the public that he was not to blame, more of what passed between him and General McClellan,* notwithstanding he and other officers had been instructed at the chief's headquarters not to give certain testimony, although 75 days had passed since the battle.

While "The Joint Committee" on "The Conduct of the War" was in session, how unbounded the power wielded by General McClellan in governmental affairs, not only at the time of Stone's arrest, but for some time before and thereafter.† On the 27th of July he wrote,‡ "*I find myself in a new and strange position here—President, Cabinet, General Scott, and all deferring to me. By* some strange operation of magic, *I seem to have become the power of the land.*" Three days later he wrote, "*They give me my way in everything, full swing and unbounded confidence.*" * * * "He professed especial contempt for the President, partly because *Mr. Lincoln* (*one of Colonel Baker's dearest and most powerful friends*) *showed him* (*McClellan*)|| *too much deference.*" While McClellan was thus so potent, being especially deferred to in every particular relating to the army, he fully exonerated Stone and reported that Baker alone was the cause of the disaster at the Bluff, and when the order for Stone's arrest was given him he had its execution suspended for ten days, informing the Secretary of War that "he did not see how charges could be framed on the testimony," but within that period he himself furnished the missing link, and the order of arrest was executed; and thereafter he did not furnish the charges nor a court to try, while Stone most positively, and very justly it would seem, claimed that McClellan possessed the power to grant a speedy trial, and that he should have exercised that power.

* See pages 190–191.
† "The Century Illustrated Monthly Magazine" for July, 1888—"Lincoln and McClellan."
‡ McClellan's own story, p. 82. || Ibid, p. 91.

CHAPTER X.

ON the assembling of Congress, in December, 1861,
the House of Representatives passed a resolution asking the Secretary of War "*whether any, and, if any,
what means had been taken to ascertain who was responsible for the disastrous movements of the National troops
at Ball's Bluff?*" *It was answered that General Mc-
Clellan was of the opinion that an enquiry on the subject
of the resolution would at that time be injurious to the
public service*—most likely that portion of the public
service in which he and Stone had been especially engaged. The investigation was made, nevertheless,
within the sacred precincts of the "Committee on Conduct of the War," where seclusion and secresy reigned
profound, whose work has since been revealed to the
public by the publication of their record. After
Stone's testimony had been taken, and that of a great
many officers having knowledge of the affair, Stone
was again called before the Committee January 31,
1862.* When the chairman had informed the committee that General Charles P. Stone was in attendance, as he stated, by order of the Secretary of War,
he was addressed as follows:

"*The Chairman.*†—In the course of our investiga-
tions here, there have come out in evidence matters
which may be said to impeach you. I do not know
that I can enumerate all the points, but I think I can.
In the first place, is your conduct in the Ball's Bluff

* Report of Committee on Conduct of War, 2, pages 426, etc.
† Senator Benjamin F. Wade, of Ohio.

(183)

affair, your ordering your forces over without sufficient means of transportation, and in that way, of course, endangering your army, in case of a check, by not being able to re-enforce them.   That is one of the points.

"*General Stone.*—I will answer that one.   I think I stated in evidence myself here very clearly and distinctly the facts in the case.   *I do not know how far the Committee may have conceived that I risked the troops there: I certainly did risk the first party sent over,*" (embracing two-thirds of all the troops and artillery that were crossed to the bluff, the other third simply being the rescuing party,) "but I think that to any military eye, I explained very clearly how I had arranged for their return.   I gave discretionary power to the next officer,* who had command of a sufficient number of troops—discretionary power, he, being the judge of the propriety of passing over and, the means he had to do so, whether he should retire what troops were over there, or whether he should advance more. That officer took the responsibility of making a passage of more troops, with a full knowledge of the facts.   And then I conceived that all responsibility of mine ended. * * *   I do not hold that I was responsible from the time I sent Colonel Baker to the crossing point, with discretionary power to pass or not to pass."   (If this should hold good, any commanding officer could imperil his troops, then turn the command over to his subordinate with discretionary power, and thereby relieve himself of all responsibility.)   How fallacious the reasoning!

"*The Chairman.*—We do not profess to sit here as a military board; we are not military men.   We do not profess to be competent judges of these matters.   But we deem that the testimony tends also to impeach you for not re-enforcing those troops when they were over

---

*See two orders heretofore given, pages 105 and 119, and Stone's testimony relative thereto, pages 154 and 155.

there in the face of the enemy, and in connection with that, when you knew the battle was proceeding, that you did not go within three or four miles of it.

"*General Stone.*—From what point should they have been re-enforced?

"*The Chairman.*—We cannot help but think that they ought to have been re-enforced, for instance, from Edward's Ferry, or, perhaps, if you had sufficient transportation, as you intimate, then right across at Ball's Bluff?

"*General Stone.*—Colonel Baker had at his disposal a force vastly superior to that of the enemy.*

"*The Chairman.*—I propose merely to state the heads. I do not desire to discuss them.

"*General Stone.*—I should like to know those heads, and I would be greatly pleased if two members of this committee, or three, or four, or the whole of them, would just take a trip up to that ground and look at it half an hour, and see if they do not become thoroughly satisfied of the impracticability and false soldiership which would have been shown if we had attempted to pass troops from Edward's Ferry to the right at that time."

It should be here remarked that immediately after the Ball's Bluff affair and previous to this testimony, the enemy had built strong fortifications defending the approaches from Edward's Ferry, and that General Stone may have been anxious for the committee to go up and look at them, although they were not there at the time the troops were across (October 21, 22 and 23.)†

---

*Colonel Lee, while a prisoner, ascertained from a Confederate officer that they had 3200 men actually engaged, against Baker's 1400 or 1500. The balance of the troops assigned to Baker were still on the Maryland shore or on their passage over where Stone was in command. After Baker fell, Stone arrived in person, and we have been informed of the ability he then displayed.

†Concerning which Major Dimmick testified (Report of

"*The Chairman.*—We are not military men, any of us.

"*General Stone.*—But you judge military men.

"*The Chairman.*—Yes, sir, but not finally. We only state what in our opinion tends to impeach them, when the evidence seems to do so, and then leave it to better judges to determine. Those two points we thought tended to impeach your conduct on that occasion. Another point is, you are apparently impeached—I say impeached. The evidence tends to prove that you have had undue communications with the enemy by letters that have passed back and forth, by intercourse with officers from the other side, and by permitting packages to go over unexamined to known secessionists.

"*General Stone.*—That is one humiliation I had hoped I never should be subjected to. I thought there was one calumny that could not be brought against me. Any other calumny that anybody could raise, I should expect after what I have received; but that one I should have supposed that you, personally, Mr. Chairman, would have rejected at once. You remember last winter, when the government had so few friends, who had this city, I might almost say, in his power? I raised all the volunteer troops that were here during

Committee on Conduct of War, 2, pages 392 and 393): "The enemy have now there very powerful forts right opposite to us. I think the first fort is about half a mile back of Edward's Ferry. When we went to Edward's Ferry first, it was only a breastwork, a few feet high. * * * It was evidently very hastily constructed, nothing but a very simple earth-work running across the road, perhaps forty paces long. * * * I think there were no guns there then, merely a breastwork. I went up within three hundred yards of it. It was apparently a breastwork from which they had retired. We were on the bluff opposite Edward's Ferry for three days, and the very day we came back they commenced strengthening that work, and they have worked on it ever since, employing from 20 to 100 men upon it. They have a fort there now, I should think about 500 feet long, pierced, I should think, for from twenty to thirty guns."

the seven dark days of last winter. I disciplined and posted those troops. I commanded them, and those troops were the first to invade the soil of Virginia, and I led them.

"*The Chairman.*—I was not so unjust as not to mention that circumstance. I have mentioned it to the Committee.

"*General Stone.*—I could have surrendered Washington, and now I will swear that this Government has not a more faithful soldier—of poor capacity, it is true—but a more faithful soldier this Government has not had from the day General Scott commanded me, the 31st day of December, 1860, up to this minute. As to any particular cases of carrying letters across the river, it is utterly false that I have had the slightest improper communication with the enemy. The charge is too false almost for a soldier to answer. I can give you every instance of communication over there. I had, unfortunately, soldiers under my command, who were prisoners in Leesburg, who were wounded, and I felt very anxious for those soldiers.

"*The Chairman.*—The next and only other point is—

"*General Stone.*—I think I should be allowed an opportunity to speak.

"*The Chairman.*—Certainly; you shall have the amplest opportunity to say all you desire. But I thought it best for me to conclude all that I have to say, and then allow you to make whatever statements you deem proper. The next and only other point that now occurs to me is, that you have suffered the enemy to erect formidable fortifications or batteries on the opposite side of the river, within reach of your guns, and that you could easily have prevented. That is the testimony.

"*General Stone.*—That is equally false."

Then General Stone went into a long explanation of

several pages, relative to the erection of these batteries and the communication he had with the enemy.

"*General Stone.*— * * * In all these matters there is, of course, but one question, Is the general loyal? is he working for the service of the United States? If he is not, then you must either replace him by some man of more ability, or, if you have him there, you must trust to his discretion. * * *

"*The Chairman.*—I believe I have stated to you all that we deemed of importance, and of course we are glad to hear your explanation."

All of the testimony taken, and the conclusions arrived at, were reported to the Secretary of War, and no doubt considered by General McClellan, and members of the Cabinet.

General Stone's apparent reluctance or inability to satisfactorily explain the cause and object of his movement, and the management of his division during the Battle of Ball's Bluff, cast a cloud upon him, and gave rise to grave suspicions, which grew apace, while many of the officers in his command, who had lost confidence in him through this movement, testified to acts which seemed to strongly indicate disloyalty upon his part. The atmosphere was full of reports unfavorable to the suspected man, and his loyalty was mercilessly assailed. At the same time officers of higher grade in his command, gave the highest testimony to his loyalty, among whom were Colonels Isaac J. Wistar, Charles Devens, James H. Van Allan, and even General Dana testified freely, without any apparent reservation in answer to the questions:*

"*Question.* Do they have confidence in him?

"*Answer.* I think the superior officers of the division have.

"*Question.* Do they doubt his loyalty?

"*Answer.* I have heard that as coming from among

* Report of Committee on Conduct of War, 2, page 457.

the men, but I had not such a suspicion myself. If I had had, no man could have reported it more quickly than I would. I came into the war to fight this matter out, and I would not put my neck into difficulties. If disloyal men are to be suffered to remain in the service, I want to leave it."

While the administration thought that the facts, the circumstances, and the weight of the evidence were rather against Stone's loyalty, still he was not given the benefit of the doubt, nor an opportunity to face his accusers, and cross-examine the witnesses. Two days before he was summoned as above, to hear the opinion of the Committee, the following order had been issued, of which Stone apparently had no knowledge until arrested:

WAR DEPARTMENT. ⎫
WASHINGTON CITY, D. C., January 28, 1862. ⎰

Ordered, That the general commanding be, and is hereby directed to relieve Brigadier-General C. P. Stone from command of his division in the Army of the Potomac, forthwith, and that he be placed in arrest, and kept in close custody until further orders.

EDWIN M. STANTON,
*Secretary of War.**

For some reason unexplained, General McClellan held this order for ten or eleven days without executing any part of it. Subsequently, in a letter written to Stone, McClellan stated, "On the evening when you were arrested, I submitted to the Secretary of War the written result of the examination of a refugee from Leesburg, and this information, to a certain extent, agreed with the evidence stated to have been taken by the Committee, and upon its being imparted to the Secretary, he again instructed me to cause you to be arrested, which I at once did by the following orders:

* Official Records Series I, Vol. V, page 341.

GENERAL: You will please at once arrest Brigadier-General Charles P. Stone, United States volunteers, and retain him in close custody, sending him under suitable escort by the first train to Fort Lafayette, where he will be placed in charge of the commanding officer. See that he has no communication with any one from the time of his arrest.

GEORGE B. McCLELLAN, *Major-General.*
*Brigadier-General Andrew Porter, Provost-Marshal.**

HEADQUARTERS OF THE ARMY, ⎱
WASHINGTON, February 8, 1862. ⎰

SIR: This will be handed to you by the officer sent in charge of Brigadier-General Charles P. Stone, who is under close arrest. You will please confine General Stone in Fort Lafayette, allowing him the comforts due his rank, and allowing him no communication with any one, by letter or otherwise, except under the usual supervision.

GEORGE B. McCLELLAN, *Major-General.*
Commanding Officer Fort Lafayette.†

That fortress being a place of durance only for men charged with treasonable acts.

Now Stone was in close confinement and all his papers were taken from him, including despatches from McClellan relative to the taking of Leesburg, of which we have read, concerning which he testified:‡

"I am sorry I have not possession of a single paper, telegraph or otherwise, of the records connected with my division. You know the way in which I was removed from my command. I was ordered to report myself here in Washington at once, and, having not the slightest suspicion of why I was required here, I left all my papers as I would have done had I been going out for a two hours' ride, and from that time to this, I have never seen a single paper of any

* Official Records, Series I, Vol. V, page 341.

† Official Records, Series I, Vol. V, page 342.

‡ Report of Committee on Conduct of War, part 2, page 488.

kind I then left behind me. * * * I make this explanation to show why it is that I cannot speak positively about the language of the despatches received and sent—why I cannot, perhaps, give the exact words."

General Stone could have produced all the communications that passed between himself and McClellan, when called before the committee, either on the 5th or the 31st of January, 1862, if he had been so inclined. He was asked various questions for the fullest information upon the whole matter, but he chose to withhold the information—telegrams and despatches—passing between McClellan and himself, and also some of his orders to Colonel Baker. In reference to the former he subsequently explained:

"The morning that I came before the committee I was instructed at General McClellan's headquarters that it was the desire of the general that officers giving testimony before the committee should not state, without his authority, anything regarding his plans, his orders for the movements of troops, or his orders concerning the position of troops. That covered this case."

In reference to the written orders he gave to Colonel Baker,* of which he said, in answer to the

"*Question.* You did not give Colonel Baker an order to cross?

"*Answer.* No, sir; I did not. Fortunately there was a written order found in his hat, in which I gave discretionary orders."

He did not give the contents of this order verbatim, but explained how he instructed Colonel Baker as to his duties under the order, nor did he make any direct reference to the second order, although he must have

* About which there was a great discussion and difference of opinion, caused by Stone using every means in his power to suppress or misrepresent them.

known it was in evidence, for previous to his last testimony, he had read all of the evidence by consent of the Committee. He neither acknowledged or specifically denied it, but stated: "I do not think a careful commander would have attempted that crossing so heedlessly. I think any careful commander would have himself gone on the field, and attempted to look before him, before he attempted to cross 2,000 men in the face of an enemy."

We have learned that of the 1400 or 1500 men and three pieces of artillery crossed to the bluff, Stone had crossed about 900 men and two pieces of artillery, and that Baker simply went to their rescue, and that Stone did not go upon the bluff himself, but gave orders to cross not only there, but also at Edward's Ferry, of which he testified, while excusing himself for not going up with Colonel Baker: "*There was another large operation and reconnaissance going on down at Goose creek, which I was watching*," where he had crossed about 4,000 men and two pieces of artillery without going upon the Virginia shore; nor did he cross, at any time until General McClellan arrived and ordered him across on the 23d. This kind of testimony did not have much weight with the committee, who reported:* "That order (No. 1)† with a communication (No. 2)‡ from General Stone to Colonel Baker, sent some time later, was found upon his body after he was killed. The two papers are as follows:

* Report of Committee on Conduct of War, 2, page 12.

† Received by Colonel Baker about 11 a. m., at Edward's Ferry.

‡ Received on the field when surrounded and about being engaged by the enemy.

HEADQUARTERS
CORPS OF OBSERVATION,
EDWARD'S FERRY, October 21, 1861.

COLONEL: In case of heavy firing in front of Harrison's island, you will advance the California regiment of your brigade, or retire the regiments under Colonels Lee and Devens, now on the Virginia side of the river, at your discretion, assuming command on your arrival.

Very respectfully, Colonel, your most obedient servant,

CHAS. P. STONE,
Brigadier-General, commanding.

*Colonel E. D. Baker, Commanding Brigade.**

[No. 2.]

HEADQUARTERS
CORPS OF OBSERVTION,
EDWARD'S FERRY, October 21, 1861, 11:50.

COLONEL: I am informed that the force of the enemy is about 4,000 all told. If you can push them, you may do so as far as to have a strong position near Leesburg; if you can, keep them before you, avoiding their batteries. If they pass Leesburg and take the Gum Spring road, you will not follow far, but seize the first good position to cover that road. Their design is to draw us on, if they are obliged to retreat, as far as Goose creek, where they can be re-enforced from Manassas and have a strong position.

Report frequently, so that when they are pushed Gorman can come in on their flank.

Yours respectfully and truly,

CHAS. P. STONE,
Brigadier-General, commanding.

Colonel E. D. Baker, Commanding Brigade.†

The second order or communication is evidently the one delivered by Major Ritman to Colonel Cogswell, who delivered it to Colonel Baker upon the bluff, and the same referred to by Captain Young while Baker was about crossing in person from the island to the Virginia shore, and also the one Wistar said Baker

* Official Records, Series I, Vol. V, page 303.

† Official Records, Series I, Vol. V, page 303.

13

had read to him,* *i. e.*, something like this : "Sir, 4,000 of the enemy are marching from Leesburg to attack you." And of which Devens said General Baker "took out and read an order which he had in his pocket, from General Stone. He then said 'that we must hold on there, that re-enforcements would come to us at the rate of about so many an hour.' I do not remember the number he gave. The order which he read was not the order in which General Stone says, 'You may expect to meet some 3,000 or 4,000 of the enemy.' But it was an order in which General Stone gives some instructions to Colonel Baker as to how to proceed,† provided he succeeds in driving the enemy. He is to be careful not to move until they are all before him; that the enemy will endeavor to draw him forward toward Manassas. That I remember Colonel Baker read in my presence to a group of officers."

This testimony points almost directly to Stone's second order, read by Baker upon the field, of which Wistar remembered something of the first part, perhaps all that had been read to him in the excitement of the moment, while Devens remembered something of the latter part, who very probably heard the whole of it read, and Devens said "that Baker then told him 'that we must hold on there,'" which means that there was to be no retreat, for Stone has testified:‡ "I directed him to hold on there (where Stone had placed Lee and Devens upon the bluff), and of course not to yield ground we had taken possession of without resistance," which Colonel Baker was preparing to make. Then came this second order, "If you can push them you may do so." That surely decided the matter with Baker, and he then ordered Wistar to feel the enemy's strength.

---

* No doubt the first part of it.

† See 11:50 a. m. order, page 193.

‡ Report of Committee on Conduct of War, 2, page 269.

upon the left, no doubt with the intention of moving by the left as soon as his re-enforcements came up.

It is very clear, after reading all of Stone's official reports and the testimony given on the two occasions before his arrest, and on the one after his release from prison, that while he apparently would not admit his full responsibility and that of his chief in this movement that he could not satisfactorily disprove it, although he attempted to evade and deny orders and dispatches by construing them so as to best suit his line of defence, that of relieving himself from all responsibility and casting it wholly upon Baker. The most that Stone would admit of his instructions to Baker with these orders was given, as we have learned, in answer to the following question:

"*Question.* Did you intend that he, Baker, should cross?

"*Answer.* I intended and instructed him to use his discretion about crossing or withdrawing the troops already over there. *If we found Leesburg had been abandoned by the enemy*, and we had nothing to do but to occupy it, *I directed him to hold on there, and of course not yield ground we had taken possession of without resistance.* But if his party found there was not a strong force there—if it was a force he could easily drive before him—he should drive it off; if it was of such a size that he could not drive it off easily, then he was to fall back. But he was to use his discretion as to whether he had the means to drive off any force which might be there. After this reconnoitering party had advanced so far, it was not an unreasonable supposition that they were in small force there; still it was a thing to be guarded against that there might be a force there, and a strong one."

Is not this sufficient evidence, without the written orders and other evidence, that Stone intended Baker should cross, and hold the position he had sent Lee over to secure on the bluff? If he had not crossed, and attempted to hold the ground on the bluff by resisting the enemy, would he have carried out the spirit and meaning of Stone's instructions as related by himself in his own defence? We must conclude that Baker was under orders to cross.*

It should be stated that some orders appeared in the public prints that were not genuine. One set forth that Stone had given orders to Baker to attack Leesburg on Sunday, the 20th, which Stone declared was false, and in reference to the order given by Stone on the morning of the 21st a statement also appeared that Colonel Baker upon receiving this order exclaimed, "I will obey General Stone's order, but it is my death warrant." That expression was very probably a growth of an imagination other than Baker's—possibly a distorted version of a social chat that occurred between Major Robert Parrish of the California Regiment and Colonel Baker shortly before the battle, as related by Major Parrish recently to the writer—*i. e.*, Colonel Baker said, "President Lincoln has given me the commission of a Major-General in the volunteer army, to be announced and used by me at my own discretion. I am now re-cruiting forces which I hope to raise to an army divis-ion, on which occasion I shall produce it. But such are the jealousies against me, entertained by the regular army officers, I do not expect to survive the first battle." As viewed in the light of subsequent events, his words seem to have been prophetic as to his death, although it does not appear that the jealousy of regular army officers contributed or in any way hastened his death.

Dr. J. H. Puleston, Military Agent of Pennsylvania, and of the Governor's staff, who went down to Edward's Ferry to look after the Pennsylvania troops, and who

---

* See Stone's testimony, "May order you to take Leesburg to-day." See Colonel Irwin's account of cipher dispatch.—*Ante.* Page 77 and post.

conversed a great deal with General Stone, testified* in reference to the disputed orders as follows:

"*Question.* Will you state what was your conversation with General Stone, and when it was?

"*Answer.* I really cannot remember how long after the battle it was. I know that General Stone was very busy writing out his report on the day I was with him. I conversed with him very freely about the battle of Ball's Bluff. I think first of all he showed me a Sunday *Chronicle* of the day before. It must have been, therefore, on the Monday succeeding the battle, he showed me *The Sunday Morning Chronicle* from Washington, with one or two dispatches purporting to have been sent by him to Baker. I told him I had already seen them. He pronounced them unequivocal forgeries; *that it was not his practice to address a Colonel as a General, etc., and sign his name with a Napoleonic "Stone."* I understood him to say very distinctly that the orders as there given were forgeries in whole as well as in part.

"*Question.* What was the import of these orders?

"*Answer.* I do not remember the wording. It was to the effect that he was to make a dash at Leesburg, or something of that kind.

"*Question.* From whom?

"*Answer.* From General Stone to General Baker.

"*Question.* To make a dash at Leesburg?

"*Answer.* Yes, sir; that was about the pith of it, showing that Baker acted with full authority, and deliberately, instead of recklessly. I then said something to him about the transportation. *I told him the point of attack generally was in reference to the want of transportation there. He entered into an explanation to show that had the transportation been properly taken care of by Baker, it would have been adequate.*

* Report of Committee on Conduct of War, 2, page 471.

This was before Stone testified that he was in command at Harrison's island during the battle.

We learn from this testimony what orders Stone classed as spurious, being those addressed to "General Baker" and signed "Stone," which we do not find among the official records. The genuineness of the orders given above Stone did not disprove, although he was given every opportunity to do so if in his power.

We have also learned that the transportation had been placed in the charge of men of the 19th Massachusetts (Colonel Hinks' regiment), by Stone's orders, many hours before Baker left his camp. They have told us themselves that they were detailed for the day to man the boats, and that Stone did not even provide them with poles for crossing, much less cables, although he had been making preparations for crossing to the island for several days, they being compelled to cut down trees for poles, and make use of them, although they were very clumsy and too heavy for that purpose, and that it took an hour and a quarter to cross and re-cross the boats over one branch, instead of ten minutes, the time allowed by Stone for crossing both branches.

Colonel Wistar further testified:*

"*Question.* Had you a guard for the boats in which you were crossing the river? Had you any men in charge of the boats?

"*Answer.* There was no guard necessary, for there were troops in them all the time.

"*Question.* Had you any detailed as boatmen?

"*Answer.* I had not. There were some detailed from one of the Massachusetts regiments. I found them there, and asked them if they were detailed for the day. They said they were ordered to remain there for the day. They transported my men. There were four or five in each boat."

---

* Report of Committee on Conduct of War, 2, page 313.

We also know that Baker, by Stone's orders, crossed to the bluff, and ordered troops to the rescue of those that were imperilled by Stone, and assisted them in holding that position by Stone's instructions. It was there he died, while making the most strenuous effort to hold the bluff, momentarily expecting a diversion or some signs of life from Edward's Ferry.

CHAPTER XI.

IN the last chapter we left General Stone in close confinement in Fort Lafayette, like other men charged with treasonable acts. Although no formal charges had been preferred against him, he was held a prisoner for about six months, and then released without comment by the power that closed the prison door upon him.

Let us see how he was released, and ascertain, if possible, why charges were not preferred, and why he was not given a trial, a full account of which we find in Hon. James G. Blaine's "Twenty Years in Congress," as follows:

"On the 24th of March, 1862, Senators Latham and McDougall, of California, the first a supporter of Breckenridge, in 1860, and the other a supporter of Douglass, with Aaron Sergeant, Representative from the same state, and a most radical Republican, united in an energetic memorial to Secretary Stanton on behalf of General Stone, a citizen of California. They stated that the long arrest of General Stone, without military trial or inquiry, had led to complaints from many quarters. * * * 'Having known General Stone for years, and never having had cause to doubt his loyalty we find it our duty to inquire of the Government through you for some explanation of a proceeding which seems to us most extraordinary.'

"To this memorial no reply was made, and after waiting nearly three weeks, Mr. McDougall introduced in the Senate a very searching resolution of inquiry, requesting the Secretary of War "to state upon whose authority the arrest was made, and upon whose complaint; why General Stone had been denied his rights under the articles of war, why no charges and specifications of his offense had been made; whether General Stone had not frequently asked to be informed of the charges against him; and finally, upon what pretext he was still kept in prison. Mr. McDougall spoke in the Senate on the 15th of April in support of his resolution, making some interesting personal statements. General Stone was arrested on the night of Saturday, the 8th of February. "On the Wednesday evening before that," said Mr. McDougall, "I met General Stone dressed as became a person of his rank at the house of the President, where no one went on that evening except by special invitation. He was there mingling with his friends, receiving as much attention and as much consideration from all about him as any man there present. * * * Only two evenings after that, if I remember aright, he was the guest, under similar circumstances, of the senior general in command of our Army (McClellan), and there again receiving the hospitalities of the men first in office and first in the consideration of the country. On, I think, the very day of his arrest, he was in the War Department, and was received by the head of that department as a man who had the entire confidence of the Government, and of himself as one of the Government's representatives.

"On that evening he was seized, taken from his home and family at midnight, carried off to Fort Lafayette, and imprisoned as are men convicted and adjudged guilty of the highest offence known to the law. * * * I undertake to say, upon good authority, that just before his arrest, he said to the present ·Secretary of War (Stanton), 'Sir, I hear complaints about my conduct at Ball's Bluff. I wish you to inquire into it, and have the matter determined.' He was assured that there were no charges against him, and the Secretary advised him in substance in these words, 'There is no occasion for your inquiry; go back to your command.' That was the day of the night he was arrested. Mr. McDougall's statement, the accuracy of which was not challenged by any one, disclosed the fact that while General Stone was a guest at the White House, and at the residence of General McClellan, the latter had in his possession the order for arrest, and had held it for several days.

"The resolution of Mr. McDougall was debated at some length in the Senate, Mr. Wade making a fiery speech in defense of the course pursued by the Committee on the Conduct of War, and Browning, of Illinois, defending the President, upon whom there had been no imputation of any kind. Mr. Doolittle suggested that the resolution be referred to a committee. Mr. Wilson, of Massachusetts, submitted a substitute, simply requesting 'the President of the United States to communicate to the Senate any information touching the arrest and imprisonment of General Stone not deemed incompatible with the public interest.' Mr. Sumner had 'no opinion to express in the case, for he knew nothing about it,' but it seemed clear to him 'that General Stone ought to be confronted with his accusers at an early day, unless there be some reason of a military character which would render such a trial improper.' Mr. Sumner had 'seen in various newspapers a most persistent attempt to connect him with the credit or discredit of the arrest.' He declared 'that from the beginning he had been an absolute stranger to it.' The arrest was made, he repeated, without his suggestion or hint, direct or indirect. He declared that he 'was as free from all connection with it as the intimate friends and family relatives of the prisoner.'

"At the close of the debate, Mr. McDougall accepted Mr. Wilson's resolution as a substitute for his, and on the 21st of April, the latter was adopted by general consent. * * * In answer to the call upon the President for information, Mr. Lincoln sent a message to the Senate on the 1st of May, saying, 'General Stone was arrested and imprisoned under my general authority, and upon evidence which, be he guilty or innocent, required, as appeared to me, such proceedings to be had against him for the public safety.'

"The President deemed it incompatible with the public interest, and perhaps unjust to General Stone, to make a more particular statement of the evidence. After saying that General Stone had not been tried because the officers to constitute a court-martial could not be withdrawn from duty without serious injury to the service, the President gave this public assurance: 'He will be allowed a trial without unnecessary delay. The charges and specifications will be furnished him in due season, and every facility for his defense will be afforded him by the War Department.'

"This message, on its face, bears evidence that it was prepared at the War Department, and that Mr. Lincoln acted upon assurances furnished him by Mr. Stanton. The arrest was made upon *his general authority*, and clearly not from any specific information he possessed; but the effect of the message was to preclude any further attempt at intervention by Congress. Indeed, the assurance that General Stone should be tried 'without any unnecessary delay,' was all that could be asked. But the promise made to the ear was broken to the hope, and General Stone was left to languish without a word of intelligence as to his alleged offense, and without the slightest opportunity to meet the accusers who, in the dark, had convicted him without trial, subjected him to cruel punishment, and exposed him to the judgment of the world as a degraded criminal.

"Release from imprisonment came at last by the action of Congress, coercing the Executive Department to the trial or discharge of General Stone. In the Act of July 17th, 1862, defining the pay and emolument of certain officers, a section was inserted, declaring 'That whenever an officer be put under arrest, except at remote military posts, it shall be the duty of the officer by whose orders he is arrested to see that a copy of the charges shall be served upon him within eight days thereafter, and that he shall be brought to trial within ten days thereafter, unless the necessities of the service prevent such trial, and then he shall be brought to trial within thirty days after the expiration of said ten days, or the arrest shall cease.'

"The act reserved the right to try the officer at any time within twelve months after his discharge from arrest, and by a proviso it was made to apply 'to all persons now under arrest, and awaiting trial.' The bill had been pending several months, having been originally reported by Senator Wilson before General Stone's arrest. The provision of the act applicable to the case of General Stone was only a full enactment by law of the 79th Article of War, which declared that 'no officer or soldier who shall be put in arrest shall continue in confinement more than eight days, or until such time as a court-martial can be assembled.'

"It was a direct violation of the spirit of this article, and a cruel straining of its letter, to consign General Stone to endless or indefinite imprisonment. Any man of average intelligence in the law—and Secretary Stanton was eminent in his profession—would at once say that the time beyond the eight days allowed for assembling a court-martial must be a reasonable period, and that an officer was entitled to prompt trial, or release from arrest.

"The law now passed was imperative. Within eight days the arrested officer must be notified of the charges against him, within ten days he must be tried, and "if the necessities of the service prevent a trial" within thirty days after the ten, the officer is entitled to an absolute discharge. General Stone's case fell within the justice and the mercy of the law. The eight days within which he should be notified of the charges against him had been long past; the ten days had certainly expired; but by the construction of the War Department, the victim was still in the power that wronged him for thirty days more. From the 17th of July, thirty days were slowly tolled off until the 16th of August was at last reached, and General Stone was once more a free man. He had been one hundred and eighty-nine days in prison, and was at last discharged by the limitation of the statute, without a word of exculpation or explanation.

"The routine order simply recited that 'the necessities of the service not permitting the trial within the time required by law of Brigadier Charles P. Stone, now confined in Fort Lafayette, the Secretary of War directs that he be released from arrest.'

"The order simply turned him adrift. He was a colonel in the regular army, and a brigadier-general in the volunteer service, and the Secretary, according to the rule of the War Department, should have given him some instructions, either assigning him to duty or directing him to report at some place and await orders. Thinking it might be an omission, General Stone telegraphed the War Department that he had the honor 'to report for duty.' He waited five days in New York for an answer, and received none; then repaired to Washington. Reporting promptly at the office of the adjutant-general, he was told that they had no orders for him, and knew nothing about his arrest.

"He then applied to General McClellan on the eve of

the Antietam campaign for permission to serve with
the army. General McClellan on the 7th of September
wrote to Secretary Stanton that he would be glad to
avail himself of General Stone's services, and that he
had 'no doubt as to his loyalty and devotion.' No
answer was returned by the War Department. On the
25th of September, General Stone, still eager to confront his accusers, applied to General-in-Chief Halleck
for a copy of any charges or allegations against him,
and the opportunity of promptly meeting them. He
reminded the General that 228 days had elapsed since
his arrest, and that if he was to be tried for any offence
those who served under him must be the witnesses of
his conduct, and that they from battle and disease were
falling by hundreds and thousands; the casualties were
so great indeed that his command was already reduced
one-half. General Halleck replied 'that he had no
official information of the cause of General Stone's
arrest, and that so far as he could ascertain, no charges
or specifications were on file against him.'

"Several weeks later, on the 1st of December, 1862,
General Stone applied to General McClellan, calling
his attention to the Act of July 17th, under which an
officer arrested had the right to 'a copy of the charges
against him within eight days.' He therefore respectfully requested *General McClellan, as the officer who
ordered the arrest*, to furnish him a copy of the charges.
General McClellan replied on the 5th of December that
the order for arrest had been given him by the Secretary
of War, who told him it was at the solicitation of the
'Committee on the Conduct of War,' and based on
testimony taken by them.

He further informed General Stone that he had the
order in the handwriting of Secretary Stanton several
days before it was carried into effect, and added the
following somewhat remarkable statement: 'On the
evening you were arrested, *I submitted to the Secretary*

of War the written result of the examination of a refugee from Leesburg. This information, to a certain extent, agreed with the evidence stated to have been taken by the Committee, and upon its being imparted to the Secretary he again instructed me to cause you to be arrested, which I at once did.'

"This discloses the fact that *General McClellan was cognizant of the character of the testimony* submitted against General Stone, and so rigidly withheld from the knowledge of the person most interested. On receipt of General McClellan's note, General Stone immediately asked for the name of the Leesburg refugee and for a copy of his statement. A member of General McClellan's staff answered this inquiry, stating that the General '*does not recollect the name of the refugee,* and the last time he recollects seeing the statement was at the War Department immediately previous to your arrest.'

"General Stone, victim of the perversity which had uniformly attended the case, was again baffled. He was never able to see the statement of the refugee, or even to get his name, though, *according to General McClellan, the testimony of the refugee was the proximate and apparently decisive cause of General Stone's arrest.* General Stone applied directly to the President asking, 'If he could inform me why I was sent to Fort Lafayette.' The President replied that "If he told me all he knew about it, he should not tell me much.' He stated that while it was done under his general authority, he did not do it. The President referred General Stone to General Halleck, who stated *that the arrest was made on the recommendation of General McClellan.*

"This was a surprise to General Stone, for General McClellan had but recently written him that he had full confidence in his devotion and loyalty. General Halleck replied that he knew of that letter, and 'that the Secretary of War had expressed great surprise at it, because he said that General McClellan himself had recommended the arrest, and now seemed to be pushing the whole thing on his (the Secretary's) shoulders.' The search for the agency that would frankly admit responsibility was rendered still more difficult by the denial of the Committee on the Conduct of the War that the arrest had ever been recommended by them, either collectively or individually. They had simply forwarded to the Secretary of War such evidence as was submitted to them.

"The responsibility for the arrest and imprisonment of General Stone must, according to the official records of the case, rest on Secretary Stanton, Major-General McClellan, and the Committee on the Conduct of the War.* It is very clear that Mr. Lincoln, pressed by a thousand calls, and placing implicit confidence in these three agencies, took it for granted that ample proof existed to justify the extraordinary treatment to which General Stone was subjected.

"General Stone is not to be classed in that long list of private citizens temporarily confined without the benefit of the *habeas corpus* on the charge of sympathizing with the rebellion. The situation of those persons more nearly assimilates with that of prisoners of war. It differs totally from the arrest of General Stone, in that the cause of the detention was well known, and very often proudly averred, by the person detained. The key of their prison was generally in the hands of those who were thus confined, an honest avowal of loyalty, and an oath of allegiance to the National

---

* We will learn that General Stone testified, "I am satisfied that this Committee did not solicit my arrest," and that he claimed that McClellan had the power to grant him a trial—he being the officer who made the arrest, should have furnished the charges; while the Secretary of War had said "that General McClellan himself had recommended the arrest."

government, securing their release. If they could not take the oath, they were justifiably held, and were no more injured in reputation than the millions with whose daring rebellion they sympathized.

" But to General Stone the government permitted the gravest crime to be imputed. A soldier who will betray his command, belongs, by the code of all nations, to the most infamous class; his death but feebly atoning for the injury he has inflicted upon his country.

"It was under the implied accusation of this great guilt that General Stone was left in duress for more than six weary months, deprived of all power of self-defence, denied the inherent right of the humblest citizen of the Republic. In the end, not gracefully, but tardily, and as it seemed grudgingly, the government was compelled to confess its own wrong, and to do partial justice to the injured man by restoring him to honorable service under the flag of the nation.

" No reparation was made him for the protracted defamation of his character; no order was published acknowledging that he was found guiltless; no communication was ever made to him, by national authority, giving even a hint of the grounds on which for half a year he was pilloried before the nation as a malefactor. The wound which General Stone received was deep. From some motive, the source of which will probably remain a mystery, his persecution continued in many petty and offensive ways, until he was finally driven, toward the close of the war, 'when he saw that he could be no longer useful to his country,' to tender his resignation.

"It was promptly accepted. He found abroad the respect and consideration which had been denied him at home, and for many years he was chief of the general staff to the Khedive of Egypt."

It is quite possible the mystery surrounding General Stone and the cause of his earlier and later persecutions

14

would have been solved had he demanded a court of inquiry as to his conduct in the affair at Ball's Bluff. How favorable the verdict of a court of inquiry would have been to his conduct throughout the whole affair no one was better able to judge than he, after he had read the testimony given against him, and we must conclude that he did not look with much favor upon any further investigation, which he of all persons knew the best that he had the right to demand.

No less an authority than Mr. Blaine has fallen into errors in his chapter devoted to General Stone and Colonel Baker. In one place he writes, "The Oregon Senator, with his ardent nature, and his impulse to take part in every conflict, had raised a regiment of volunteers principally composed of men from the Pacific coast"—while it is a well-known fact that Colonel Baker's regiment, called "The First California Regiment," was recruited in Philadelphia, and at one time marched sixteen companies strong, all composed of Pennsylvanians excepting company "G" from New York city and company "R" from Washington, D. C., and was finally accredited to the State of Pennsylvania in the War Department, and became the 71st of the Pennsylvania line, about twenty years before the publication of Mr. Blaine's book, having been raised promptly for three years' service in pursuance of a special order from the War Department, dated May 8th, 1861, as shown.

While Mr. Blaine's chapter is replete with all the incidents attending the chequered career of General Stone as seen from the halls of Congress, it is not without a bias almost as strong as though it had been written by Stone himself, clearly not in keeping with the just appreciation of all the facts and testimony adduced by the Committee—nor is it in accord with all the official reports of record, into which Mr. Blaine may not have delved very deeply—otherwise we may fairly presume that in justice to the illustrious dead he would not have quoted the contents of Stone's official communication as veritable facts, *i. e.*, "He called attention to the distinct violation by Colonel Baker of his orders and instructions." * * * He found it "painful to censure the acts of one who gallantly died on the field of battle," but justice to himself required "that the full truth should be made to appear," etc.

Before leaving this article we will note another error, into which Mr. Blaine had been led by an official report from Stone's headquarters. He writes, "The details of this disaster were greatly exaggerated. The official summary of losses, made up with care, showed that the total number killed, including both officers and men, was 49; wounded, 158; missing 714, of whom a few were drowned, and the great mass taken prisoners. This carefully prepared "official summary of losses" bears the impress of Stone's manipulation or intentional neglect, in which the losses to the 1st California Regiment are given as follows: Officers killed, 3; enlisted men, 10; officers wounded, 3; enlisted men, 37; total, 53—while the actual casualties were over 100, prisoners 213, to the 1st battalion of this regiment alone, making their casualties average about twenty per cent. of their number engaged. Colonel Banes, who was present with the "Philadelphia Brigade," writes in his history, "of 520 men of the 71st who entered this engagement, 312 were lost"—killed, wounded and drowned, 99; prisoners, 213—the greatest total loss that befell the regiment in any action. And it is only fair to presume that the 15th and 20th Massachusetts regiments suffered in about the same proportion, while the three or four companies of the Tammany regiment, and the artillerists that crossed, lost officers and some men. The casualties commenced at 7 a. m., and only ended when the remnant had been taken prisoners, at 10 p. m.

When we compare the true percentage of losses here with that of the battle of Waterloo, one of the most desperate and bloody fields chronicled in European history, where the killed and wounded were less than twelve per cent., and with that of the great battles of Marengo and Austerlitz, sanguinary as they were, where the loss was less than fourteen and a half per cent., we should not regard it as so slight an affair. Thus we may conclude that here again he has unwittingly, but most manifestly done a great injustice to Colonel Baker's old regiment, which, to a greater or less extent, must share with their old commander the praise and censure alike, relating to this battle.

Captain Vaughan, who, with ten men, crossed under a flag of truce the day after the battle, to bury our dead upon the field, reported to General Stone through Colonel Hinks,* that he had "succeeded in burying forty-seven bodies, which he reported to be about two-thirds of the number lying upon the ground, but night coming on, he was unable to bury the remainder." That would indicate seventy bodies of our men that he saw exposed to view on the bluff, and while a number more had fallen in the woods and underbrush not exposed to view; this only relates to the men who were killed in the field. General Stone was informed two or three days after the battle by flag of truce that six of our wounded had died at Leesburg, and that all of our dead had then been buried. It is also in evidence that about thirty of the wounded men were drowned by the sinking of the scow, and that others had been shot while attempting to swim across the river (many dead bodies having washed ashore or lodged upon the rocks at different places down the river), while a great many of the mortally wounded taken from the field died during the day and night, swelling the dead roll

* Official Records, Series I, Vol. V, page 313.

to perhaps one hundred and fifty, and it is not unreasonable to suppose that the number of wounded
would be increased in about the same ratio. General
Stone reported forty-nine in all had been killed,
and a hundred and fifty-eight wounded, giving the
balance as missing; and General Evans' grossly exaggerated report fixed our killed, wounded, and drowned
at thirteen hundred, which almost equals the entire
force engaged; while their historian writes, "This enterprise brought on a conflict among the most sanguinary
of the war, in view of the numbers engaged." They
also having lost quite heavily, Comte de Paris, then at
General McClellan's headquarters, placed our dead at
two hundred and twenty-three; wounded, two hundred
and fifty; and the loss of the enemy at three hundred,
of whom one hundred and fifty-three were killed.

It would seem that this official report was strictly in
keeping with most of the other reports that passed
under the surveillance of General Stone, and through
him were forwarded to the Department at Washington.

CHAPTER XII.

GENERAL STONE APPEARS BEFORE THE COMMIT-
TEE AGAIN—SUPPLIES OMISSIONS AND COR-
RECTS SOME OF HIS MISSTATEMENTS.

GENERAL STONE has now been released from prison over six months, during which time he continued his efforts to ascertain what specific charges if any were on file in the War Department against him. All his efforts proved futile. There was still a refuge to which he could flee, and seek redress—the court of inquiry—if he had wished to invoke its friendly aid to determine all these questions and allegations in a trial by his brother officers, ready to do him full justice. He may have sagely concluded that discretion was the better part of valor, that he would endure the ills he had, be they ever so humiliating, trusting to the sympathy of the public, which had been aroused over his imprisonment without formal charges, and a release without trial, rather than face a trial by his own peers of all the facts and circumstances connected with the battle, and in the mist and confusion surrounding the whole affair, escape with the sympathy of the nation, to pose as a martyr.

On application to the Committee on Conduct of War he was shown every courtesy, and was permitted "in consideration of the peculiar circumstances attending his arrest" (of which the committee disclaimed all direct responsibility),* "to examine all the testimony

---

* They having "reported to the Secretary of War that the testimony upon the points to which his attention had been called was conflicting. They made no recommendation as to what should be done, one way or the other merely reported to

which they had taken" relative to the whole matter; and finally, on the 27th of February, 1863, after Mc-Clellan had been relieved from command of the "Army of the Potomac" almost four months, General Stone appeared before the Committee and corrected some of his former misstatements, and supplied many important omissions, notably among which are parts of dispatches from General McClellan, *i. e.*, "*I may order you to take Leesburg to-day. Shall I push up one or two divisions from this side ?*" To which General Stone replied, "*I think I can take Leesburg,*" and thereby declined the close co-operation of these two divisions.

General Stone appeared before the Committee.

"*By the Chairman :* If there is anything you desire to state to the Committee in addition to what you have already stated, you will please state it. What the Committee desires is to get at the truth as nearly as possible."

"*Answer.* I have observed that a great deal of blame has been cast upon me for leaving a small body of troops on the Virginia shore,* opposite Edward's Ferry, on the night of Monday, October 21, 1861. * * * The moment I had given the orders for the retiring of these troops, I reported by telegraph to General McClellan at Washington that 'we had met with a severe repulse on our right," and that "any advance from Dranesville must be made cautiously, but that I was doing the best I could to secure the left" (where it is evident that attention was not nearly so imperative on the Maryland side as at the right, which he had just left. The sequel proved that he was withdrawing his forces upon the left from a victory within their grasp), "and him that the testimony was conflicting" and "that in the opinion of the Committee a prompt investigation should be instituted."—Report of Committee on Conduct of War, 2, pages 17 and 18.

* About 4,500.

to retrieve * * * I received orders from General Mc-Clellan to this effect, 'Hold all the ground you now have on the Virginia shore if your men will fight, intrenching if necessary. You will be re-enforced.' * * I telegraphed to General McClellan, urging that re-enforcements should be sent to Goose creek on the Virginia side, supposing all the time that General Mc-Call was not far off. The response to that, which I think I received about 11 o'clock on Monday night, was the first intimation I ever received that McCall had not all the time been near me. That dispatch informed me that no re-enforcements could reach me from the Virginia side, but that Banks would re-enforce me from the Maryland side.''

General McCall testified that he was then in his camp at Langley, 28 miles from Leesburg, and that ''Ball's Bluff could not have been reached, even from Dranesville, under 17 miles by any road.''

General Stone: ''*Question.* How far was General Banks from you?''

''*Answer.* He was about fourteen miles in my rear.

''*Question.* Did that first dispatch from General Mc-Clellan, promising you re-enforcements, contemplate they should come from General Banks?

''*Answer.* Yes, sir; I suppose so; but at the time my idea was that McCall was close by me. * * * I think that by this statement I must remove any unpleasant impression with regard to my improperly exposing troops to disaster at Edward's Ferry, *since I acted under the instructions of my superior officer,* and also under the constant impression that our forces under General McCall were near us on the Virginia side of Edward's Ferry.''

Could not Stone have entered a plea almost, if not quite as strong, for his troops at Ball's Bluff if moved by a sense of justice?

''*Question.* How happens it that you failed to make

this statement concerning these orders on your former examination?

"*Answer.* Because I did not deem it proper to give any of the orders of my superior officer which he had not himself previously published, or authorized me to use. The morning that I came before the Committee I was instructed at General McClellan's headquarters that it was the desire of the General that officers giving testimony before the Committee should not state, without his authority, anything regarding his plans, his orders for the movement of troops, or his orders concerning the position of troops. That covered this case.

"*Question.* Did you understand that to apply to past orders and transactions, as well as those to be expected in the future?

"*Answer.* I did, because I could not know, and did not know what orders to others were given contemporaneous with those I received, and I might create wrong impressions by giving the orders I had received from my commanding-general unless there were at the same time produced cotemporaneous orders given to other generals; and I presume that the Chairman will remember that I stated when giving my testimony before, that *I could not give any orders from my commanding-general except such as he had made public.*

"*Question.* Did General McClellan approve of the crossing at Edward's Ferry, and at Ball's Bluff, on the 21st of October, 1861?

"*Answer.* I received a despatch from General McClellan, in reply to one which I sent him,* informing him of the crossing of Colonel Baker and General Gorman. That despatch to me commenced with these words, "*I congratulate you and your command.*" I took that congratulation on the fact of having crossed as an approval of the crossing, and as I had received no information whatever concerning General McCall,

---

* See page 162.

in my own mind I supposed that it was but a simple
thing of General McClellan's in connection with any
other movement he might be making.''

How apparently inconsistent is this last sentence
with other parts of Stone's testimony as to his depend-
ing upon McCall being near; one might suppose that
Stone meant to go it alone, and take all the glory to
himself, when he said, ''I think I can take Leesburg.''

'' *Question.* Was General McClellan informed of your
means of transportation for crossing troops?

'' *Answer:* Some time during the day, and I think it
was in the same despatch in which he asked me for information of the apparent force of the enemy, and I
should think that that despatch must have reached me
about noon, General McClellan asked, 'what means
of transportation I had.' I replied to him by telegraph
stating the number and character of the boats at each
crossing, at Edward's Ferry and at Harrison's Landing.
In connection with that I would say that from my despatch of the previous evening (Sunday), General Mc-
Clellan might have supposed that those boats were of
somewhat larger capacity than they really were. In
that despatch, after reporting the demonstration I had
made, I reported *that I had means of crossing 250 men
in ten minutes at two points.* This estimate was made
from a trial which I had made on Sunday at Edward's
Ferry of the boats there, which were of the same character as those used at Ball's Bluff. The management
of those boats at Edward's Ferry was very perfect.
The men were marched on in a very orderly manner,
guards were placed, and the men were detailed in advance for the poling of the boats.''

The 19th Massachusetts men claimed that they had
been detailed for duty upon the island by Stone, and
to man the boats at Harrison's Island,* but had not
been furnished with poles, much less ropes. Colonel

* Where Stone testified he was in command during the battle.

Tompkins said there "were no planks there (Edward's Ferry) and no ropes, and the boats had to be shoved across with poles." General Gorman asked Philip Hauger for poles, to which he replied, "I told him that there were none within two miles and a half suitable for boat poles. He said the men on the other side were in a very perilous condition, and he was afraid our boys on the other side would be lost. I told him there was a canal flat lying in the river, and that no one was using it, and I could raise men and poles enough to take that up, and with that I could bring over more than with any three boats up there. He said, "For God Almighty's sake do it as soon as you can.' I took it up there, and made nine successful trips across the river with it."

Stone continuing, said, "The time, according to the watch, required for poling these boats across on Sunday evening, according to the best of my recollection, was for one of the boats exactly five minutes, and for another of the boats seven minutes, from the time of pushing the boat from the Maryland shore to the time when the men landed on the Virginia shore. But the estimate made on Sunday night was very nearly what proved to be correct at Edward's Ferry on Monday, and would have been the capacity of the boats if well-managed opposite Harrison's Island."

What an inconceivable misstatement, in face of the testimony of Gorman's Quartermaster Foote, and other officers who crossed, and had charge of the transportation at Edward's Ferry! Foote testified,[*] "I will state at this point the river is about 450 yards wide, with a current about five miles an hour. For about 150 yards from each bank the bottom is soft, but in the centre of the river it is rocky. We could make the trip in *about one hour and ten minutes*," and that by using a canal boat secured by his orders, which would

[*] Report of Committee on Conduct of War, 2, page 364.

hold more men in the aggregate than all the other boats put together, he was enabled to cross the whole brigade before evening. Thus the means of transportation at Edward's Ferry was very much greater than at Harrison's Island.

COLONEL JAMES H. VAN ALLAN, one of Stone's warm supporters, testified:* "I wish I could say that I knew there was sufficient transportation right at hand in the canal. I do say, with all my regard for General Stone, that if there was not, *the order to cross the river was an improper one,* and I do not think that General Stone's defense is strong upon that point in his report; for although he says there was a scow and two boats there (Harrison's Island), and that they could carry across so many men in so many minutes, I do not think that that is a sufficient justification for sending such an expedition across, for I maintain that transportation should have been ready there, to take the whole command across at one and the same time. And more than that, I say he should have looked to having transportation enough to re-enforce the men upon the other side, because he could not tell how many of the enemy we had to meet."

"*Question.* General Stone, what prevented your sending over a much more formidable force than you did send?

"*Answer.* It was this: the disposition of the larger portion of my command was turned over to Colonel Baker on Monday morning.† At Edward's Ferry a much larger number would have been sent over had there been the troops there to be sent. My first intention at Edward's Ferry was not to send over as many as I did." (He had crossed the 1st Minnesota and 2d New York,

* Report of Committee on Conduct of War, 2, page 459.

† While Stone remained with the smaller portion, although he was in command at Harrison's Island, and on the Maryland shore at both crossings.

one skirmishing company of the 19th Massachusetts, and a company of sharpshooters, cavalry, and two pieces of artillery, between 10 and 11 o'clock a. m., which were followed immediately thereafter by the 34th New York, raising his forces across the river to about 2500 men, before Baker could have arrived at Harrison's Island, and taken command. And Stone has told us that "there was another large operation and reconnaissance going on down at Goose creek, which I was watching" (*before Baker left him with orders.*) "But when I found the crossing taking place in force at Ball's Bluff (where Stone had crossed about 900 men and two pieces of artillery, which Colonel Baker attempted to re-enforce in compliance with Stone's orders), I then commenced passing over troops more rapidly at Edward's Ferry" (the 7th Michigan, and perhaps a remnant of the 34th New York, the only troops he had there that had not crossed). "Time was lost in passing the men over in the morning at Edward's Ferry" (until the transportation was improved, although they had commenced to cross at daybreak), "and time was also lost from the necessity of bringing up one entire regiment from the lower picket. At the commencement of the affair, the 34th New York was some six miles below Edward's Ferry,* and they had to be marched up before they could be transported over. There were also not so many over at Edward's Ferry early in the day" (about three times as many as at Ball's Bluff) "because I did not wish to use the 7th Michigan Regiment, as they were poorly armed. They were excellent men, but I deemed it unfair to put them into battle with the poor arms they had.

"*Question.* Was the demonstration which you made across the river on Monday morning made in concert or co-operation with McCall, according to your understanding?

* Which arrived about 10 a. m.

"*Answer.* When I first ordered men across on Monday morning, I did so entirely without reference to any co-operation on General McCall's part, except so far as this, that I thought I should, by that small movement, more fully carry out the instructions of the day before, and also aid whatever project the general-in-chief might have had in sending McCall up to Dranesville, because the general's orders evidently pointed to the desirableness of *Leesburg being forcibly evacuated* by the enemy. The Committee will see that I was obliged to proceed very much on my own ideas of what was taking place elsewhere. It may have been 12 or 1 o'clock on Monday, but whether in a despatch by itself, or in connection with some of the despatches which I have already mentioned, I cannot say, for it is now thirteen months since I have seen any of those papers at all. In a despatch General McClellan informed me as follows: 'I may order you to take Leesburg to-day,' and whether it was in that despatch or in another I cannot say, but in one dated at Fort Cochran or at Arlington, the general asked me this question, '*Shall I push up one or two divisions from this side?*' I thought a moment, and concluded that if there was a slight force in front of us, then my force and McCall's would be all-sufficient; and if that was not sufficient, then it was too late for any other divisions to come up. I therefore replied to him, '*I think I can take Leesburg,*' still under the impression that McCall was near me, and that General McClellan's question referred to other divisions near Washington, other than McCall's.

"*Question.* If you were to make a demonstration upon Leesburg, or to take Leesburg, as seems to have been contemplated as possible, what military reason could have induced the retiring of McCall's division from Dranesville back to their original camping ground before the demonstration was made?

"*Answer. With my present information, I can see no good military reason for it.*

"*Question.* Had you been apprised of the retirement of McCall's division before you crossed over, would it have made any difference in your arrangements?

"*Answer.* Had I known on Sunday night at 10 o'clock, when I gave the order to Colonel Devens to go over and destroy the Rebel camp, which was supposed to be on the other side, that General McCall's division was not at Dranesville, I should then have made the order to return, and return rapidly after accomplishing that duty, an imperative order, and I should also have accompanied the expedition myself, because that would have been the sole object of that movement. I desire to state here that in my previous examination before the Committee, I stated that had I tried to move troops from Edward's Ferry up to Colonel Baker's position, it would have been one of the most hazardous things possible to be attempted. I stated to the Committee that I saw three guns go down into the position between the fortification on the Leesburg road and Ball's Bluff. Those I saw with the glass."

How completely this wonderful gun canard has been exploded by the ample testimony from both sides, the reader is now aware, and therefore the gun and masked battery fabrication must be settled as a story not founded on fact;* and even if the guns had been there supported by 1,000 men, our best generals have told us that it was Stone's duty, under the circumstances, either to engage them with his vastly superior force, or to go to the assistance of Colonel Baker when he knew his forces were engaged.

"*Question.* Suppose McCall's division had been ordered to advance on Leesburg, instead of retiring

* Colonel Elijah V. White, of Leesburg, to whom we have referred, an undoubted authority of approved veracity, has written the author recently that "nothing but the Confederate forces were between Gorman's and Baker's, and that about 2 o'clock p. m. nearly all of our people were withdrawn from before Gorman," thus corroborating the other information to those points.

back to his camp at Washington, what would probably have been the result?

"*Answer.* Had he arrived at Goose creek by 12 o'clock on Monday, the capture of the entire Rebel force at Leesburg, *I should think, must have been certain.* Had he arrived at Goose creek on the afternoon of Monday, *the disaster could not have occurred,* and probably the same result would have been achieved, that is, the capture of the whole or greater part of the Rebel force then at Leesburg." (It might very truthfully be added that had General McCall been at Goose creek, in command of Stone's forces, a victory would have been achieved, and the enemy driven with great loss. If McCall's forces were necessary, why did not Stone ask for their close co-operation, instead of saying, '*I think I can take Leesburg,*' when offered assistance.)

"It may appear strange that after a reverse like that of Ball's Bluff the general commanding the troops engaged there, should not have asked for a court of inquiry. The reason why I (General Stone) did not ask for a court of inquiry, as I most undoubtedly should do under such circumstances, was this: while General McClellan was present at Edward's Ferry and after he had examined into the affair, he showed me a telegram which he had written to the President to the effect that he had examined into the affair of the 21st, and that General Stone was entirely without blame. That was as strong an expression of opinion from my superior as I could have obtained from any court of inquiry. It was, therefore, neither necessary, nor would it have been respectful after the expression of that opinion by that high military authority, to have asked for a court of inquiry. Not only was it given by this high authority, but it was sent to the highest authority, and as a soldier I had no right to ask for justification except of my superiors. If they were satisfied, I could ask for no other justification."

(How startling the revelation, when we find that General McClellan appeared before the committee the very next day, and testified that he had made no formal investigation, that his dispatch exonerating General Stone was based upon Stone's statements and hearsay evidence, and that he now thought that *Stone was to blame* for giving Colonel Baker permission to cross without furnishing him with sufficient transportation —and further that he was to blame for not throwing his troops at Edward's Ferry either upon Leesburg, or upon the enemy engaging Colonel Baker's forces. Thus the exoneration Stone claimed to enjoy, when read by the light of McClellan's testimony, was swept away by the same hand that gave it ; and if Stone was sincere in his expression, and desired a court of inquiry, he was then relieved from all ethical embarrassment as to such application. But he seems to have rested his case upon the fact that his chief had once exonerated him, and that no one would prefer charges against him, and therewith he was content, without demanding a court of inquiry. No doubt he wisely concluded that it was better to

> " bear those ills we have,
> Than fly to others that we know not of.")

" Again on another occasion when Mr. Conklin of the House of Representatives made a speech in which my conduct was severely criticised, in connection with the affair at Ball's Buff, I telegraphed to the aide-de-camp of General McClellan as likely to know the wishes of the General, stating that I had noticed Mr. Conklin's speech and desired to know if I should apply for a court of inquiry. The reply was, 'No !' I then asked if it was desirable that I should write a statement which should expose the mistakes in Mr. Conklin's account of the affair at Ball's Bluff. The reply was : 'Write nothing ; say nothing ; keep quiet.' "

When the Committee had concluded the re-hearing
15

of General Stone in his own defense as to all the evidence taken, they were apparently still convinced that
to properly account for his generalship and conduct in
the whole affair would be a difficult matter ; but in
view of the fact of his imprisonment, and that efforts
had been made by many to hold them alone responsible
for all that had taken place in reference to his arrest—
and perhaps having concluded in the meantime that
they had erred as to Stone's disloyalty*—they re-
frained from giving further expression to positive
opinions, preferring to "allow each one to form his own
conclusion from the testimony they had been able to

* General Stone testified, Report of Committee on Conduct
of War, 2, page 501 : "*I then wrote to General McClellan.* * *
*I stated to him that the officer who arrested me claimed to act by
his (McClellan's) authority ; and therefore I claimed from him
the charges which caused my arrest. To that General McClellan replied that * * * when he spoke to the Secretary of War
upon the subject, he was informed that the Secretary did it at the
solicitation of the Committee on the Conduct of the War. I em-
phasize the word solicitation*, BECAUSE I AM SATISFIED THAT
THIS COMMITTEE DID NOT SOLICIT MY ARREST.' This coming
from one who studied his case more closely than any man then
living must have weight ; thus leaving that responsibility with
General McClellan, who had said "that he did not see how
any charges could be framed on the testimony," but who thereafter supplied the missing link. Stone further testified: "When
General Halleck was general-in-chief, he told me that the Secretary of War had told him that it (the arrest) was done on the
recommendation of General McClellan. I stated to the general-in-chief that that surprised me greatly, for only a short time
before I had seen General McClellan, and he had informed me
that he had arrested me on the peremptory order of the Secretary of War." * * * "General Halleck said that he knew that
such a letter had been written, and that the Secretary of War
had expressed a great surprise at it, because he said that General McClellan had recommended the arrest, and now seemed
to be pushing the whole thing on his (the Secretary's) shoulders."—Report of the Committee on the Conduct of War, 2,
page 500.

obtain;" and then they finally submitted the whole testimony, *including their former opinions without reversing them*, adding thereto, "In connection with the battle of Ball's Bluff two points remain to be considered: First, whether a crossing was justifiable under any circumstances, considering the very inefficient means of transportation at the command of General Stone. * * * In regard to the first point, all the testimony goes to prove that the means of transportation were very inadequate. In reference to re-enforcing Colonel Baker (the second point), the testimony is very conflicting. There is no question that it was known that the forces at Ball's Bluff were engaged with the enemy." (We have learned that General Stone had his chief of staff upon the field of battle during the heat of the engagement, and that his aid, Captain Candy, and an orderly, spent the day in transit back and forth.) "The firing of musketry was distinctly heard at Edward's Ferry on both sides of the river. The only question is whether re-enforcements should have been sent under the circumstances, and whether there was any sufficient reason why they were not sent" (as against General Stone's testimony.) "Other witnesses testified most positively that so far as they were able to judge, there was no obstacle whatever in the way of our troops passing up on the Virginia side from Edward's Ferry."*

General Stone having been released by the limitation prescribed by statute without charges having been preferred against him, became a free man without a vindication of any kind, with the unreversed opinion of the Committee on the Conduct of War ringing in his ears: The evidence "may be said to impeach you" for "order-

---

* See testimony heretofore given by Generals McClellan, Lander and Dana, Colonel Tompkins, Majors Mix, Bannister and Dimmick, and Philip Hanger, also Colonel Barksdale's report and Colonel White's statement.

ing your forces over without sufficient means of transportation," "for not re-enforcing those troops when
they were over there in the face of the enemy," "when
you knew the battle was proceeding, that you did not
go within three or four miles of it." "We can not help
but think that they ought to have been re-enforced, for
instance, from Edward's Ferry, or perhaps, if you had
sufficient transportation, as you intimate, then right
across at Ball's Bluff." This committee—the Joint
Committee on the Conduct of War,—appointed in December, 1861, during the second session of the 37th
Congress, consisted of Senators Benjamin F. Wade,
of Ohio; Zachariah Chandler, of Michigan; and
Andrew Johnson, of Tennessee; and Representatives
D. W. Gooch, of Massachusetts; John Covode, of
Pennsylvania; George W. Julian, of Indiana; and
M. F. Odell, of New York.

CHAPTER XIII.

LET us briefly review some of the important points and facts that have been made to appear, and after learning what a marvellous combination of circumstances occurred, see if it has not been clearly shown that all the movements were made with one object in view—the capture of Leesburg—notwithstanding the reports of Generals McClellan and Stone did not disclose that fact, but would rather make it at first appear that there had been no preconcerted plan or special object in view, that the disaster was caused by rashness and disobedience of orders; and finally, if there was not an attempt to mislead and stifle all investigation without allowing the truth to be made apparent.

We have learned that General McClellan arrived at Edward's Ferry, and after conferring with General Stone, sent the following telegram to the President, "I have investigated the matter, and General Stone is without blame. Had his orders been followed, there could or would have been no disaster." And he had filed in the War Department the following: "The disaster was caused by errors committed by the immediate commander, not General Stone."

Then followed Stone's official reports, casting the whole blame of the disaster upon Colonel Baker, and charging him with rashness and disobedience of orders most unjustly; and his (Stone's) testimony before the Committee on the Conduct of War of January 5, 1862, withholding the information which would have made the full truth to appear, a part of which testimony General McClellan used in his own defense, who says in his report:* "General Stone says he received the order from my headquarters to make a slight demonstration at about 11 a. m. on the 20th, and that in obedience to that order, he made the demonstration on the evening of the same day.

In regard to the reconnaissance on the 21st, which resulted in the battle of Ball's Bluff, he (Stone) was asked the following questions:

"*Question.* Did this reconnaissance originate with yourself, or had you orders from the general-in-chief to make it?

"*Answer.* It originated with myself, the reconnaissance.

"*Question.* The order did not proceed from General McClellan?

"*Answer.* I was directed the day before to make a demonstration, and that demonstration was made the day previous.

"*Question.* Did you receive an order from the general-in-chief to make the reconnaissance?

"*Answer.* No, sir."

General McClellan having previously reported, "The first intimation I received from General Stone of the real nature of his movements was in a telegram as follows:

"EDWARD'S FERRY, October 21, 11:10 a. m.
"MAJOR-GENERAL MCCLELLAN: The enemy have been engaged opposite Harrison's Island, our men behaving admirably.
"C. P. STONE,
"*Brigadier-General.*"

Now let us consider some more of General McClellan's testimony given before the Committee,† as follows:

* Official Records, Series I, Vol. V, page 34.

† Report of the Committee on the Conduct of War, 2, page 508.

" *Question.* Was it (the affair at Ball's Bluff) not of such a character as demanded an inquiry?

"*Answer.* I do not think it demanded any more direct inquiry than the examination of the reports.

" *Question.* Had you any idea of occupying Leesburg.

"*Answer.* If I had known definitely that the enemy had gone from there, I probably should have occupied the place.

"*Question.* I think you have stated already that you gave General Stone notice that you had retired McCall.

"*Answer.* I think that I did. That is my recollection ; but I am not certain. I remember sending dispatches very freely from that vicinity."

We have learned that General Stone has testified, "I received a dispatch from General McClellan to one which I sent him, informing him of the crossing of Colonel Baker and General Gorman. That despatch to me commenced with these words, '*I congratulate you and your command*"—and that about 12 or 1 o'clock on Monday * * * "in a dispatch General McClellan informed me as follows : 'I may order you to take Leesburg to-day,' and in the same or another dispatch, ' Shall I push up one or two divisions from this side?' (no doubt McCall and Smith's divisions): I thought a moment and concluded that if there was a slight force in front of us then, my force and McCall's would be all-sufficient ; and if that was not sufficient, then it was too late for any other division to come up. I therefore replied to him, ' I think I can take Leesburg,'"—which was followed by a dispatch in cipher, to which General Stone replied : "I have received the box, but have no key," since explained by Colonel Irwin to have contained: "Take Leesburg."

General McClellan further testified:

" *Question.* What would have been the effect of precipitating Smith and McCall's divisions upon Leesburg at the time Stone was making this demonstration? Would it not have prevented the disaster at Ball's Bluff, and probably led to the destruction of the enemy there?

"*Answer.* I do not think they would have remained to make a fight.

"*Question.* You say you did not expect General Stone would cross—what did you expect he would do, under the order you gave him? what definite object was contemplated by it?

"*Answer.* I did not contemplate any crossing of the river by that order—merely to show a force in the vicinity of the river." (It must be observed that McClellan here confines himself to his order of the 20th, to make a demonstration.)

"*Question.* If the divisions of McCall and Smith had continued to occupy their positions at Dranesville, it would have been easy to have protected the men that Stone had across the river, would it not?

"*Answer.* Not easy; it was a long day's march (16 miles by the roads, and 12 miles as troops would march, to Ball's Bluff). I did not know that General Stone's troops were engaged until too late."

General McCall commenced to retire from Dranesville about 10 a. m. of the 21st, and Stone's dispatch of the same day informing McClellan of his troops being engaged is marked 11:10 a. m. No doubt McClellan understood from Stone's dispatch given above* that these two divisions, would not be needed. We have learned that when McClellan placed Stone in command of his division, August 12th, 1861, he gave him the privilege of crossing the river to capture or disperse any small party, and then said, "I leave your operations much to your own discretion, in which I have the fullest confidence." Thus he seems to have intrusted to Stone the taking of Leesburg.

* "I think I can take Leesburg."

General McCall testified that the Confederates under General Evans were at Goose creek while he was at Dranesville, and that "had I been ordered forward, I have not the slightest doubt that I could have defeated Evans, and captured his whole command," at the same time expressing some fear that he might have been attacked in turn from Manassas before reaching his camp..

It is a well known fact that Colonel Baker expected an advance from Edward's Ferry, notwithstanding General Stone's opinion to the contrary; for as the flag of a Confederate regiment appeared from the opposite woods early in the action, he ordered his men to stop firing, fearing that they might be firing on our own men, but the firing was soon resumed. Previous to this, when Lieutenant Wade reported troops moving in on the left, Colonel Baker said they must be Gorman's men from Edward's Ferry.

If Stone had advanced his troops from Edward's Ferry, a decided victory would have been achieved. We have been told that while McClellan was greatly distressed, "that he had not a word of censure" for Stone when they met just after the battle, and we have learned that he fully exonerated him at once.

It must be fairly presumed that the dispatches testified to by Stone from McClellan as above had existed, or McClellan would have specifically denied them while testifying before the Committee on two different occasions, after Stone had given their contents to the committee. Nor did McClellan deny them in his official report given above. These are the dispatches which Stone claimed were taken possession of with his division papers, when he was secretly arrested, and that he never saw them again.

Let us consider the peculiar position occupied by General McClellan at that time before the public. It may assist us in coming to a conclusion in the premises. We find that "General McClellan was called to the active command of the army at and around Washington on the 27th of July, 1861. He brought to the service youth, a spotless moral character, robust health, a sound theoretical military education, with some practical experience, untiring industry, the prestige of recent success in the field, and the unlimited confidence of the loyal people. Having laid the moral foundation for an efficient army organization, he proceeded with skill and vigor to mould his material into perfect symmetry. * * * It was (soon) known as the Grand Army of the Potomac, whose existence was a wonder. He was busily engaged not only in perfecting its physical organization, but in making a solid improvement in its moral character. He issued orders that commended themselves to all good citizens, among the most notable of which was one which enjoined 'more perfect respect for the Sabbath.' He won 'golden opinions' continually, and with the return of every morning he found himself more and more securely entrenched in the faith and affection of the people, who were lavish of both. His moral strength at this time was prodigious. The soldiers and the people believed in him with the most earnest faith. His short campaign in Western Virginia had been successful. He had promised on taking command of the army of the Potomac that the war should be 'short, sharp and decisive,' and he said to some of his followers while the President and Secretary of War were standing by, 'Soldiers! We have had our last retreat, we have seen our last defeat; you stand by me, and I will stand by you, and henceforth victory will crown our efforts.' These words found a very ready response from the soldiers and the people. They were pondered with hope, and repeated with praise." Such was the bright picture in which McClellan marshaled his forces, and was about leading them to victory. Just at this time the unfortunate affair at Ball's Bluff occurred, and at the same time the brevet Lieutenant-

Generalship was almost within his grasp. On the 1st of November, 1861, General Scott retired from active service, and on his recommendation General McClellan was made Commander-in-Chief of all the armies of the Republic. How unpropitious a time for an investigation of the affair at Ball's Bluff, which might not add to General McClellan's already brilliant prestige! If it had been shown that he had been over-cautious or derelict in military duty, it might have impaired his popularity and usefulness as a commander, upon whom the public then depended for the salvation of the country. While General McClellan was thus crowded with cares, and so busily engaged as the active commander, he exonerated General Stone upon his own statements, without looking very closely into the matter. When embarrassments and difficulties growing out of this affair encompassed McClellan and Stone through public indignation, Stone was arrested by his chief for disloyalty, concerning which we read in Stone's defence:* "Mr. Stanton's order for Stone's arrest was issued on the 28th of January. It was not executed until the morning of the 9th of February; what happened in the interval has never been told." It is soon done. General McClellan asked that General Stone might be heard in his defense. (We have learned that General Stone had been heard at length on the 5th of January.) The Committee assented and General Stone was examined on the 31st (rather had delivered to him the Committee's opinion in full from the testimony taken, which is generally done before sentence is passed). Meantime, the execution of the order was informally suspended in deference to General McClellan's expressed statement to the Secretary of War that he did not see how any charges could be framed on the testimony.

In a few days the missing link was supplied by a

* "Battles and Leaders of the Civil War," Part 10.

refugee from Leesburg, with a vague and utterly groundless story. Of this missing link General Mc-Clellan testified before the Committee, giving his agency in the matter which caused the arrest,* *i. e.,* "I satisfied my own mind by personal examination of the sincerity of this refugee, and then showed the statement to the Secretary of War, upon which he directed me to give the order to arrest General Stone immediately, and send him under guard to Fort Lafayette. The order was carried into execution that same evening." May not Stone then have felt as did Wolsey when he exclaimed—

> "Had I but served my God with half the zeal
> I served my king, he would not in mine age
> Have left me naked to mine enemies."

It has been made painfully apparent that neither General McClellan nor General Stone was anxious to have a court of inquiry convened for the consideration of affairs relating to the battle of Ball's Bluff. McClellan must have realized that he had made at least two mistakes: one in placing Stone in so important a command without more closely supervising and supporting his movements ;† and another in exonerating him upon his own statements, and retaining him in command after the battle, without making a thorough investigation, which his despatches surely indicated that he had made—and perhaps still another of a grave nature in causing the arrest of Stone for disloyalty without preferring against him charges, or granting him a trial. While many pretences of confidence and faith in Stone's ability to command were made after this affair, it is very evident that he was not again

---

* Report of Committee on Conduct of War, 2, page 510.

† McClellan had selected the wrong man for the position when he said, "I leave your operations much to your own discretion, in which I have the fullest confidence."

placed in any important command from the time the Committee on the Conduct of War went behind Mc-Clellan's official despatches and Stone's official reports, into the true inwardness of the whole affair.

While Stone was an impressive martinet at division headquarters, as a captain or leader upon the field of strife he seems to have been a complete failure, as weak and inconsiderate as he was scholarly and accomplished.

All men are not born leaders, as we learned in the late war to our cost; and it must be said that General McClellan labored under the disadvantage of having to select from material that had not been tried in important commands. After Stone was released from arrest he again took the field, and was finally reduced from brigadier-general of volunteers to his old rank of colonel of the 14th infantry.*

We find Stone hugging to his bosom the delusive phantom of an exoneration given by McClellan, after its force and virtue had been annulled by the hand that gave it, opening the door for an investigation if Stone desired it; and according to Stone's expressed opinion it became his duty then to demand a court of inquiry, but he did not, although he had plenty of leisure, not having been assigned to duty until 1863, when he served as chief of staff to General Banks in the Department of the Gulf, and participated in the Red river disaster. Having re-entered the service under a cloud, he was subjected to various persecutions, which continued until he was finally driven to resign his commission as colonel, which was promptly accepted, and he sailed for distant shores without demanding through a court of inquiry an opinion or expression

---

* General Grant remarked when abroad to Reverend William L. Bull, while conversing upon the Ball's Bluff affair, "that misfortunes generally attended General Stone, and that he seemed to have been born under an unlucky star," as related to the author.

upon his guilt or innocence, having stoutly claimed that it was McClellan's duty, who had him arrested, to have confronted him with the charges, and to have seen that he had a speedy trial. And General Stone also testified before the Committee* in answer to the

"*Question.* I will now ask you as a military man, who had the power to bring you to a trial?

"*Answer.* When I was arrested, the general-in-chief, General McClellan, had that power. I know I should claim that power if any man under my command was arrested."

What a terrible blunder the second—committed by General Stone in dissimulating and in giving a false coloring and mystery to the whole affair, when he charged the disaster upon the brave Baker, which no doubt was largely the cause of his arrest and also the cause of his subsequent imprisonment and suffering—like a two-edged sword, it cut both ways.

When the mind of the public had become less sensitive to the appalling effects of war, other military blunders occurred, probably quite as false and far more disastrous, for which little if any better excuse could have been given than Stone could have truthfully given, had he at first made a frank and generous avowal of the whole affair just as it had occurred. How different would have been his fate had he shown the candor and manliness which Burnside did, of whom Lossing writes: "The disaster at Fredericksburg touched Burnside's reputation as a judicious leader very severely, and for a while he was under a cloud. Prompted by that noble generosity of his nature which made him always ready to award full honor to all in the hour of victory, he now assumed the entire responsibility of the measure which caused a slaughter so terrible, with a result so disastrous. That generosity blunted the weapons of vituperation which the friends of the late commander of the

---

* Report of Committee on Conduct of War, 2, page 502.

army of the Potomac and the enemies of the government were too ready to use.''

Some importance was attached to the battle of Ball's Bluff from the fact that it was the first engagement of forces from the Army of the Potomac with the enemy, in which they gallantly repulsed a force much larger than their own upon the ''sacred soil of old Virginia,'' and held the ground by hard fighting for hours thereafter—thus dissipating the oft-repeated story current after the battle of Bull Run that the army had been demoralized and would not fight.

The Confederate Colonel, Thomas M. Griffin, who was in the charge upon the left, where they lost heavily, reported: ''The Federal forces fought well. A number were killed by the bayonet by my men''*—in an action where almost 4000 Confederates were engaged against less than 1500 of our forces thus, wringing even from the enemy meagre though merited notice for gallantry so different from the prevailing stories of their writers, *i. e.*, ''that a whole brigade would take to their heels at the sight of a Confederate regiment advancing to the charge.''

General McClellan officially reported: ''The affair in front of Leesburg on Monday last resulted in serious loss to us, but was a most gallant fight on the part of our men, who displayed the utmost coolness and courage. It has given me the utmost confidence in them,'' and had read in general orders, ''The Major-General commanding the Army of the Potomac desires to offer his thanks, and to express his admiration of their conduct, to the officers and men of the detachment of the 15th and 20th Massachusetts, *First California Regiment*, and Tammany Regiment, the First United States Artillery and Rhode Island Battery, engaged in the affair of Monday last near Harrison's Island. The gallantry and discipline there displayed deserved a more

* Official Records, Series I, Vol. V, page 366.

fortunate result; but situated as those troops were—cut off alike from retreat and re-enforcements, and attacked by an overwhelming force—5000 against 1700—it was not possible that the issue could have been successful. Under happier auspices such devotion will insure victory."*

After General George A. McCall, by force of circumstances over which he had no control, was dragged into this affair, he made diligent enquiry to know how it all came about, who testified:†

"*Question.* Then what was the object of ordering Stone across the river while you were ordered back?

"*Answer.* I do not think it was intended to order Stone across the river. I never did believe it.

"*Question.* How did he go—without orders?

"*Answer.* I cannot say that he did altogether without orders." (It must be here observed that neither McClellan nor Stone had given to the public at this time various despatches herein given, of which McCall had then no knowledge.) * * * "I think either that Colbourn misunderstood the General's order, or that Stone gave too broad an interpretation to it—a little of both, I think. I have never been able to account for Stone's movement, *which was certainly a very injudicious one.* * * * He should not have undertaken it, because he had not the means of crossing. I should not have undertaken it under so vague an order, nor would I have done it if I had had a positive order. *I would not have thrown away those men.* * * * If Stone had reported that he had the means of crossing the river, then there would have been no mistake in giving such an order. *Stone has misstated*, unintentionally no doubt, one or two things in his report. It proved afterward that he had not the means to cross at

* Official Records, Series I, Vol. V, page 291.

† Report of Committee on Conduct of War, 2, pages 260 and 261.

all. He could not have crossed in the face of the enemy."

We may be morally certain that had Stone been in Baker's place, and Baker in Stone's, the Confederate right and rear would not only have been explored, but felt the force of heavy crushing blows from Edward's Ferry long before the hour of Baker's death had arrived, causing them to fall back upon Leesburg; and we must finally conclude that while this movement originated with General McClellan, having for its object the forcible evacuation of Leesburg *by his bloodless frightening strategy*, which there totally failed in its mission, *the cause of the defeat and disaster must rest principally upon General Stone*, whose false generalship and criminal neglect have been made apparent. He prepared the transportation, took the offensive at Edward's Ferry and the bluff, and gave Colonel Devens the fatal order to wait on the Virginia side for re-enforcements, then sent Colonel Baker to the front on the right with instructions "to hold on there, and of course not yield ground we had taken possession of without resistance," and when he learned that there were 4000 of the enemy between Colonel Baker's small force and Leesburg, he showed no uneasiness on that account, but merely pointed out to Colonel Baker the way to pursue the enemy, and then gave him authority to move forward—*while he himself did nothing* * *with much the larger National force* on the Virginia shore, although he must have known that Baker was in great peril. Had Stone followed up his offensive movement of the morning with his two columns, not more than two miles apart, as he should have done after he had crossed, there would have been no disaster, and Lees-

* As written by a well known military authority, "the army that takes the offensive must keep the offensive," this is even more true in tactics than it is in strategy. Nothing is always the very worst thing a hostile column can do.

16

burg might have been captured, although it could not have been held long without the support of a general advance.

Perhaps the least creditable part of the whole affair, over which we would gladly cast the veil of charity, is the dissimilation practiced by Stone in shuffling himself to the bottom, and turning up the pallid face of his brave subordinate as the reprehensible officer who brought on the action, through rashness and disobedience of orders, and who was wholly responsible for the disaster. Although Stone had been exonerated by his chief, it was he who thereafter largely assisted in closing upon him the prison door.

Stone does not seem to have been devoid of feeling, and may have undergone the punishment of a mental hell. "Thus conscience does make cowards of us all."

It has been said that while at a review of the Army of the Potomac he was heard to exclaim, "Do you see those men looking at me? Don't you hear what they are all saying? Ball's Bluff! Ball's Bluff!" And the echo of those words kept ringing in his ears until his recent death. Thus the affair palled upon him like an ever-present nightmare, besetting him with a spirit of unrest.

Happy for Stone had he fallen in Baker's stead on the pine-clad bluff of the Potomac, before fulminating his charges, and seeking shelter from his blunders beneath the bullet-pierced and blood-stained mantle of his valorous subordinate! His name would have found rest "among the dearest though most mournful recollections of his country, and that country would have been spared" the scandal of an apparent false imprisonment for treason, and Stone's memory the one dark spot that blurs his former good record.

Of these actors all have now passed from the stage of life, and will become notorious or distinguished in the pages of history, among whom the memory of

Baker will stand out conspicuously for statesmanship, valor and honorable service to his adopted country, as enduringly as the Potomac which surges aloft its endless requiems to the immortal memory of the heroes there slain.

INDEX.

AUTHOR'S INTENTIONS, 7, 8, 53, 74.

BAKER, SENATOR E. D., Sketch and Portrait of, 9. Replies to Breckenridge, 15. Speech in New York, 19. Commissions not Accepted, 74. Forecast of Defense, 53. Stone's Charges and Misstatements Answered, 61, 78 to 93. Map of Battle Field, 94½. At Stone's Quarters, 114, 115. Baker given Orders to Cross, 101. His Orders from Stone, 106,119, 193. His Instructions from Stone, 61, 80, 101, 154, 155, 195. On the Island, 90, 117. Takes Command, 89, 110, 116, 156. Misled by Stone as to Transportation, 63. He Goes to Post of Danger, 159. His Presentiment, 196. All Going Well up to Baker's Death, 76, 177. Dying Declaration, 17, 55, 162. Mentioned by McClellan, 180. His Generalship Endorsed, 161. One of our Best Commanders, 177. General Grant on Ord, 75. On Stone, 237. McClellan Ordered Stone to "Take Leesburg," 77. One Thousand more Troops and Victory, 78. Stone in Command at both Crossings, 61, 76, 77, 128, 138, 170, 171 to 174. A Commander wanted no Orders Given, 127, 129. Baker Cool and Gallant, 82. Moves up his Reserves, 86.

BATTLE LINES FORMED, 83, 84, 86, 93, 94, 117. Engaged, 164, 165, 144, 145. Reserves Moved up, 86. Left strongly

Posted, 85. Centre well Posted, 83. Right well placed, 83. See Maps, 94½. One Thousand more Troops and Victory, 78.

BARTLETT,* CAPTAIN WM. F., Mentioned, 82, 83, 110, 158.

BALL'S BLUFF CLIFF, Scene of, 157½.

BANKS, GENERAL N. G., Despatch, 69. Opinion of, 159.

BOWE, MAJOR, of Cogswell's Regiment, in Charge of Transportation when lost, 92.

BURNSIDE, GENERAL A.E.,238.

BARKSDALE, COLONEL WM., Report of, 149. Mentioned, 150.

BURNS, GENERAL W. W., Address of, 23.

BANNISTER, MAJOR DWIGHT, Testimony, 134. Stone in Command at both Crossings, 138.

BANES, COLONEL C. H., Statement, 211.

BLAINE, HON. JAMES G., Mentioned, 200, 210, 211.

CASUALTIES, 211 to 213. Wistar, on Same, 165, 175.

CONKLING, HON. ROSCOE, Mentioned, 225.

CONFEDERATE STAFF, Official Statements, 149. The Enemy very much Shattered, 175.

COMTE DE PARIS' OPINION, Stone to Keep a Watch on Leesburg, 70. Did not Guard Against Attack, 120. His Imprudence, 87.

CALIFORNIA REGIMENT, Enlisted, 12. Early Service, 33 to 38. Repulsed Confederates, 147, 166. Took Prison-

* General Bartlett.

(245)

ers, 165. Casualties, 211 to 213. Percentage of Losses Compared, 211 to 213.

CROSSING, Length of Time Consumed in, 62, 63, 73.

"COMMITTEE ON THE CONDUCT OF THE WAR," Members of, 228. Opinion of Stone's Conduct, 183 to 188, 226, 227. Stone's Orders Authenticated by Committee, 193. Committee did not Solicit Stone's Arrest, 208, 226. Do not Affirm Opinion of Disloyalty, 226, 227.

CHARGES AGAINST BAKER, and Answers Thereto, 78 to 93.

CANDY, CAPTAIN, Scouts sent by Stone, 88, 89. Bears Despatch to Stone, 100, 104. 118, 138. Mentioned, 137, 170.

CONFEDERATES AND MOVE-MENTS OF, 84, 85, 92, 110, 146 to 151. Charge Ordered, 147. Very much Shattered, 175.

COGSWELL, Colonel, Report of, 83, 84, 85. Mistaken in Report, 86, 164, 165. Bears Despatch to Baker, 163, 164, 193. Given Charge of the Artillery, 166. Orders a Retreat, 169. Boats lost, 73, 92. Surrenders, 151.

DANA, GENERAL N. J. T. Testimony, 63, 124. Stone in Command at Both Crossings, 128. As to Stone's Loyalty, 188, 189.

DEVENS,* COLONEL CHARLES, Ordered to Remain on the Bluff, 79, 88. Boats lost, 73. Orders, 95, 96 to 99. Opinion of Transportation, 157, Ordered to Retreat, 169. Testimony as to Baker's Order, 194. As to Stone's Loyalty, 188,189.

DIMMICK, MAJOR, Testimony as to Fortifications in the Way, 139, 185, 186.

EVANS, GENERAL N. G., Confederate Official Report, 146.

EDWARD'S FERRY, Troops at,

148. Map, 94½. No Orders Given, a Commander Wanted at, 127, 129.

FALSE IMPRESSIONS, Produced by Stone's Reports, 61, 80, 81, 142, 143, 160.

FOOT, QUARTERMASTER H. R., in Charge of Transportation, 169, 219.

FIRST THREE YEARS' REGIMENT, 12.

FEATHERSTONE, COLONEL, 17th Miss. engaged, 147.

GRIFFIN, LIEUT. COLONEL, 18th Miss. Found the Enemy Strongly Posted, 84, 85.

GRANT, GENERAL U. S., Opinion of Stone, 237. Of General Ord, 75.

GORMAN, GENERAL, "Sleep in Leesburg To-night," 136. Mentioned, 219.

HINKS,* COLONEL E. W., On Transportation and Place of Crossing, 58, 64. Had Rope Stretched Across, 73. Mentioned, 91. His Orders for Transportation, 170, 171.

HOWE, QUARTERMASTER Church, Messages from Stone to Devens and Lee, 99 to 101.

HARVEY, CAPTAIN, Baker's Assistant Adjutant-General, Rallied the Men, 168. Was Killed, 169.

HALLECK, GENERAL, Interviewed by Stone, 226.

HANGER, PHILIP, Testimony on Transportation, 65 to 67, 140.

HUNTON, COLONEL, 8th Va. Engaged, 84, 85, 86, 146.

IMPRESSIONS PRODUCED by Stone's False Reports, 61, 80, 81, 160.

JENIFER, LIEUT. COL., Confederate Report of Action, 84.

KELLEN, CHAPLAIN ROBERT, Message, 115. Testimony, 156.

LANDER, GENERAL F. W., Testimony, 128. A Com-

* General Devens.   * General Hinks.

mander Wanted, 129. Could Take Leesburg, 130. Sketch of, 130. Opinion of Movement, 160.

LEE,* COLONEL WM. R., Testimony. Baker Cool and Gallant, 82. Disaster Caused by Insufficiency of Transportation, 92. On the Bluff, 101 to 105. Number of Confederate Forces Engaged, 92.

LOYALTY OF STONE Questioned, 186 to 189. But not Affirmed, 226, 227.

MONUMENT at Gettysburg, 26 to 28.

MAP Showing Positions of Troops between 1 and 2:30 p. m., and 2:30 and 5 p. m., 94½.

McCLELLAN, GENERAL GEO. B., All-potent, 182. Order to stone, 59. Despatches, 69, 70, 71, 118, 162, 170, 177, 222. "Take Leesburg," 77. Offered Stone Two Divisions, 222. His Generalship, 161. Exonerated Stone, 177, 178. Changes his Opinion, 178. Stone should have Attacked, 180. McClellan's Prestige at Stake, 233. His Opinion Missing Link Found, 199, 236. Arrest of Stone, 189, 190, 199, 208, 226. He Supplies Evidence, 189, 235. Did not Advise Stone of McCall's Withdrawal, 77, 216. His Testimony, 230 to 232. As to Stone's Loyalty, 188, 189.

McCALL, GENERAL GEO. A., His Opinion of the Transportation and of the Crossing, 240, 74, 92, 216, 223, 224, 232, 233.

MARKOE, CAPTAIN, JOHN, on Skirmish Line, 164. Brings Prisoners off, 165.

MERRITT, CAPTAIN C. M., on Transportation, 72.

MIX, MAJOR JOHN, Testimony to have a Dash at the Enemy, 121.

MISSING LINK SUPPLIED by McClellan, 189, 199, 235, 236. ORDERS, said to be Spurious, 196, 197.

PARRISH, MAJOR ROBERT A., Conversation with Colonel Baker, 74, 196. Mentioned, 30, 36, 38, 44.

PULESTON, DR. J. H., Despatches Spurious, 196. Transportation Sufficient, 197.

PICKETT'S MEN at Gettysburg, 27.

PRISONERS Fired upon from the Cliff, 151.

REVERE,* MAJOR PAUL J., Disaster Resulted from Insufficiency of Transportation, 92. On the Bluff, 102.

RITMAN, MAJOR GEORGE L., Statements, 63, 67, 143. Mentioned, 115, 193.

RETREAT ORDERED by Cogswell, 169.

RICHARDSON, CAPTAIN J. H., Testimony, 58.

STONE, GENERAL CHARLES P., Sketch of, 48. Builds Fortification to Defend Crossing, 64. Orders from McClellan, 59, 70, 77. Ordered Devens to Remain on Bluff, 88. Orders Baker to Cross, 101. Instructs Baker, 61, 80, 101, 154, 155, 195. His Flotilla, 65 to 67. In Command at both Crossings, 61, 76, 77, 128, 138. His Aide, Captain Candy, and Scouts, return, 89. He arrives after Baker Fell, 171 to 174. His Despatches to McClellan, 68, 70, 71, 118, 162, 170, 177, 222. His Charges Against Baker, and Misstatements, 61, 78 to 93, 219. Testimony, 181. McClellan's Opinion of, 178. Stone thinks Transportation Sufficient, 197, 219. Supplies Omissions, 215, 217, 222. His Arrest, 190. "I think I can

* General Lee.

* Colonel Revere, killed at Gettysburg.

take Leesburg," 222. His Transportation Mentioned, 62, 65 to 67, 70, 71, 80, 157; 169, 170, 197, 218, 240. Not Advised of McCall's Withdrawal, 77, 216. Effect of Withdrawal, 224. Stone does not Demand a Court of Inquiry, 224, 225, 237. Reduced to rank of Colonel, 237. Resigns his Commission, 237. Baker one of our best Commanders, 177. All going well up to Baker's Death, 76, 177. Stone Thought he had been Relieved of all Responsibility, 155, 156. A Commander wanted no Orders Given, 127, 129. He should have Attacked, 180. Stone's Loyalty, 186 to 189, 226, 227.

STEWART, STONE'S ADJUTANT-GENERAL on the Field, 76, 170. Gave Orders in Stone's Name, 170.

SLEEPING SENTINEL, 39.

SUMNER, HON. CHARLES, Mentioned, 202.

STANTON, EDWIN M., Order of Arrest, 189. Said McClellan Desired it, 208, 226. McClellan All-potent, 182.

SCOUTS Sent by Stone to the Bluff, Mentioned, 88, 89, 100, 104, 118.

TOMPKINS, COLONEL C. H.

Testimony of, at Edward's Ferry, 130.

TRANSPORTATION. Mentioned, 62, 63, 65 to 67, 70, 71, 80, 157, 160, 169, 170, 173, 197, 218, 219, 220, 240, 241.

TOPOGRAPHY of the Country, 64, 65. Of Harrison's Island, 60. Of Edward's Ferry, 64.

VAN ALLAN, COLONEL J. H. Effect of Stone's Reports on, 81, 160. Opinion of Transportation, 220. As to Stone's Loyalty, 188, 189.

VAUGHAN, CAPTAIN, Report of the Dead Buried on the Field, 212.

WISTAR, GENERAL ISAAC J. Sketch and Portrait of, 29. Orders, 43, 113, 115, 163, 194. Addresses, 16, 176. His Testimony, 62, 113, 163, 174, 175, 193, 194. Opinion of, 144, 174, 175, 198. As to Stone's Loyalty, 188, 189.

WARD, LIEUT. COLONEL, 15th Mass. Ordered to Re-enforce Devens, 79, 88. On the Bluff, 101, 104.

WHITE, COLONEL ELIJAH V., Confederate, Statements of, 86, 151, 152, 223.

WADE, LIEUT. Co. D, California Regiment, Report of, 143.

YOUNG, CAPT. F. G., Testimony of, 107, 114, 193. Message for Colonel Baker, 109.